THE
DESERT
PRINCE

Secrets of the Sands

The Lost Scroll of the Physician
The Desert Prince

SECRETS OF THE SANDS

THE DESERT PRINCE

WITHDRAWN

ALISHA SEVIGNY

DUNDURN
TORONTO

Publisher and acquiring editor: Scott Fraser | Editor: Jess Shulman
Cover designer: Laura Boyle
Cover illustration: Queenie Chan
Printer: Marquis Book Printing Inc.

Library and Archives Canada Cataloguing in Publication

Title: The desert prince / Alisha Sevigny.
Names: Sevigny, Alisha, author.
Description: Series statement: Secrets of the sands ; 2
Identifiers: Canadiana (print) 20200200623 | Canadiana (ebook) 20200200666 | ISBN 9781459744325 (softcover) | ISBN 9781459744332 (PDF) | ISBN 9781459744349 (EPUB)
Classification: LCC PS8637.E897 D47 2020 | DDC jC813/.6—dc23

We acknowledge the support of the Canada Council for the Arts and the Ontario Arts Council for our publishing program. We also acknowledge the financial support of the Government of Ontario, through the Ontario Book Publishing Tax Credit and Ontario Creates, and the Government of Canada.

Care has been taken to trace the ownership of copyright material used in this book. The author and the publisher welcome any information enabling them to rectify any references or credits in subsequent editions.

The publisher is not responsible for websites or their content unless they are owned by the publisher.

Printed and bound in Canada.

VISIT US AT

 dundurn.com | @dundurnpress | dundurnpress |  dundurnpress

Dundurn
3 Church Street, Suite 500
Toronto, Ontario, Canada
M5E 1M2

"NORTH?" REB ECHOES. The scribe looks like he's just tumbled off the back of a donkey. "You wish us to go north after Princess Merat?"

"Yes," I say. My heart and mind are still racing from our confrontation with the Queen of Egypt. "If we hurry, we may catch up to the Hyksos chieftain and his men. Did you not hear Queen Anat? The princess was given to him just before the queen herself arrived here."

"You mean when she arrived here to kill us," Reb points out. "Why should we trust anything the queen says? She came to take the scroll and send us to the underworld." He gestures at the mastaba that houses my parents' bodies, that would have held our bodies if not for the intervention of young Prince Tutan and Ahmes.

"It is a good thing she only accomplished the first task," Paser says cheerily, still holding the surgical blade Ahmes gave him.

By the gods' good graces, the physician's knife and the prince's royal command were enough to stop Crooked Nose from entombing us alive. Ahmes and Prince Tutan are now on their way back to the palace to check on my brother, Ky, who is still recovering from the risky surgery Ahmes performed only hours ago.

Crooked Nose, Queen Anat's favourite solider, is with them. He will have the unpleasant task of informing Her Highness that her plan to leave us dead has been thwarted. By her only son and heir to the throne, no less. As the cruel soldier is responsible for the fire that killed my parents, I do not feel all that sorry for him.

"If we are to catch up to the Hyksos chieftain and rescue the princess, we must get moving." Paser glances up at the sky.

"Say we do catch up to them," Reb says, crossing his arms. "What are we supposed to do? Walk up to the chieftain and say, 'Greetings, we would like the princess back'?"

"Maybe we can convince the Hyksos tribe to let us join them," I say, though my stomach lurches at the outrageous thought. "Healers are always needed."

Reb snorts. "You really think our rivals will welcome three young physicians into their midst?"

"Why not?" I speak with more confidence than I feel. "Our skills will be of use to them, especially if there is a battle coming."

"And if they do not welcome us among them?" Reb asks. "What then?"

"We grab the princess and run," I say grimly.

"Run where?" Reb throws his hands up in exasperation. "We cannot come back to Thebes."

"We can go to their port city of Avaris," Paser interjects. "That is likely where they are taking Merat anyway."

"You wish us to go to the Hyksos capital?" Reb is aghast. "Into the very heart of their territory?"

"I have family there," Paser says. We look at him in shock and a shadow crosses his face. "I'm not sure whether we will be welcome, but they are my blood, and it is our best chance."

A flicker of hope ignites in my chest. "Do you think they might help us?"

"There is no guarantee," Paser says. "But from what I know, the port city is vast, with many people from distant shores. If the gods are willing and we find Merat and free her, we might be able to disappear into the crowds." He hesitates. "Or board a ship for another land."

My stomach falls even further at the thought of crossing the seas to unknown worlds.

"The chieftain and his men will probably kill us before that happens," Reb says, ever optimistic. "Especially if they hear we are there to steal away his future wife."

"A possibility," I admit. "But our deaths are certain if we stay in Thebes. Queen Anat will see to that."

"We will not last a moment out there, away from our home." Reb motions at the world beyond the city borders. "We are scribes, not nomads. How can we make our way north to the Hyksos unaided? We will be swooped up by the queen's men, faster than the falcon seizes its prey."

"You forget something, my friend," Paser interrupts again, and I look at him, grateful for his support. I am not sure I would be so bold in my plans were it not for his calm strength at my side. "There is someone who can take us there."

Reb pales in the moonlight. "You cannot mean —"

"The Hyksos spy," I breathe. "The one they caught in the marketplace. Paser, you are brilliant! He can show us the way."

"What makes you think he will help us?" Reb scoffs. "Besides, even if we could free him from the Place of Confinement — which we cannot — it would only have Pharaoh's men joining the queen's in hunting us like rats for betraying both him and the kingdom."

"It is our only choice." I look back at the mastaba, then at my friends. "We do not have much time. We should gather up anything that might assist us on our journey."

"Did you take some of the blue lotus flower you gave your brother this evening?" Reb, assessing that I am quite serious, seems truly alarmed. "In addition to this terrible plan, which will likely see us all killed —" he looks at Paser, who shrugs, then back at me "— you wish us to free an enemy spy right after we rob the tombs of our ancestors? Of your very parents, Sesha?"

"While our ancestors may have need of these objects in the afterlife, we need them now, in *this* life," I insist. "My parents will not begrudge us borrowing a few items."

"We will be cursed," Reb protests.

"We already are," I say, tart as unripe berries. "I have lost my parents and my home, and now I must leave my brother behind. The gods can take nothing more from me. I do not ask you to join us, but if we are to have any chance of escaping, we must be on our way."

2

RESTING MY HEAD AGAINST my mother's coffin, I collect my courage. It is quiet in the room. Paser and Reb are searching the other tombs for anything that might be of use on the long and dangerous journey ahead. I say a brief goodbye to my parents.

"I will not be back for some time, Mother," I whisper.

If ever.

"We are going to find Merat." I smile, thinking of my friend. "You remember the princess? She has a most irrepressible spirit." My smile fades. "Know I will honour your memory every day with my life. I will never forget you and Father." Wishing I could look upon my mother's face once more, I close my eyes to recall the image of her eyes, the colour and sweetness of honey, her wide smile, and the soothing sound of her voice. I picture her singing to my brother when he was young and had woken suddenly from a restless dream.

If only this were a dream I could wake from as easily.

Will Ky think I have abandoned him? I would give anything to see my brother once more, to explain why I am leaving Thebes, why he is safer without me. I take a deep breath. I must trust that Ahmes will relay my message to Ky: I will come back for him as soon as I am able. I must also trust that Prince Tutan's affection for his best friend is enough for the queen to leave Ky alone. Despite her threats otherwise, I pray she will not harm my brother just to get back at me. After all, he is only a child.

I am not a child. His stubborn words come back with the bittersweet realization that he no longer *is* a child. Perhaps he has not been one since that night our parents died, despite my best efforts to keep him so.

"Sesha." Paser stands in the doorway, holding a waterskin, the long woven strap slung over his broad shoulder. "We should be on our way. Khonsu will only shine a few more hours before Ra chases him from the sky."

"Coming," I say, picking up the objects I hurriedly gathered from the crypt. A scalpel, a scarf, some loose gemstones that once adorned a bracelet Father bought Mother — these are the remnants I have to remember them by, items that may make all the difference to our survival. These plus my father's obsidian blade and his priceless scarab amulet, which hangs from my neck. There is much more I wish I could bring, but we need to travel light. The burden on my soul at leaving my brother is heavy enough.

I kiss my fingertips and brush them along the length of my parents' intricately painted coffins as I walk between them, leaving the room and their physical remains for what may be the last time. Our chances of reaching the Hyksos unscathed are slim, maybe non-existent, making it unlikely I will ever return. As Reb pointed out, we are scribes, not nomads.

But there is no other option.

Pausing at the exit, I am unable to resist one last glance at their final resting place. And though I hope they are somewhere in the Field of Reeds, laughing and having a wonderful time, a part of me hopes their spirits will be with me always.

"What did you find?" I ask Paser and Reb to distract myself from the fact that we have just become tomb robbers and are currently on our way to release an enemy spy from confinement. That, and out of simple curiosity.

"In addition to the knife Ahmes gave me, I have a water container." Paser holds up the waterskin. It looks to be the bladder of a rhino. "And some silver for trading."

"Praises," I say in admiration. "Reb?"

"I did not take anything." He is defiant, fists at his sides, eyes a bit wild. "I do not wish to be cursed for defiling the graves of my ancestors."

"That is your choice." Though, ten ankhs to one he will not turn down a drink from the waterskin once we are on our way.

We walk in the dark, as furtive as stalking cats, toward the pits. Khonsu has disappeared behind clouds left by the earlier storm, which passed as quickly as it began. Good for our travels, catastrophic for the crops and the kingdom, which desperately need the rains. The threat of famine looms over the landscape, an invisible cloud of its own.

As we draw closer to the pits, we move even more slowly so as not to fall into one of the gaping holes and break our necks, or any other body part essential for a quick escape. We carry no torch; fire will only call attention.

"That one," Paser says softly, pointing into the blackness. It is quiet, and though we tread lightly, our footsteps make a soft crunching noise in the dirt.

"Who's there?" a voice shouts, high pitched and tremulous. "It is I, Nebifu, High Priest. I am being

held here in error. Let me out and you will be reward-
ed handsomely by the gods!"

We ignore Reb's uncle and keep walking. No noise
or pleading comes from the spy's cavity, which is just
to the left of where we stand. In fact, it is ominously
quiet. In unison, we peer over the edge of the pit.

"Pssst," I call down into the hole.

No answer.

"Do you think he is dead?" Reb whispers, sounding hopeful.

Paser, on my right, shrugs. "It depends if they've
been feeding him or not."

"Maybe this is the wrong hole?" I say, a little louder. At that there is a scuffling noise and a voice starts
speaking in the startled tone of someone just woken,
wondering who is there and if they are dreaming.

"Peace." I make my voice soothing, like my mother's.
"We mean you no harm."

A short bark of laughter from the pit suggests he
does not believe us.

"He speaks our language," whispers Reb.

"Of course he does, they all do," I whisper back.
"The Hyksos people have been in our lands for many
years. Our language is theirs now. Besides, what good
is a spy who cannot understand what is said?"

"How shall we get him out?" Paser asks as we stand
there, looking down into the pit.

"The rope." I look around, something prickling at the back of my memory.

Reb scuffs his toe in the dirt, then clears his throat. "I, uh, threw it into Nebifu's pit when we were here earlier."

Eye of Horus. I had forgotten that. The High Priest had not been kind to his nephew, and Reb had returned the favour, leaving him in the pits where he had been put on Pharaoh's command. The king did not look well on the priest for keeping Egypt's most sacred treasures hidden from him and proclaimed it an act of betrayal. Presumably, Pharaoh does not know of his wife's collusion with the priest, though Nebifu swears he and the queen were only keeping the country's priceless heirlooms safe. She does not want them used to provide for the common people, or even more insultingly, as tribute for the Hyksos who rule in the North. *She'd rather use her daughter as an offering instead*, I think indignantly while scouring the area for another rope.

Have faith, Merat, we are coming for you.

Further searching reveals nothing we can use to fish the spy out. Then I remember the scarf. Quickly, I unwrap it from around my head and dangle it down into the hole. The clouds part, clearing away from the crescent moon, and though it is still dark, a little illumination makes its way into the pit. A man stands there, rubbing his eyes and blinking up at us as if he cannot quite believe what he is seeing. The scarf hangs several royal cubits above his head.

"Jump," I say. The moonlight shifts, glinting off white fragments of something deep in the pit.

He jumps, high, but not high enough to reach the end of the scarf. Trying again, he grunts with effort, but misses. There is a clattering sound when he lands, and I finally recognize the ivory shards glinting in the moonlight.

Bones.

3

"WE WILL HAVE TO GET NEBIFU to throw the rope back up to us," Paser, ever logical, says after a few moments of this.

"He will only do that if he thinks we will free him." Reb folds his arms. "Which I made very clear I will not do."

"We may not have a choice," I say, glancing over at Nebifu's pit. Besides, even if the scarf is long enough to reach the spy, it might not be able to bear his weight. Reeling the scarf back up, I make up my mind.

Reb and Paser follow me over to Nebifu's pit.

"Nebifu," I call.

"Yes?" he says, his voice frantic. "Who's there?"

"It is I, Sesha, Daughter of Ay."

"Gods be praised, Sesha, you have come to your senses. Hurry and free me, child!" The desperation in his tone hits me, along with an unpleasant odour. I suppose there isn't a separate latrine in the pit.

"Very well." I take a hesitant step closer to the edge. "Throw me the rope and we will set you free."

"Do I have your word?" he cries in a warbly voice.

"Yes."

"Swear it! Swear it on the names of your father and mother."

"We could always say we are going to free him and then not do so." Reb looks over my shoulder into the dark pit.

I sigh, weighing the risks, and reach my decision. "Despite my previous claim, it seems there *is* something I possess that can be taken from me. And, fortunately for Nebifu, I would like to keep my word." I take a few more steps toward the hole. "I swear on my family name, if you throw up the rope, you will go free." I hope I am not making a mistake.

The High Priest sobs his thanks as a knotted end flies up out of the pit. Instinctively, I lunge to catch it. A firm hand grabs my other arm from behind, keeping me from toppling into the pit. With the way this day is going, I would have likely ended up face first in a pile of Nebifu's excrement. As it is, I miss the rope.

"Careful." Paser releases my arm. He takes my hand in one of his and holds Reb's in his other to extend our reach.

"Thank you." I take a steadying breath, then turn back to the pit. "Again," I urge Nebifu. This time he throws the rope higher. I stretch, fingers straining, seeking, grasping. Rough fibres graze their tips, but I am unable to get a grip.

Reb and Paser have their feet planted solidly in the earth. "Once more," I say, and Nebifu throws the rope a third time.

Again, Reb and Paser yank me back from the brink. I fall on my bottom, dazed. Looking down, I am surprised to see the rope in my hand, having no recollection of catching it. The boys cheer, already looking around for something to tie the end to. I stand and brush myself off, wincing. Paser and Reb, unaware that they almost detached my arm, come back carrying a large brick between them, straining under its weight. They drop it with a heavy thud.

"Will this do?" Paser pants.

Rust-coloured splotches stain the brick and I try not to dwell on what it might have been used for. The Place of Confinement brings back memories of my days on the streets and the feeling of a churning stomach after eating something foul. There is sweat on my brow and a lump in my guts as hard and heavy as the brick.

This place is home to many uneasy spirits.

Paser ties the rope around the big square block, knotting it expertly. "We must hold it secure so he can climb up."

Reb inhales through his nostrils and throws the other end of the rope back down to Nebifu. "He does not deserve this," he mutters, looking down at the hole. We brace ourselves and hold the line taut, Paser as anchor, me next, Reb in front.

There is much grunting and wheezing as Nebifu slowly hauls himself out of his prison. We lean back, using our weight to keep the brick from sliding toward the pit. At last, a hand claws its way up and over the edge, fingernails torn and bleeding.

"Hold on," Reb says between gritted teeth, leaning his weight back farther while walking forward, moving one hand over the other, gripping the rope, maintaining the tension, until at last he reaches the edge and grabs Nebifu's quivering arm. With a few grunts of his own, he manages to heft his uncle over the lip.

Nebifu lies on the ground, babbling to us, to the gods, to any creature who cares to listen to his tearful exclamations over his regained freedom. He has tied the rope around his waist, and now Paser helps him unknot it. One prisoner free, one to go.

Paser then walks over to the brick and, bending forward, biceps straining, begins to push it over to the spy's pit. Reb joins him, their feet kicking up dirt behind them as they use their weight to move the brick. Nebifu finally sits up, taking note of his surroundings and the boys' efforts. Confusion crosses his face.

"What are you doing?" he demands as they stand, Reb rubbing his shoulder, the scar left by his uncle stark in the moon's light. Paser ignores Nebifu and picks up the rope, tossing it down to the spy. Nebifu gasps. "You cannot be serious? You are freeing the criminal?"

"Do you also consider yourself a criminal, then?" Reb asks. For someone reluctant to free the spy, he seems to enjoy Nebifu's outrage at our intentions. "Because only moments ago, you two shared the same fate. In the eyes of the pharaoh, you are no different from him."

"We are nothing alike." Nebifu puffs out his chest, apparently affronted by the comparison. "I have served the kingdom faithfully. That man is a spy, a foreigner. He is not a native son of our Black Land." He spits. "His kind are dogs."

I think of Anubis, the dog who saved my brother and me in the market; loyal, intelligent, and brave, I wish he were here right now. But he is with Ky, protecting him, watching over him, which is more than I can do. I walk over to help Paser hold the rope so the prisoner can climb it, as Nebifu did. "Dogs are honourable creatures," I say, passing by the fallen priest.

Let us pray this man is as well. Or we may all live to regret our next actions.

4

ALTHOUGH THE HYKSOS SPY was in the pit longer than Nebifu, he scales the rope more deftly and quickly than the out-of-shape priest. He stands at the edge, alert, hands raised in a defensive position, eyeing us as if we might push him back in. His eyes and hair are as dark as the night; the beginnings of an unkempt beard shadow his full lips and high cheekbones. He looks a few years our senior, maybe seventeen or eighteen years old, with a lean, muscular body, almost as tall as Paser. His skin is streaked with dirt and he smells no better than Nebifu.

"We mean you no harm," I say, glancing at Paser, wondering if he's also having second thoughts about this course of action. Will we be able to control him?

"Why have you freed me?" the spy rasps. I do not know what I am expecting, but overall — aside from the filth and the stench, which, to be fair, is unavoidable after a week in a pit — he is completely ordinary. I suppose this is a good thing to be, as a spy.

"We need your help," I begin, glancing at Nebifu. I do not want to say too much in front of the priest. Now that he is free, there's no telling if he'll go running to the queen.

"You cannot do this!" Nebifu rises to his feet and walks toward the stranger, arms raised, finger wagging. "He is a defiler and a criminal. His people are a plague on our lands!"

The spy ignores him. "Do you have any food or water?" He licks his cracked lips. His clothes are filthy, hanging off him in rags. "I've drunk little and eaten nothing but a few pieces of mouldy bread since being thrown in the pit."

I look at Paser and Reb, who both shake their heads. Now that he speaks of food, I realize it's been some time since I last ate well, consumed as I was with copying the priceless scroll, with Ky's surgery, with Queen Anat's treachery. My stomach rumbles loudly, and the spy's mouth tugs up at one corner.

"No," I say, licking my own lips. "But I know where we can find some."

"Where?" Reb asks with his usual skepticism. "Everything was collected for the Festival of the Inundation."

"Exactly," I say, turning to confer with him and Paser. "It is all assembled in one spot: the storehouse near the palace grounds. Everyone should be sleeping off the effects of the celebrations by now." The brief rains, desperately needed, will have given the people reason to rejoice at the festival's success in appealing to the gods. The security around the storehouses will not be as stringent as it might have been, which is fortunate because, despite the danger, we must find food and drink or we will not have the energy to go anywhere. "Let us divide the tasks. I will go to the storehouses. Paser, you and Reb can take him" — I gesture at the spy — "to find a boat. The fastest way to move is on the river."

"Do you think splitting up is wise?" Paser murmurs, taking full stock of the spy, who sways slightly. Weakened by hunger and thirst, he is manageable now, but we will need to rely on our strength as a trio to keep him in line.

"We must have supplies for our journey, or we will not get far," I say. "And we must be on the river before Ra rises if we want any hope of escaping." Paser's muscle and Reb's wiry strength will, hopefully, be enough to prevent the Hyksos from doing anything … unanticipated while they look for a boat.

"You said you need my help." The spy eyes us, chin raised. "What do you wish of me?"

I turn to face him directly. "We want you to take us north, to your people. Our friend was taken by one of your chieftains and we wish very much to find her. For this, we give you back your life."

"You cannot trust him!" Nebifu, who has been spluttering in shock these past few moments, starts in again. "He will betray you the second he gets the chance."

The Hyksos gathers himself, looking coldly down his proud nose at Nebifu. "I swear on the lives of my family and my gods, I will see you safely to my people. Once there, though …" He lifts a shoulder. "You are on your own."

"That is acceptable," I say, crossing my arms.

"It is likely they will kill you," the spy adds, not looking at all bothered at the thought.

"We will take our chances." I eye him warily. Besides, we have no other options.

"I am coming with you," Nebifu says to us.

"To the palace?" I say. That does not seem like a wise course of action.

"No." Nebifu grimaces. "North."

"I will not travel with this man." The Hyksos narrows his gaze. "He will try to slit my throat the moment my eyes close. Not that this flaccid pasty maggot would succeed." He waves a dismissive hand at Nebifu. "But there is the principle of the matter."

Nebifu's mouth drops open in shock. "How dare you! I am High Priest of all the land —"

"Was," Reb interjects.

Nebifu ignores him. "A man of my position and esteem would not stoop to commit a crime so hideous."

"In my experience, it is those kinds of men who commit them the most," the spy says. "Particularly when it satisfies their interests. Many powerful people, accustomed to getting their way, will not hesitate to ensure their own success."

I think of Nebifu sitting on a mountain of treasures back at the temple. There is no way to know if he is telling the truth when he says he was protecting them for our kingdom.

"I am sorry, Nebifu," I say. We need the Hyksos spy more than we need the priest.

"I will go to the pharaoh!" he cries, finger wagging in the air again as if he is berating an errant student. "I will tell him of your plans. He and the queen will know what you are up to —"

It happens so quickly, I do not have time to blink. The Hyksos grabs Nebifu's finger and tugs hard, pulling the priest off balance so that he stumbles to the edge of the pit, arms flailing. Before he can get his balance back, the spy kicks Nebifu squarely in the bottom, sending him over the edge of the pit with a screech

23

that would have been comical had it not ended with a thud and yelp of pain.

We stare at the Hyksos in shock.

"I am very hungry." He smiles, showing excellent teeth. "Shall you go and find us something to eat?"

5

I AM ALONE AGAIN.

It seems unreal that it has been only a matter of hours since I left the palace after Ky's operation, at his insistence, to seek answers from Nebifu. Then, I was confused but essentially oblivious, free to come and go. Now, after learning of the queen's involvement in secreting the kingdom's treasures away from her husband, I am a threat and must be careful. My mother's scarf, still smelling faintly of smoke, is wrapped tightly around my head to hide my face, only the slits of my eyes showing. I need to move unseen, in and out of the shadows, if I do not want to be recognized. I am counting on the fact that after days of vigorous partying, everyone, guards included, will be resting before continuing with the celebrations.

Holding my breath, I approach the area where the vengeful fruit vendor and his wife attacked me on the way to the Place of Confinement. Tightly clutching the strap of the waterskin slung across my body, I squint to make out their shapes on the ground. The luck of Shai, god of fate, is with me — the vendor and his wife are no longer here.

Were it not for Paser and Reb knocking the pair out with bricks, I would most likely be dead, as payment for the outrageous crime of taking a little food to feed my brother. Newly orphaned, near starving, and unsure of whom to trust, we kept away from the eyes of the palace for a whole moon and did what was necessary to survive. Coincidentally, it was Crooked Nose who discovered us as a result of that very theft and brought us before the royals.

As it has turned out, my instincts to avoid the palace were correct, though not for the reasons I thought. It is the queen, not Pharaoh, I need to fear. We all do now. My life will be in the hands of my friends, and theirs in mine, on the journey ahead. And in the hands of the Hyksos spy. Strengthening my resolve, I reflect on past events and on our upcoming journey: I managed to keep my brother and myself alive in the city with only my wits — if we find Merat and escape to Avaris, I can do it again.

Taking the servants' route into the palace grounds, the very place I should be avoiding, I grab a basket discarded nearby and put it on my head, lowering the front so I can see just where my feet are walking. It is quiet, though not everyone is sleeping. A group of servants ahead talk among themselves as they make their way to the storehouse, which is just off the physician's chambers. Behind them I spot a familiar form and dart behind a palm, rage clouding my vision.

Crooked Nose.

Lowering the basket and hazarding a quick peek around the tree, I watch him stalk toward the storehouse, likely in search of the same thing as me. Attempting to bury children alive on the queen's orders must work up an appetite. My blood bubbles, as much for the part he played in my parents' death as for my inability to do anything about it. I bite my lower lip to keep from screaming in frustration. It will not do for my temper to get the upper hand. We need food.

With Crooked Nose prowling around the storehouses, there is no help for it — I must seek out food inside the palace. Hoisting the basket back onto my head and pulling it low again, I slink toward the outer doors to the main kitchens. Every step farther inside the premises adds to the risk. However, it is not only my rumbling stomach that has me willing to take it. It is the thought of Ky. I stop in front of the wing that houses the physician's chambers and look up.

There.

A light shines in the small high window, and my heart leaps. I am so close. Perhaps there is a way I can see my brother? Not to speak to him, no; the queen might have placed guards outside his room. But I need reassurance that she did not immediately return to the palace to exact revenge for my crimes, as she threatened to do. I make for the cluster of date palms outside the window. One in particular leans forward at a slight angle, making it easier to climb.

Without stopping to think, I dart to the slanting tree and drop my empty basket at its base, along with the empty waterskin. Moving quickly, before anyone can walk by, I hike up my dress and scuttle up the palm, rough bark scraping my hands and shins. It feels neverending, but I know only seconds pass before I reach the leafy fronds and can hide in their partial cover.

A candle burns in the room, but it is difficult to see much. I need to get closer. Now that I am here, it is impossible to refuse the temptation of saying goodbye in person. A hazardous gamble, but one I am compelled to take. It may be the last opportunity I have to speak to my brother. Besides, the queen probably still thinks we are trapped in the mastaba. Crooked Nose would not want to tell her the news of our escape on an empty stomach.

I scamper back down the palm, throw the waterskin over my shoulder, and grab the basket, placing it on my head. After adjusting the scarf, I sneak quietly inside the palace. Security is always more relaxed during festivals — even guards deserve a break during the Inundation. The halls are dark, but it will only be a short while before Ra surfaces from the underworld to light up the day.

There are sleeping bodies everywhere, and I tiptoe around snoring servants and the guests who did not make it back to their quarters. After what feels like an eternity, I reach the physician's private chambers, where I left Ky resting, and slip inside.

The room is empty.

6

ALARM SPREADS THROUGH MY BODY, flickering like the candle on the table.

Where have they taken my brother? Was I grossly mistaken in assuming the queen would not come back for him? After everything he has been through, that we have been through, it cannot end like this. Despair rises along with Ra, whose first rays penetrate the room. A sound at the door has me whirling, prepared to beg, fight, or die in the effort to discover what has happened to Ky.

A servant stands there, looking at me blankly. It is my friend Bebi. "Can I help you? If you are looking for the physician, he is tending patients on the main floor."

Heart still pounding, I unwrap the scarf from my head.

"Sesha?" Bebi blinks as if she is having a vision.

"Where is Ky?" I ask urgently, moving toward my friend. Back at the mastaba, Ahmes said he'd left my brother in her care while he and Prince Tutan came to find us.

"Kewat and I moved him to the handmaidens' quarters." She yawns. "We are taking turns tending him and he is doing well."

Relief floods my body and I grab Bebi, hugging her tight. She emits a surprised squeak.

"Thank you," I say.

"What is happening?" she asks, apparently sensing my heightened emotions. I forgot she has no idea of anything that passed at the tomb.

The light in the room grows brighter. I am running out of time. I wrap my head back up. "I am leaving Thebes."

She blinks again. "Why?"

"There is no time to explain and doing so will only put you in danger." I look around, searching for anything that might be of use on our journey. I grab a small jar of honey, some bandages, a needle, and a pair of tweezers and shove them into a satchel left here during Ky's surgery, one that once held brains in the not-too-distant past. "Please tell Ky I came back to say goodbye, and that I love him."

"I do not understand."

"Farewell, Bebi. You have been a good friend. I leave my brother in your care." With that I lean over and kiss her on the cheek, then walk out the door.

"Wait!" she follows me. "Why won't you tell me what is going on?"

"It is complicated," I whisper, glancing down the hallway, calculating. I am not sure if her presence will help or hinder my escape.

"Can I help?"

"You do enough by caring for Ky." Walking quickly, I keep my head down. I do not wish to endanger another person because of their connection to me. Bebi hurries to keep up.

"There must be something I can do," she insists, and I remember the reason I came to the palace in the first place. Food.

I stop and look at her. "Can you find me something to eat? Something that will travel well?"

"Yes," she says.

I hand her the waterskin. "See if you can fill this as well."

No one will question her. People might not question me either, but it is best not to take any more chances. Shai may be growing weary of accommodating me.

I follow her through the hallways toward the kitchen. She slips inside and returns moments later with a fresh loaf of bread, some dried fruit, cheese, and dates, which I add to the satchel. The waterskin is heavy, and she helps me adjust the strap so it rests against my left hip, the satchel on my right.

There is a rumble of voices down the hallway. Soldiers.

"I must go now," I say, keeping my voice and my head down. "Many thanks to you, my friend."

"Stay safe, Sesha. May the gods be with you." I hear a loud bark of laughter and I hunch my shoulders up higher. Soldiers stumble in, looking for food. A discreet look assures me that Crooked Nose is not among them, but it is time I am on my way.

"Take care, Bebi," I whisper, turning to leave. Then I remember something. Unclasping the scarab necklace, I take it from around my neck and fasten the protective amulet around hers. "Please give this to Ky."

"I will," she says. And because I have already said goodbye more times than I can bear, I turn and walk out into the first light of morning.

7

I MEET UP WITH THE OTHERS on the bank of the Nile, close to where some of the fishermen's boats are tied, bobbing on the dark waters.

"Were you able to find food and drink?" Reb asks eagerly.

"Yes," I say, holding up the bag and full waterskin. The Hyksos holds his hands out for the liquid, swallowing hard.

"Wait," Paser says as I move to pass him the barley drink. "Sesha, give me your scarf." Confused, I place the satchel and waterskin on the ground before unwrapping the scarf from around my head and passing it to him. "Hold out your hands," he says to the spy, who gives him a wry look of acknowledgement. "I am sorry, but we cannot take any chances." Desperate for a drink, the Hyksos reluctantly does as he asks, and Paser binds the spy's wrists together in front of him.

I split the bread into four equal portions, noticing my own hands are shaking a little. *Well, it is no wonder after the night you've had*, a familiar voice chides gently.

A wave of relief sweeps over my body, like the sand across the dunes. My mother is still with me. Even after I defiled — as Reb called it — my parents' tomb and abandoned my brother, though I do so to go after our friend.

Now that the ancient scroll my father was transcribing has been found — though it and the copy we made lie with Pharaoh and the queen — and Ky's life-saving operation is done, Father's spirit must feel he can rest for a bit. My mother's, however, seems to be taking issue with her eldest child wandering off in the company of a stranger whose only established quality is a talent for treachery.

I suppose we are no slugs in that area, either, I think, glancing at the Hyksos's tied hands while distributing the food to the boys. Paser lifts the waterskin to the spy's mouth and the Hyksos drinks deeply. He then offers him some food, which the spy is able to bring awkwardly to his mouth despite his bound wrists. I feel a pinch of guilt as the spy clumsily pops a date into his mouth, not bothering to chew before swallowing it whole, but Paser is smart to be cautious.

"Is the plan still to travel by boat?" Reb asks, mouth full.

"We should go as far as we can by the river," the Hyksos says. "It will not be long before they discover I am gone — which will be as soon as the morning duty guard comes by to pelt me with scraps. Or to urinate in my pit." He cups his palms for another date and Paser obliges. The eye-watering scent of ammonia wafting from his thin frame suggests the guard relieving himself happened more often than the tossed scraps. I swallow. By the end of the journey my bones will likely be as prominent as his.

No matter. One can survive for some time without food, as evidenced by our new companion. Our bigger problem will be finding fresh water. We will survive only days without it. Less, in direct sunlight. We pass around the waterskin again. It will not last long with the four of us sharing. The plan to stay on the Nile is a sound one, not only for a swift escape, but for access to water, which is not as safe to drink as beer, but something at least. Away from the river, things get very dry, very fast. Not far from the Nile's banks lies the Red Land, Deshret, endless unforgiving desert.

"I wonder how far we will get before we are caught," Reb says. He swallows a piece of cheese as Paser passes him the waterskin.

"Look on the bright side of the pyramid, my friend." Paser grins.

"Which is?" Reb takes a drink, then wipes his mouth with the back of his hand before passing the waterskin to me next. Bebi filled it to the brim with the barley drink, which tastes delicious as it slides down my parched throat. I put it to the Hyksos's mouth, who drinks thirstily, then give it back to Paser.

"What comes next will be an adventure. We scribes are the ones who record the great stories on temple walls. But this time, *we* will be the ones to live it first-hand." Paser claps Reb on the back, shoulders the waterskin, and stands tall. It is easy to see the training his grandfather, a respected soldier of the previous pharaoh's army, instilled in him. Erect posture and a strong build are not qualities scribes are known for, making Paser's bearing stand out even more. These attributes will serve him well in his new career as traitor and fleer from the queen's army, as we all are now.

No, my mother corrects me. *Not traitors. Survivors.*

"Which one are we taking?" I whisper, looking down at the boats. They range in size, many of them simple but well made.

"That one." Reb nods at a large wooden craft that looks recently built.

"No." The Hyksos shakes his head. "The sail is down." He points to a beaten skiff with a small sail and two sets of oars; its ends curve up out of the water. "We will take that one."

"At least the current will be on our side." Paser strides over to the boat, followed by the Hyksos, who seems much improved after having something to eat and drink. He is resilient, I will give him that. "One advantage of travelling north."

"The only one," Reb mutters.

"That, and we will see the princess soon," I say, giving him a gentle nudge toward the craft that we mean to … borrow. The sun is almost fully up, roaring like fire in the sky, red-orange streaks slicing through gold.

It is beautiful.

Despite the urgent need to depart, we take a few moments, holding our hands up to the warmth, acknowledging and praising the deity that delivers us from darkness each day.

The spy, too, drops to his knees, staring up in reverence at Ra in his glory — though I doubt that is what the Hyksos people call him. I suppose a sun by any other name is just as warm.

"I never thought I would see it again," he says, voice soft. "Thank you for my life."

I look at Paser, unsure if the Hyksos's sincerity is a trick. Paser shrugs one articulate shoulder to indicate that, sincere or not, we are in this together, for now.

Paser climbs into the boat, followed by Reb and the Hyksos, who doesn't seem to need his hands to balance. I step onto the rickety craft after him. Paser uses Ahmes's knife to saw at the knotted rope, which would take an eternity to untie. I join in with my father's obsidian blade. Every fisherman has his own secret combination of knots to deter thieves, but it is nothing crystallized volcanic glass cannot handle. Luckily for fishermen, this rare item is not normally in the general public's possession.

"And we are sure this boat is sound?" Reb eyes the rickety wooden planks held together by worn ropes.

There is an angry shout in the distance. "It will have to be," the Hyksos says, looking over his shoulder, "as the owner is on his way to express his disapproval over its abduction."

We look up to see an agitated form running toward us, shouting and calling for help. Unfortunately, his loud cries attract some attention and three figures run up over a small hill in the distance.

Soldiers.

8

"HURRY!" I URGE PASER, who gives the rope a final saw with the blade. It breaks at last. I sit on a wooden board behind the Hyksos and grab the oar on my left; Reb is beside me, grabbing the one on his right. Paser gives the craft a hard push off the dock and plunks down in front of Reb, reaching over the Hyksos to take an oar in each hand.

We pull away just in time. The man reaches the dock and shouts for the soldiers who are coming to see what all the commotion is about.

"Thieves!" the man shouts, shaking his fist at us.

"Apologies," I shout back over my shoulder, paddling even harder.

"If you untie me, I can help row," the Hyksos offers.

We ignore him, paddling in earnest away from the infuriated man, who is now yelling at the soldiers to do something about his stolen boat. I see one of them hold a hand up to his eyes and squint into the sun, as if to memorize our faces, taking in the Hyksos's bound hands. It will not be long before they put things together and realize who we are and what we are doing. Meaning it will not be long before more soldiers are after us.

As we row frantically downriver, I notice the water is much lower than usual. On the banks beside us, I can see the stark line where dark grey sediment meets light grey, marking the ideal level for this time of year. Last night's rains were nowhere near enough to reduce the threat of famine.

The river is mostly quiet as we move, the normal traffic lessened by the celebrations. Only after an hour of exhausting effort do I somewhat relax. By then my arms are burning and my clothes are soaked with sweat, as if I've jumped into the river.

"I need a few minutes," I say finally, ashamed of my weakness.

"Thank Ra," Reb groans, arms flopping to his sides. Paser, too, pauses, catching his breath, and we let the boat drift on its own accord. "I cannot feel my arms."

"You will feel them tomorrow." The Hyksos gives us a grin that is surprisingly full of good cheer for someone who's bound as a hostage and smells strongly of urine.

Paser shields his eyes from the morning sun as we approach a bend in the river. "There is a boat ahead," he says. "A big one."

"It looks like a cargo ship, probably coming with more supplies for the festival," I say, scanning the river. "We have nothing to worry about. Word cannot have spread that quickly."

Resuming our paddling, we keep our heads down as the cargo boat approaches. It is much larger than ours. As it passes, our little craft bobs in its wake.

"Greetings, Sewedt!" a voice shouts. "How are the fish biting this morning? I see you have some friends with you."

We freeze mid-stroke. I lower my head, gazing at the bottom of the boat. Paser raises a hand in friendly greeting, and I can almost feel the crew member of the cargo ship squinting his eyes.

Another shout: "You there! Where is Sewedt?"

"You mean my brother?" the Hyksos shouts back, keeping his bound hands between his knees. "He is enjoying himself, letting us collect his catch to repay him for his hospitality while we visit for the festival."

Paser, Reb, and I exchange looks. I hope the sailor does not know the fisherman well.

"Sewedt has no brother!"

The Hyksos shrugs. "It was worth an attempt."

"Thieves!"

We begin paddling again, freshly motivated in our efforts.

Thunk.

A large arrow sticks up from the bottom of the boat, its stem quivering like my exhausted arms. We gape at it in shock.

"Untie me!" the Hyksos shouts, holding his wrists out, breaking the spell. "Untie me now!" Paser hesitates for half a second, looking at me. I give a quick nod and he grabs Ahmes's thin blade, lying beside him. A few forceful saws at the linen frees the spy, just as another arrow hits the deck.

"Jump!" I shout and the four of us dive overboard.

The water is cool and refreshing after our frenzied paddling. And whatever else happens, I am thankful Paser cut the Hyksos's bindings.

I kick to the surface and gulp down a deep breath of air, blinking water from my eyes. Spinning in circles, I frantically look around for the others.

There.

Paser and the Hyksos are off to my right, the big boat sailing on placidly behind them. Despite the outrage of Sewedt's sailor friend, a cargo ship destined for the palace will not stop for a fisherman's nicked craft. But Reb still has not surfaced. I shout his name. Paser and the Hyksos both dive under the bluish-green water. I also sink down, my arms pushing water upward as I let my body be heavy. Keeping my eyes open, I try to see something, anything, that looks like Reb.

Nothing. I come back up, but I do not see Paser or the spy. I let myself sink back under. Many Thebans can swim, but, of course, there are exceptions.

No. Reb *can* swim. I recall the beer-vat incident on my first day at temple. Is there any way an arrow could have found its mark before we dived into the water? I need air, so I surface again, scared of what I might see — or worse, what I might not see.

Thank Ra.

The spy has Reb. Paser surfaces as well and splashes over to the pair. Reb appears dazed, but whole. There is a lump on his head I can make out from here.

"Can you make it?" I shout. Reb nods. The Hyksos releases him and they swim over to the boat, which fortunately did not capsize when we jumped off. I climb aboard first and lean over the edge to help hoist Reb over. Paser and the spy push him up from below.

We collapse on the floor of the boat, panting from our exertions. Lying on my back, I look over at Reb. "Are you well?" I ask. He is pale, and the lump is an angry purple welt, knotting up like the fisherman's rope.

"Yes ... I hit my head on one of the oars ... when I jumped," he says, gasping for air. Paser and the Hyksos clamber over the edge of the boat and join Reb and me in coughing up enough of the Nile to fill a *shaduf* bucket.

"You saved me," Reb sputters to the Hyksos. "My blessings to you."

"It is I who am blessed," the Hyksos says, still coughing. "Without you three, I would have been tortured and killed. I spent hours in that hole fearing I might never again see my people. But you have given me back my hope. As long as I am alive, I will be reunited with them." He grins, water running off him in rivulets. "I also appreciate the bath."

Reb snorts, and a giant glob of mucous lands on the deck. Laughter intersperses the coughing as we try to get our breath back. Hope. What a thing to carry around with you. If a Hyksos spy can feel hope among his enemies, then I, too, can hold on to the hope we will find Merat and I will one day see my brother again. Overwhelmed with gratitude at being alive and intact on the fishy-smelling, snot-covered boards of a boat, I turn to the spy once in control of myself. "You have our thanks, uh ..." I stop, realizing we do not even know his name.

"You may call me Pepi," the Hyksos says, rapping his chest twice over his heart.

I nod. "Thank you ... Pepi." Speaking his name, it is the first time I think of him as something other than a spy. He is a person, with a family, like me.

"If we are to travel together, we must be able to trust each other," Pepi says, pushing the dark hair out of his now serious eyes. "Or we will be dead within a day or two."

I nod again, though Paser and Reb exchange a wary look as they resume their positions at the oars, Paser sliding Ahmes's knife through his belt. My eyes fall on the scraps of linen that were once my mother's scarf, now lying tattered and wet, stained with dirt. I pick up the sorry remains of the garment and put them in my satchel. Nothing should go unused.

The sun rises higher and higher. Its reflection bounces off the water's rippling surface as we paddle the great river in the company of a Hyksos spy, unsure of our final destination or if we will indeed reach it, knowing only that we go to save our friend.

9

BY MIDDAY IT IS TOO HOT TO PADDLE. We pull over to the bank for a rest, making our way carefully through the reeds. After a hasty look around for any dangers hiding in the tall grasses, we pull the small boat onto shore. I am exhausted and need to rest, having not slept since ... I cannot remember. The night before the festival and Ky's surgery? I flop down under some of the trees, eyelids heavy.

Paser walks over to me, looking just as tired. "Rest, Sesha. Reb and I will watch the Hyksos, to make sure he does not escape."

"We should take turns," I mumble.

"We will. But there should always be two of us, should he decide to run. We have nothing to bind his hands with, nor do I think I could do so after he saved Reb in the river."

"He did swear on his family he would guide us north," I say, eyes closing despite my efforts to keep them open. Paser says something in a low voice but I do not catch it, falling asleep before he finishes his sentence.

I wake groggy. Hungry, thirsty. Sensations I have not felt with such intensity since our month on the streets, when my brother and I had to scrounge for food and drink. The other three are asleep under the shade of a few scraggly palms. Paser and Reb must have nodded off after the spy did. I stand up and look around, but all is quiet. Walking to the boat, I grab my satchel, which I stashed under an oar. There are a few shrivelled raisins and I savour my share, longing to shove them all in my mouth, but saving some for the others.

The sun is slowly sinking as Ra begins his descent to the underworld. We have slept away most of the afternoon, our worn bodies soaking up sleep like the land soaks up the quick rains. I scan the horizon, looking for clouds, but the skies are clear. The too-brief shower the night before has been the only rain in weeks. Isis's tears seem to have dried up. Another sensation I am familiar with.

The ground crunches softly behind me as the spy makes his way down to the water. He scoops his hands into the river and greedily takes a drink.

"Careful." I eye him warily, wondering if I should wake the boys. "The river can make you sick." Walking over to the trees, I pick up the waterskin resting beside Paser's slumbering form. Taking my chances, I decide to let him and Reb sleep, and I carry the skin back down to the riverbank. I hand it to Pepi, who nods his thanks and drinks thirstily. Having been held in the pits for the last week with little to eat or drink, his body needs it more than ours.

Pepi lowers the skin, looking at me. "You are very kind."

I look down, uncomfortable with his compliment. "My mother taught me to be so."

He hands me back the waterskin. "Even to an enemy?"

"We are allies, for now," I say before taking a sip.

"For now," he agrees as I offer him another drink. "So, tell me, who is this friend we chase after? She must mean something to you all, to risk your lives."

"It is the princess," I say, gauging his reaction.

The hand bringing the waterskin to his mouth stops in mid-air. "Princess Merat?"

"She was given by Pharaoh and the queen to one of your chieftains against her will," I say as he takes a drink. He passes the waterskin back to me.

"How are the princess's marriage arrangements the concern of three young scribes?"

I blink. "How do you know we are scribes?"

He nods at my fingers, calloused from my frantic transcription of the scroll. "Your hands." He glances at Paser. "Your companion confirmed it himself when he spoke of writing stories on walls and having adventures."

The spy misses little. "Princess Merat is our treasured friend," I say simply.

"What will you do when you find her?"

"I do not know," I admit, putting the stopper back in the waterskin. "Perhaps the Hyksos can be persuaded to release her?" I am careful not to mention our plan to flee with her to Avaris if they do not.

If only we had something of value to offer in her stead. The scroll would come in handy now. The information it contains is extremely powerful; it saved my brother's life and can save countless others. My fingers clench, remembering the feel of the reed as I completed my father's transcription. Despite my strong attachment to the document, I would give it up in an instant for Merat. But the papyrus lies with the queen now. She snatched my father's and my copy of the surgical manual out of my hands, back at the tomb. Pharaoh still holds the original, the one I found for him, written over a thousand years ago by Imhotep, Egypt's great physician and brilliant architect of the first pyramids. Dealing with trauma often seen in battle, particularly to the head and the spine, it would be critical for the success of any military campaign, where lives are at stake. Which, according to Pharaoh and his Grand Vizier, Wujat, may be something the Hyksos are considering, betrothed princess aside.

"Say you find the princess," Pepi says again, interrupting my thoughts. "Would you not go back to Thebes?"

I hesitate. I told Ahmes to tell my brother I would be back for him, yet I cannot think how to accomplish this without risking death.

"We cannot return for some time," I say, then swallow. "According to the queen, we are a threat to *Ma'at*" — universal balance — "to her, and the kingdom. Even now, her soldiers will be after us."

"How did you betray her?" Pepi's voice is curious, soft.

"Only by learning the truth." Feeling restless at the thought of pursuit, I stand and walk closer to the water's edge, plucking a few green shoots to gnaw on. I think about the fact that she prefers to secrete her family's riches away, rather than use them to help her people. That science — a threat to the priests and her family's status as gods — and magic are merely different facets of the same jewel. "Having freed you does not help our situation." I look out at the water, imagining a boat full of Queen Anat's soldiers, Crooked Nose at its helm. "It is complicated."

"Things often are," Pepi says, coming to stand beside me. "And yet, sometimes they are in fact quite simple. In betraying your queen, were you acting on your own good conscience?"

"Yes." Queen Anat considers the act of preserving the scroll to be a form of disobedience because it threatens her family's omniscient power. To her, parcelling out her precious heirlooms, whether to the Hyksos as grudging tribute or to the Nubians in exchange for supplies, is unthinkable. What did she say? *Famines come and go — it is an unfortunate, yet handy, way to rid the land of … excess. My family will be just fine.* Maybe I did not think much about it before my time on the streets, but people should not starve simply because of the circumstances of their birth. Nor because of anything that befalls them along their way. Tragedy can strike anyone, at any time. Ky and I met others like us, doing whatever they needed to survive.

"I know what it is like, how acting on your conscience can bring you into conflict with higher powers," Pepi says. I am about to inquire further, but he comes back to the matter at hand. "So, we are off to find the princess," he muses, without any sign of judgment.

Yet the more we speak of it, the more laughable it seems that three young scribes, as Pepi so accurately put it, can extract the pharaoh's daughter from a fierce warrior tribe. Our course of action was not carefully planned; it was forced on us by the queen and circumstance. There was no time to fully consider it, or the consequences. And so here we are.

"Yes." I clear my throat. "We think Merat might like some company."

He laughs, startling me. His face changes, making him look much younger. Almost my age. "You are loyal friends."

"We are." Paser stands a few paces behind us, body taut. Reb still sits under the palm, yawning and stretching. "Can we be assured of your loyalty, *friend*?"

"I gave you my word." Pepi's voice is as cool as the wind that has picked up. He looks out at the sky; it grows a dusky blue. "It will not be long before the stars are out. And the creatures who hunt along the Nile will wake for their dinners." He nods at the boat. "We should be on our way."

Paser looks over his shoulder. Maybe thinking of aggressive hippos. My own eyes go to the thick reeds, looking for any telltale swish.

"Let us leave, then," says Reb, who walks over to us. His stomach growls like a lion. "But first I must eat." I pick up the satchel and pass him his share of squashed raisins. "Sesha, you are funny. Where is the rest?"

"That is all we have left."

His stomach lets out another grumble of protest at my admission. It occurs to me that although Reb has had to deal with many things, being nephew to Nebifu, he has never had to deal with hunger. There is always food in the temple, the priests and their families often sampling the offerings. And while junior scribes do not eat so well as the higher officials, they do not go without, either. It is surely an unfamiliar feeling for Paser as well.

The Hyksos is already on the boat, picking up a papyrus net. "Perhaps you can catch us some fish for our dinner?" He spreads the net wide, hands apart, the two ends pinched in his fingers.

We walk into the water to get into the boat, the Nile lapping at our legs. Reb grumbling along with his stomach, Paser behind me with the satchel, the pair passing the waterskin back and forth. Something tells me my friends will soon become closely acquainted with the sensation of hunger — real hunger. Though not a comfortable feeling, it is good motivation for survival.

I T IS NIGHT — NOT A SAFE TIME to be travelling along a river, when the chances of crashing into another boat are highest. But the light of the heavens above is dazzling, providing a few cubits of visible distance ahead. I pray there is no one else as desperate or as foolish as us, also moving at night, whether up ahead or close behind.

The Hyksos nods at the stars, digging his oar deep into the water. "We will follow them."

"Follow them where?" Reb says. "Can we not just take the river?"

Pepi looks over his shoulder at us. "I thought you wished to find the princess."

"We do," I say. "We believe the chieftain has taken her north."

"Tell me, what did this chieftain look like?" Pepi says.

I picture the enormous man storming from the festival, outraged at Merat's rejection of him in front of the court. "He was as large as the rhino whose horn he wore around his neck, with fierce weapons at his belt. His dark hair was thick and unruly, and he had a most impressive beard." Something not seen on average Thebans, who are fastidious about removing unwanted body hair.

"As I thought," Pepi says, satisfaction in his voice. "We will not go much farther by river. We are too visible, and she will not take us where we want to go."

"And where is that, exactly?" Paser asks.

"Into the desert."

"I think there is still water in my ears." Reb shakes his head vigorously and smacks his ear with an open palm. "I thought you said 'the desert.'"

"I did," Pepi says, calmly paddling.

"Why in the name of Osiris would we do that?" Reb asks, scowling. He has not been successful in netting any fish; the growls erupting from his stomach are likely scaring them away. He becomes more irritable with each stroke.

"That is where the main Hyksos camp lies. The chieftain you speak of is its leader."

"In the desert?" Paser looks over at Pepi beside him.

It sounds like he, too, thinks there is water in his ears.

"There is a hidden oasis there," Pepi says, tilting his head up to examine the stars. "That is where your friend is."

"How do you know this?" Paser demands.

The spy gives him a pointed look. "It is my business to know these things."

"Have you been to this oasis before?" Reb asks.

"Yes." Pepi does not elaborate.

I look up at the lights in the sky. They stretch as far as I can see, their shapes and patterns familiar, and though I know them well, I did not study them as closely as those who specialize in reading the heavens. My focus has been on the things below: the scripts or the patient in front of me.

"If this oasis is hidden, how will we find it?" I ask Pepi, uncertain. *And once we find Merat, how will we escape it again?*

"They will guide us." He nods toward the sky. "And my spirit knows the way."

"Does it also know we are sinking?" Reb inquires, looking at the bottom of the boat. It is rapidly taking on water.

I look around for something to scoop up the water with, but there is nothing. I grab the waterskin. "Hurry, drink as much as you can." I take a healthy swig myself and pass it around to the others. We finish it in seconds, and I kneel on the bladder, squeezing the air out, then release the pressure to let it suck up the water pooling at our feet. It does not work as well as we need it to.

Paser, Reb, and Pepi begin to row furiously for land. We are in a wide section of the river, the bank a way off. I do not feel like another swim today. Especially one in the dark, where it will be difficult to see where we are going.

The waterskin idea is as useless as an ox without legs.

"Find the leak, Sesha!" Paser shouts.

I drop the skin and swish my hands around the bottom of the boat. The water is getting deeper.

"I cannot!" I shout back in frustration.

"Harder," Pepi urges Reb and Paser to row, while I frantically search for the source of the inflow.

The water is now up past our ankles and shows no signs of slowing. Where is it coming from? And so quickly, from nothing?

"One of the bindings below must have snapped," Pepi shouts, paddling without looking back at us.

"Hurry," I say, eyes seeking out the shoreline, hands scraping along the bottom of the boat, trying to find the leak. It feels like we are going nowhere.

"There!" I shout and point at the shadow of a large patch of reeds ahead. In an instant, something gives way below and water starts bubbling up, like someone releasing wind into the bath basin.

"Faster!" Pepi shouts.

They paddle hard. The reeds do not seem to be getting any closer. The boat is now listing to one side, unsteady and wobbly. The edge is only a cubit above the river.

"Jump!" Paser shouts.

"Watch your head," Pepi warns Reb before jumping.

Reb shoots him a dark look, though he glances around carefully before he dives in.

The waterskin floats past Paser in the boat. He grabs it and jumps. Kneeling, I frantically search for the stowed satchel. My hand clamps over the strap. Standing, I throw it over my shoulder. Then I jump after the others, swimming in the direction of the reeds.

"This feels familiar," Reb calls, just up the river to my left.

I turn to swim on my back, watching our little craft sink under the dark water. We can add destruction of property to our list of sins. For scribes trained to record and uphold the laws of the kingdom, we seem quite good at breaking them.

As the reeds draw nearer, I long to put my feet on solid ground. The satchel is heavy and cumbersome. It weighs me down and I cannot swim as freely as I'd like.

"Almost there," Paser shouts over his shoulder. He is the strongest swimmer and has pulled ahead of Reb and Pepi, the waterskin bobbing on the surface behind him. The three of them reach the first of the reeds, and then I am also there. The reeds are spaced out in clumps at first but soon grow thicker. We stop before we become too entangled, treading water.

"Here." Paser hands Reb the waterskin, then lets out a huge breath and sinks down, arms up over his head as he tries to touch bottom. The patch of reeds is enormous. Paser breaks the surface and shakes his head. No bottom.

"We need to go around," Pepi says.

"Which way?" Reb asks, head swivelling in the almost dark.

"This way," Pepi says decisively, swimming to his right.

"Land is closer if we go directly through," Reb argues.

"So are the crocodiles," Pepi says.

"The most dangerous ones swim in the middle of the Nile," Reb says, treading water, looping the strap of the waterskin around his arm. "The smaller ones who prefer the reeds are not as bothersome."

Pepi does not look convinced. Pharaohs often keep the smaller crocodiles as pets, and they do seem mostly harmless despite being representatives of Sobek, the mighty crocodile god.

"I am going through," Reb decides. He begins making his way to the thick of the reeds. Paser follows Reb and I swim after them. I must go with my friends.

Pepi sighs and shakes his head, but follows us as we move slowly through the reeds, pushing them aside in an attempt to make our way to land. It is darker in the patch and we do not move with agility. There is a big splash, far off to the left.

"Go," Paser says, voice low. But it is impossible to move quickly through the tangled mass of grasses.

"This way," Reb calls, nodding toward a small opening directly to the right that allows for more freedom of movement. The reeds seem to be thinning.

"Bottom," Reb cries, just as my own foot strikes rocks.

There is a shout. I turn to see the top of a croc's domed head sticking up from the water, the only part visible besides its yellow eyes. It is about three arm lengths away from Pepi.

Paser, Reb, and I scramble up onto the bank.

"Swim!" I shout at Pepi. I pray to Sobek that the animal is only investigating the creatures swimming though its territory and is not hungry — crocodiles can go ten full moons without eating.

The croc trails behind Pepi, who's almost reached us. It opens its mouth and yawns, showing lethal teeth.

We scurry farther up the bank, screaming at Pepi to swim. While faster in the water, a crocodile loses its advantage on land. If only Pepi can make it to shore. He is almost to us. Suddenly, the creature disappears under the water. Pepi reaches ground, finds his footing, and turns, bringing his arms high over his head. The crocodile sticks its snout out of the water and Pepi's fists come together, slamming down on the croc's nose while our jaws hang open, wider than any crocodile's.

11

PEPI RACES THE REST OF THE WAY out of the water, and the stunned croc swims away as if offended by the assault; it had only been trying to investigate the disturbance in its domain. We sink to the ground, breathing hard.

"Are you all right?" I ask Pepi, barely believing what just happened. It's a good thing the crocodile was only curious.

"I am fine." But when he holds up one of his hands I see a deep gash bleeding profusely. "Just a small cut," he says.

"Come," I say, digging around in the soggy satchel at my side. "This is an ailment that I will treat."

I pull a thread from one of the linen scraps and wet one end with my mouth, then insert it through the eye of the needle, the approaching dawn aiding my vision.

"You may want to look away," I advise Pepi, but he does not. He watches without flinching as I stitch up the cut.

"Where did you learn to sew such a fine line?" Pepi does not take his eyes off the needle. "From the mother who taught you to be kind to your enemies, perhaps?"

"No. From my father." I allow myself a brief smile. "He was royal physician to the pharaoh and his family, the best healer in the land," I say proudly, knotting the last stitch. I bite the thread to sever it.

Pepi inhales sharply and I look up at him. "Are you well?"

"Just a little pinch," he says, looking a bit pale. Odd — the stitching hadn't bothered him.

Taking the jar of honey I found in Ahmes's chambers, I remove the wax seal and spread the sweet substance over the wound while murmuring a brief incantation. Using another of the wet linen scraps, I bind Pepi's hand. My patient taken care of, I fish around in the satchel for the tweezers to address the splinters in my own hand, courtesy of the bottom of the boat.

Paser, seeing what I am about, walks over and reaches for the tiny instrument. Reluctantly, I surrender it and hold my left hand out. He begins to extract some of the larger pieces of wood in my palm, bending his head over my hand. I prefer not to view the proceedings and look up at the lightening sky. Watching people pull slivers from one's body is only slightly worse than not watching. Father asked his patients to look away, as I did with Pepi. Unlike the spy, I take my father's advice.

"Will we find another boat?" Reb asks.

I hiss, not at his suggestion, but at Paser's most recent extraction. It feels like fire coming out.

"No," Pepi says. "We are close to a village with a small market. We can make our way there and get what we need for our journey."

"What will we barter with?" I ask to further distract myself. Paser takes my other hand in his, beginning his efforts anew.

"What do you have?" Pepi says, eyeing the satchel.

My free hand automatically goes to my neck for my father's scarab amulet. But I'd left it with Bebi to give to Ky. Though it would come in handy, I am relieved the necklace is safe with my brother. I pray it protects him better than it did my father. More than done with the splinter removal, I wave Paser off and pick up the bag. As I stick my hand in, my body gives a small, involuntary shudder, remembering a time when I touched brains, a cruel joke by another scribe.

"The silver is gone," I say, digging around.

"It is probably at the bottom of the Nile," Reb says.

"Along with Ahmes's blade," Paser adds with regret.

I take everything out, upend the satchel, and give it a vigorous shake. The precious stones from my mother's bracelet fall to the ground. I drop to my knees and pick them up, relieved and amazed they were not also lost during our swim. The fiery orange and stunning green-blue stones sparkle in the early morning light. They are valuable, not only in terms of what they can buy, but because they were my mother's. The only physical pieces I have left from her.

"Perhaps someone will barter with us for these," I say past the lump in my throat, holding them out. I do not know why I feel so sad. This is why I took them in the first place: they are small and easy to travel with and can be used as payment.

"Those will do well." Pepi walks over and holds his injured hand out. "May I see them?" He seems to sense my reluctance. "I know what we need. I will buy the items. One is less memorable than four, especially as our escape will have been noticed by now."

Paser, Reb, and I exchange glances. He means that soldiers are definitely in pursuit.

Paser crosses his arms over his broad chest. "How do we know you will not leave us once you have what you need to flee?"

"I said we must trust one another," Pepi reminds him. "I saved your friend's life in the river. I also listened to him and followed you all through the reeds, which could have ended worse than this." He holds up his bandaged hand. "I did this as a show of faith, despite knowing the suggestion was most stupid."

"Paser will go with you," I say, wondering if we are wasting precious time by arguing. I can tell Pepi is growing impatient, but he gives a curt nod.

"As you wish."

I place the gemstones in Paser's palm. "Get a fair exchange."

"I will do my best," he promises. He picks up the waterskin and walks toward the water's edge to fill it.

"And what are Sesha and I to do while you barter?" Reb calls to Paser.

"You can look for some edible herbs and plants," Pepi suggests. "Every bit of food for our journey helps."

Reb does not look pleased at this suggestion. "I have to pick flowers while he gets to engage in trade?"

Paser stands up with the container, ignoring him. He is overly familiar with Reb's complaints. "Are we ready to go?"

"Yes," I say.

Reb lets out a sigh to rival the desert winds.

Paser looks at Pepi. "Lead the way, friend."

We follow behind Pepi, the sky growing brighter with each passing step.

"Check if they have sandals to spare," Reb says after several minutes. "My feet are not as calloused as Sesha's."

I frown. "I was not aware of your fascination with my feet, Reb."

He grins. "One can't help but notice their bottoms are like the hide of our friend crocodile."

"We cannot all be as delicate a blossom as you," I say archly. "A moon on the streets of Thebes fighting for your life will toughen anyone's soles." Among other things.

Reb falls silent. The boys know little of my time after the fire, before arriving at the palace. I do not really like to speak of it.

"You could rub some almond oil on them to make them smoother," Paser suggests. "If we find some."

I roll my eyes to the heavens. "Thank you both, but my feet are not my primary concern at the moment." They would come last on a list, were papyrus not so precious, after water, food, finding Merat, Ky's safety — I look at Pepi's back in front of me — a trustworthy guide. "Do you think you can fill that waterskin with something cleaner than river water?" I ask him.

"We will do our best," Pepi says. "But there are never any guarantees about what will be on offer."

"Sesha's gems should be enough to pay for more than we can carry," Reb says, smacking his lips together. "I cannot wait to fill my belly."

"Remember," Pepi says over his shoulder, "you and Sesha need to stay away. People remember new faces, especially young ones. Paser and I will be quick."

"Will they not ask you questions?" Reb asks.

"They will," Pepi says, looking straight ahead. "Which is why we will have a story ready."

"What kind of story?" Paser asks, walking past me to catch up to Pepi, who looks back over his shoulder with a brief smile.

"You tell me. You are the scribes."

12

REB AND I MOVE THROUGH TALL GRASSES behind the collection of buildings. The village is small, just a few dwellings. The market will be even smaller, *if* there is anything for sale. Pharaoh said he's depleted much of the available resources. There has been frequent famine in the past hundred years. Things were better for a short time, but now it seems they are turning worse again.

"Do you think they will have any fruit?" Reb says with longing. At the temple the scribes would just be starting their midday meal.

An odd grumbling sound greets my ears.

"Calm your stomach. They will be back soon enough. Here." I cast my eye around and pick a few shoots off the ground. "These are edible." Spotting a small trail, I follow it for a few steps, then stop abruptly.

"That wasn't my stomach," Reb calls from behind.

A large donkey stands in front of me, chewing placidly at the grasses around him. Or her. I am not intimately familiar with the creatures.

Reb walks over to me, admiring the beast. "At last, some good fortune!"

"You want to take it?" I say, surprised. "It likely belongs to the people here."

"That hasn't stopped us so far," Reb points out. "Besides, the people here are traitors."

"What do you mean?"

"They must know who Pepi is."

"He is a messenger, with news of Princess Merat's engagement." That's the story we decided on. By the time the real messenger arrives with word, we will be far into the desert. And, by the gods' good graces, still alive.

"I am certain they know he is a spy." Reb eyes the donkey, who takes no real notice of us. "They could even be in league with the Hyksos. He is probably selling us, along with the gemstones, as we speak."

"That may be a bit of a jump," I say. "Besides, Paser is with him. And Pepi wants to get back to his people."

"Does he?" Reb turns to look at me. He is not as tall as Paser but still taller than I am. His eyes glitter darkly, like the Nile at night. "We know nothing about him. Surely the chieftain who came for Merat would know that one of his own was being held in the pits. You'd think he would try to free a member of his tribe." Reb walks slowly up to the donkey. "If this is the mark of the loyalty the Hyksos show each other, then we'd best be wary." He puts his hand out cautiously, touching the donkey's coarse brown hide. The sturdy beast's long ears tilt back, flickering as Reb strokes it slowly. "I am thinking we should liberate this magnificent animal."

"It is not tied," I point out.

"Then it is not stealing if it chooses to come with us," Reb reasons. "I might not take from my ancestors' tombs, but this is another matter."

I cross my arms. "And how are you going to charm it into coming with us? A complimentary look at his teeth?"

"Maybe you are not the only one who can enchant an animal," Reb says, clicking his tongue at the donkey.

"If you're referring to the snake, I did not enchant it." I puff at a piece of hair that sticks to my cheek. It is very hot today. "It thought I was an enemy and was mimicking my movements."

"How is that not enchantment?"

Suddenly, I hear voices. I duck in the bush, pulling Reb down with me. We do not want to be seen.

Especially if Reb has his way and this donkey is about to go missing.

"… around here somewhere …" a voice says.

We scramble farther back into the scrub, but it is no use. We will be caught if the owner of the voice comes any closer.

"There you are, you demon," says another voice, this one sounding overjoyed. Pepi comes into view. He stops when he sees Reb and me and turns quickly, blocking the man behind him from seeing us. "Friend," he says to the man, "I have assured myself of my animal's good health. Thank you for caring for her while I was away. Let us go and find some beer and food." Pepi puts an arm around the older man's shoulder, guiding him back in the direction of the village.

"There is not much," the man mumbles. "Everything we have went to the palace." They walk off, leaving Reb and me with the donkey, who brays loudly at her master's desertion.

"Looks like you got your wish, Reb," I say. "We seem to have acquired another travel companion."

We leave the town, walking not far from the Nile's banks. Pepi and Paser managed to fill the waterskin with barley mash and find a few small loaves of stale bread. They begged two small melons and some wilted cabbage, which we have added to the onion shoots Reb and I collected. They also found several linens in varying lengths and sizes, thin papyrus belts, and, most wondrously, four sets of sandals. The village boasts an esteemed sandal maker and son in residence, which means there is always an extra pair or two around — maybe not in perfect condition, but serviceable enough. Our steps make a rhythmic slapping sound of foot against papyrus. *Pfflip. Pfflop. Pfflip. Pfflop.*

"We will need to conserve what we have," Pepi says, walking beside the donkey, whom he calls Nefer. The name means "beautiful," an attribute I would not personally ascribe to the donkey, though it is said that beauty is a most subjective quality.

"Sesha." Paser holds his hand out. "We did not need all of them." I open my palm and two of my mother's gems fall into it.

"Thank you, Paser." My throat is tight. He smiles and catches up to Reb, who stares at Nefer's back as if picturing himself on top of it. I put the turquoise and carnelian in my satchel. It is silly that a few stones make me feel so much better, but they do. Carrying them with me makes my heart lighter. They are protective stones, talismans for the journey ahead.

I walk at the back of our caravan, wondering about the impossibility of what we are doing. Going blindly after Merat into the desert, led by a man known to us as a spy. Paser, Reb, and I had the good fortune to grow up more privileged than most, as children of scribes and priests. And surviving the streets of Thebes was one thing, but to survive the Red Land? Where Set, the god of chaos, rules and havoc reigns in the brutal sands and unrelenting heat. Dangerous creatures and angry gods, all waiting to hasten one's way to the afterlife —

"Sesha."

I look up. Paser is staring at me.

"Are you well?"

"I am," I say. "Just admiring my new shoes." Which are not a terrible fit, all things considered. "Soon my feet will be as smooth as Reb's bottom."

They all burst into laughter, including Reb, and we continue walking, talking of insignificant things.

13

WE HAVE NOT SEEN A SIZABLE LANDMARK in some time and are beginning to leave behind the sparse green shrubs that dot the sands. Ra is almost at his full height.

"We will stop soon," says Pepi. "There are rock formations ahead where we can make camp for a few hours. After that, we will travel only at night, by the stars. It is too hot to walk far in the desert."

"He tells me what I already know," Reb says, wiping his brow. Each of us is robed in one of the faded linens from the village. We used the remaining pieces to cover our heads, securing them with a papyrus belt, fabric trailing down over our shoulders. Even Nefer gets a large swathe folded across her back.

"As the beasts laze in the day, so too will we. Moving

instead of sleeping at night will keep us warmer, as well as safer from the smaller, but no less lethal, creatures that come out after dark." Pepi looks over his shoulder at us. "We should stop speaking now. I find the desert kills those who talk most the quickest."

At last, the rocks Pepi spoke of come into view. The flies and bugs buzzing around our faces are intolerable. I wave them off at first but eventually give up, adjusting my linen head covering so only my eyes show. I feel sympathy for Nefer, who twitches her long black ears in annoyance at the insects but is unable to do much more than wheeze and shake her head every so often.

Pepi holds up his hand. "We will stop and rest here for a few hours."

"Thank the gods," Reb croaks, throat sounding as parched as mine feels.

"Look around for sticks we can lean against the side of the rock. This will block the worst of Ra's rays."

"Do you not call the god by another name?" I ask Pepi, my mouth dry, while we cast our eyes about for sticks.

"My ancestors have lived on this land, at the delta, for many years. In addition to your language, we've adopted many of your gods and traditions along the way. We identify your Set with our chief god, Hadad."

This surprises me. The Hyksos, rulers of foreign lands, stay mainly in the North, in their capital of Avaris, and though some do make their way to Thebes, Pepi is the first I have met. He is not what I expect. He speaks as eloquently as a temple scribe, calls his donkey Nefer, our word for *beautiful*, and shows respect to the gods as we do. Though the chaotic Set would not be my first choice as chief god.

Between the four of us, we collect enough sticks to create a small shelter. We lean them against the sandy stone to build a welcome, if slightly gapped, barrier from the unrelenting heat.

There is barely room for all four of us. Sweating, we get settled as best we can, lying down, side by side. Nefer brays loudly and Pepi shifts slightly, allowing her to poke her nose and head into the spotty shade of the shelter. The rest of her body is exposed, though being on the north side of the rock offers some relief from the sun, as does the folded linen draped across her back. Paser passes around the waterskin. We each take a drink that seems much too short, but we need to ration what we have. Paser puts the stopper back in and slings the strap over his shoulder. By unspoken agreement he and Reb will share the carrying of the barley drink. It goes unsaid, but I know they think there is less chance of Pepi abandoning us if he does not have access to liquid. The satchel with the food and medical supplies, including my father's blade, lies between Paser and Reb. I am squeezed between Paser and Pepi.

It is very tight quarters.

"Try to rest." Pepi rolls over onto his side, stroking Nefer's nose. "We will move again when the sun is down."

"How will we wake?" Paser asks, leaning back against the rock face.

"I will wake." Pepi's voice holds no doubt.

"But will he be here when we do?" I hear Reb whisper in Paser's ear.

Paser does not respond, and I close my eyes, exhausted from the heat and the walking, unable to think of anything but sleep.

I wake with a shiver. The temperature has fallen drastically. The space on my left is empty. Heart quickening, I sit up, rubbing the gritty sand out of the corners of my eyes. Reb and Paser continue to snore lightly on my right. I stick my head out of our crude shelter and see a strange outline.

Pepi leans back against the donkey, looking up at the sky, purple grey in the west, fading to a deep violet in the east. He is studying the stars, which are beginning to reveal themselves in great numbers as night settles upon us. I leave the warmth of Paser's side and go to sit with the spy.

"How long until we reach the oasis where the princess is?" I ask.

"Roughly two more nights," says Pepi, scanning the horizon. "If there are no sandstorms or any other … complications."

I try not to dwell on what other complications he might mean and instead think of seeing Merat in three days' time. She will be most surprised. My heart swells as I imagine the look on her face. I hope she is being treated fairly and that the chieftain does not hold her public rejection of him too strongly against her.

"How is your hand?" I ask Pepi.

"Well enough," he says, holding it up, still bound in the dirty linen.

"You need a fresh bandage," I say, getting up to go back into the shelter. I grab the satchel, careful not to wake Paser and Reb, who both sleep like the dead, their breathing rhythmic and deep.

Rejoining Pepi, I take a relatively clean strip of linen and the jar of honey from the bag.

"May I?" I ask, reaching for his hand. He shrugs and lets me unwrap the dirty strip. The wound looks decent, aside from some mild seepage, and seems to be sealing, crusted over with dried blood. I apply some more honey and murmur another incantation to prevent the gash from festering, then rewrap Pepi's hand. He nods his thanks and settles back against Nefer, who gives off a little heat.

"It would be nice to have a fire," Pepi remarks, crossing his arms over his chest. "It was very cold in the pits."

"How did you come to be there?" I ask, remembering Reb's speculations. I put a little of the honey between my toes where the sandals rub. The sticky substance feels wonderful. Nefer turns her head, long pink tongue darting out.

"Someone might have betrayed me," he says with little emotion, as if stating the hour of day, a simple observation.

"Why were you in Thebes?" I let Nefer lick the sweetness from my fingers. As the donkey does not mind that the honey was just between my toes, I decide not to mind her tongue, which is warm and wet and tickles. A laugh escapes me.

"I was gathering information." Pepi looks at me intently. "A currency worth more than gold or silver."

"You wished to know how the city fares?" Paser says, making his way out of the shelter. I must have woken him when I retrieved the satchel.

"Yes." Pepi does not deny it.

"For what reason?"

"The interests I represent want to know such things."

"And whose interests are those?" Reb, also emerging from the shelter, yawns.

"That is not your concern, young scribe," Pepi says, but his tone is not unkind.

Reb scowls at being called young by someone only a few years his senior — though there is much about Pepi that makes him seem far older. As if he has seen things others have not.

"Shall we eat?" I interrupt. Reb's scowl vanishes and we split the limp cabbage and a loaf of bread, chewing slowly, wanting to make it last. Encouraged by the cool air and the smell of our food, small critters begin to make themselves known through their quiet rustles and skittering across the sands. I am reminded that although sometimes the desert can seem lifeless, many animals find a way to survive.

May we be among them.

14

IT IS FULLY NIGHT AND WE TREK under the dazzling stars. I am tired and long to rest. My body protests at treating day as night and night as day. My feet ache.

Pepi had gathered a few of the sturdier sticks from our shelter and tied them in a bundle, presumably for firewood. They lie horizontally across Nefer's back. I go through a mental list of the rest of our dwindling supplies. The waterskin is a third empty. One stale loaf, some onions, two melons. The honey, the obsidian blade, the turquoise and carnelian, a pair of tweezers, a needle, some linen — everything else was lost to the river or has been eaten. Pepi says we have three days and two nights before reaching the oasis. We will have to make our supplies last.

We talk more in the evenings than during the day, when the soaring temperatures encourage us to keep our mouths shut so we do not lose precious moisture.

Despite not-so-subtle prodding from Reb and Paser, Pepi does not reveal any more information about the mysterious interests he represents. I imagine he has been through tougher interrogations. In fact, Pepi seems particularly good at turning these attempted questionings around.

"I heard the priest call you 'my son,'" he says to Reb after one such fruitless inquiry. "Yet you left him in the pits — not once, but twice."

"He is my uncle," Reb says. "But having the same blood does not guarantee someone will treat you well." Pepi makes an encouraging noise and Reb continues. "He thinks I am lazy and stupid and that hitting me will make me less so." Reb's voice is raw, and I wonder if it is from the dust in the evening air or from suppressed emotion.

"You are not stupid," Paser says to his friend, putting a hand on his shoulder.

"Then why can I not write the scripts as you do?" Reb's voice cracks. "They sometimes look reversed to me, and it takes me twice as long as you and Sesha to read or draw them."

Surprised, I glance at Reb. I did not know he had trouble, but with his admission several pieces fall into place: his acting out in class, his uncle's frustration and anger.

Paser appears to know of Reb's troubles and reassures him. "That does not mean you are stupid. You just see things differently."

"I, too, see things from a different perspective," Pepi offers. "It can be a gift. I also know about pleasing higher powers." His tone is wry. "Or rather, displeasing them."

I look down at the sand. I was blessed with a father who treasured me, one who saw as much value in me as in my brother. After my time at the temple and with Nebifu, it is easy to see why he faced criticism for training me to become a physician like him, and for other radical ideas that many of the priests were resistant to, such as learning from our neighbours to the north. Yet he was not afraid to speak out and do what he thought was right.

"Nebifu will survive the pits. The queen will fish him out." Reb says this with bitter confidence. "He was helping her protect Egypt's treasures." He seems to consider his next few words, and when he speaks them, his tone is accusatory. "Much has been pilfered over the years to pay tribute to your rulers in Avaris."

Pepi's posture stiffens but he lets Reb's comment pass, and we continue walking in silence.

I contemplate Nebifu's motivations. Was he really under Queen Anat's orders to protect the treasures? Or was he hoping to secure them for himself? Will Pharaoh feel betrayed by the queen's actions? Or will she persuade him that she was doing the right thing in preserving her family's legacy? For that matter, was she? I shake my head, which is throbbing as much from unanswered questions as from lack of water. Things were easier when I was a child and it was clear what was right and what was wrong. The more I learn of the world, the muddier its waters become.

It is during a period of quiet reflection that Reb begins to sing, softly at first, then louder. It is a temple song, one I am familiar with. His voice is unexpectedly beautiful, and I listen to it for a few minutes before joining in. Paser, too, begins to sing and the three of us continue into the fading night, our voices spiralling up to the heavens above.

The sky is lightening. The giant red disk will soon come up from the underworld to light the day. We have entered a sea of sand, waves cresting higher and higher, with no end in sight. I am exhausted, but Pepi pushes us to keep moving before it is fully morning, as there is no shelter here. I have a feeling he thinks someone or something may be following us. He glances over his shoulder frequently and stops to scan the horizon behind us.

"Do you know where we are?" I ask, peering anxiously at the dunes from under my hand, trying to see what he sees. It looks the same in every direction.

"The sands shift. It is wise not to look to them," Pepi says. He points at the sky, at the birds soaring overheard. "We will follow the animals. They know the way to water."

We trudge on, the sun peeking above the horizon. The red-orange dawn will soon give way to the bright light of morning. I focus on putting one foot in front of the other, trying not to think of water, possible pursuit by the queen's men, or even a hungry lion stalking us — a ready-cooked meal. At last Pepi lets out a triumphant shout, and I look up to see a few bedraggled palms around a tiny dot of something that is not beige or brown. Even though we are exhausted, our pace quickens.

I give Pepi a sidelong glance. "Did you know this was here?"

"I was praying to find something like this soon." His smile is tired but full of relief. "There are a number of spots throughout the desert like this, where the water appears."

"Where does it come from?" Reb asks, scanning the sky.

"From under the ground," Pepi responds. "Natural springs bubble up in places. They might be nothing more than a small pond, as this one appears to be. Or they can be larger, like the oases used as stopping points along the trade routes. The Nile itself is one giant oasis. We are headed to a lesser-known one, where there is a substantial Hyksos camp."

"How do you know these routes so well?" Paser inquires.

"I have been travelling the desert my whole life," Pepi says.

"See?" I tease Reb, feeling uplifted at seeing the specks of green and blue. "Are you not happy we freed him from the pit?"

We reach the shade of the small knot of palms, startling some birds from their perch. Maybe even the same ones we followed to get here. I drop the satchel under a palm and head straight to the pond's edge, eager for a drink. I want nothing more than to dive into the water.

My foot sinks deep into the wet sand. Then my other foot vanishes, my leg sinking to mid-calf. I try to lift my back foot up and bring it forward. It does not budge, and my movements make me sink even more. Struggling to free myself only gets me more

stuck, but I am in almost up to my waist before I realize what is happening.

"Sesha, stop moving!" Pepi shouts.

Quicksand.

15

"STAY CALM," PEPI INSTRUCTS.

"That's easy for you to say." Panic rises as I sink farther, the sand now almost up to my chest. "You are not being swallowed by the desert!"

"The sands will not swallow you." Pepi and Nefer have stopped a palm tree away. Paser strides by them, extending his hand to pull me out. Pepi grabs his arm and yanks him back.

"What are you doing?" Paser says angrily, shaking off Pepi's grip. "I mean to give her my hand."

"And then you will be stuck as well," Pepi says. "Listen to me, Sesha. Stop moving. The more you fight the sand, the more it will pull you in, sucking the strength from your body." He points at the sun, which is climbing higher into the sky, the heat of the day rising along with it. "The danger comes not from below, but from above."

"What am I to do?" I ask, holding my arms at shoulder height. The soupy clay slurps at my body, making it almost impossible to move.

"Bring your legs to the surface," Pepi instructs. "You will need to crawl out."

I try to lift a leg, but the sand will not release it. My limbs feel heavy, like they no longer belong to me but are becoming part of the desert itself. "It's not working!"

"Steady your breathing," Pepi says, his voice calm. "Lean forward onto your chest. You need to spread your weight out evenly."

His instructions go against every instinct I have. The last thing I want is to put more of my body into the sand, but I try to calm my breath and do what he says.

Leaning forward, I push down on the crust of the quicksand. It is slightly firmer, but still my hands begin to sink. I lift them back up, not wanting them to disappear beneath the muck, too.

"Reb!" Paser shouts, taking off his head covering and gesturing for Reb to do the same. "We will tie them together." Pepi takes off his as well. Paser knots the belts together, forming a rope. Pepi ties one end around Nefer's body.

"Catch, Sesha!" Paser says, letting the rope fly.

His aim is direct, and I catch the linen in my clay-covered hands. Pepi gives Nefer a swat with his hand and the donkey steps forward, one dainty hoof at a time. I let the rope take some of my weight and try to float my legs to the top. It feels like they are encased in granite blocks.

"Come to me," Pepi coaxes Nefer, who stops and flicks her tufted tail, not overly concerned with my predicament. Pepi throws his hands up in frustration. He grabs the satchel and pulls out some green onion, clicking his tongue at the indifferent donkey. He waves the onion in front of her. Nefer sniffs at it and takes another step forward. I cling to the makeshift linen rope, praying for the thick clay to release me. Nothing happens.

"Move your legs in small circles, to let some water trickle down. This will lessen the sand's suction," Pepi says, continuing to walk backwards with the onion. Nefer takes another few steps forward. The rope slides through my muddy grip until I am left holding nothing but a few threads. Tears come to my eyes.

"Try your back," Pepi urges, locking eyes with me, his expression encouraging. Float on my back in quicksand? But I am running out of options. Letting go of the linen strings, I lean backwards, trying to bring my legs to the surface. I think I feel them rise closer to the top, but it is not enough.

"Sesha!" Paser frees one of the sticks from the bundle across Nefer's back. "Put this under your hips for support, so you can raise your legs higher." He throws the branch and it lands beside me. I grab it and push it deep into the muck under my bottom. This keeps my hips from sinking and lets me bring my legs up a little more.

"Good," Pepi says. "Now stroke, to propel yourself out."

Lying almost completely flat, I hold my head out of the thick silt. I spread both arms wide and push myself backwards, hands digging into the sucking sand. Cubit by cubit, I wriggle myself back toward the edge of the quicksand by bringing my arms behind me and shoving the mud forward. At last, my fingertips graze firmer ground.

Mustering my remaining strength, I roll onto my side and up over the lip of the deadly circle. Panting hard, I crawl slowly, inching farther away from the pit that held me firmly in its grasp only seconds before. Paser, Pepi, and Reb grab me and haul me to solid ground, laughing and cheering while I try to catch my breath. I am covered in mud and must resemble some hideous beast. Nefer brays loudly at all the commotion, tail swishing.

"So much for your sandals," grins Paser, giving me a tight hug.

Regaining some air, I manage a casual shrug. "They were giving me blisters."

The sun climbs overhead, scorching everything below. I see why getting stuck in quicksand is so dangerous. Not because you sink completely, but because your energy and strength evaporate quickly in the sweltering sun, leaving you to starve or dehydrate, shrivelling like dried fruit.

Once again we make our way down to the small pond. Pepi allows us to go in briefly so we can wash and cool ourselves after our early morning exertions before we settle down to sleep. With great attention to where we step, we enter the water in our clothes, which will dry fast enough. The pond is not deep or wide, and I sink onto my knees, voluntarily this time, as does Pepi.

"Wait," he says, sniffing the water. He cups some of it to his mouth, then immediately spits it out. "Do not drink from here," he warns. "The water is too salty and will only increase your thirst."

We stare at him in disbelief. "But what about filling the waterskin?" Reb asks, holding up the container.

"With careful rationing we should have enough," Pepi reassures him, yet he looks as desolated as I feel.

I close my eyes briefly. It will do no good to cry; it will only make me lose more moisture. Grumbling, Reb wades out farther, Paser behind him. At the least it feels good to rinse off the sweat and dirt.

"How did you know I should spread my weight across the sand?" I ask Pepi, trying not to think about the tantalizing liquid surrounding me. Liquid we cannot drink.

"As I said, I have travelled the desert all my life. Both its gifts and its hazards are well known by my people," Pepi says, with one eye on the merciless sun. "That's enough," he calls to Paser and Reb. "We need to get into the shade."

Before Pepi and I leave the pond, we reach down to scoop up cool mud from its bottom and smear it all over our bodies. Paser does the same, then walks out of the pool, giving himself a shake, hair flying. Reb goes for one last dunk and comes back up, spouting a defiant arc of water from his mouth. He gags and splutters at the salty taste and Pepi shakes his head.

Back under the shade of a scraggly palm, Nefer chews on even sadder-looking grass, which looks surprisingly appetizing, for grass. I am starving. We have not eaten much these past days and my struggle in the quicksand has whipped my stomach into a storm rivalling any Set could cast.

Paser pulls the last loaf of dry bread and the fruit out of the satchel.

"We should save them for later tonight," I say, despite wanting nothing more than to shove the entire sandy loaf in my mouth, which would be watering were it not so dry. "We need the energy for our trek."

"Sesha is right." Pepi plucks some of the limp grass Nefer chews on. "Let us rest now. When the sun goes down, we will search the oasis at dusk for anything to supplement our rations."

Despite my hunger, sleep tugs at me like a child at her mother's arm, insistent and impossible to ignore.

Giving the area with quicksand a wide berth, I choose a spot under one of the trees. There is not much shade at the small oasis, about a dozen palm trees in all. Flopping down in my wet clothes — which will cool me at least a short while — I settle in to sleep. The last thing I see before my eyelids flutter shut is Pepi, one hand shielding his eyes and a frown furrowing his brow, scanning the desert behind us.

16

I DREAM OF WATER, OF FOOD. The smells from the market fan my hunger, like fronds at a flame. I see the vendor and his wife, Ky held firmly in their grip.

"Sesha!" he cries out to me. The frizzy-haired vendor's wife turns into Queen Anat, who laughs in our faces. Tutan is there now and shouts at his mother to release Ky. His shouts become louder and angrier, and now Tutan sounds more and more like Reb.

"Away with you, beast!"

I shake my head to clear it of the lingering dream. It is dark, but I can just make out Reb, clapping his hands at a growling, hunched shape with four legs. In the confusion of awakening, I think Anubis has found us. Rubbing the sleep from my eyes, I sit up eagerly, squinting into the night.

It is not Anubis.

A wild hyena has the satchel in its mouth, ears pressed back against its head. Wide eyes glint in the moonlight as it shakes the bag vigorously and some of the contents fly out.

Our food.

"Leave it!" I command. If the hyena does not understand my words, at least it catches my meaning. It growls, deep and low in its throat.

My shout wakes the others. Pepi scrambles around for stones to throw while Paser races forward, joining Reb in shouting at the wild animal. The hyena growls again. It will not be intimidated into dropping what promises to be its best meal in months, judging by its scrawny hide. Pepi launches a stone, and with an indignant yelp, the hyena races off into the night, the satchel still clutched in its jaws, dragging on the ground.

Paser and Reb run after the thieving animal. Pepi whistles loudly. I'm not sure if it is directed at the hyena or at the boys, signalling to them to return before they are lost to the vastness of the desert. Nefer stomps her feet and brays in a most hysterical fashion.

"Calm yourself," I say crossly, feeling sick at the loss of our food. Nefer brays again loudly, then snorts and tosses her head. Perhaps there are more hyenas nearby. One on its own is no real cause for alarm, but a pack of the vicious creatures … or maybe it is something else she senses. Something bigger. To distract myself from these thoughts, I scold Nefer. "Now you make a fuss? Where were you when that mongrel was stealing our food?"

Pepi walks to where the satchel's contents lie scattered on the ground. I join him to see what we can salvage. Grief hollows out my already-empty stomach, not only over the loss of our remaining food, but also over the loss of the few precious items we carried with us. And over the bag itself. Despite the gruesome contents it once held, I love that satchel. It was my physician's bag; carrying it reminded me of my passion and duty: healing others. Must I lose everything that has value?

Pepi and I drop to our knees. Khonsu, still a crescent, does not offer much help. As I swirl my hands through the sand, something slices my finger. I pick it up. My father's obsidian blade. The tightness around my chest loosens a cubit.

Pepi stands and cups his hands, calling for Paser and Reb to return. He turns to me. "They must not go far, or they will not find their way back."

I grip the blade and search for any other items that might have fallen from the satchel, hands brushing over the cool ground. The cut left by the knife is deep; the sand stings and grates as it enters the wound. Wincing, I stick my finger in my mouth, then spit out grains of sand.

Pepi strides after Paser and Reb, shouting again for them to come back. I set the blade on a rock and continue sweeping with my hands, not wanting to give up. Nothing. As my eyes adjust to the dark, I make out a small shape. I pick it up, thinking it a rock.

By the gods, it is the honey.

Continued searching produces only a few grimy linen strips. The tweezers and needle are lost, as are my mother's gemstones, the talismans for our journey. I do not want to think about the implications of this. I hear Reb and Paser coming back with Pepi, all three cursing the hyena who is feasting somewhere, likely feeling he has entered the Field of Reeds.

"What now?" Reb kicks the base of a palm. At least he still has his sandals. I have none. Nor food.

"We keep walking," Pepi says.

"We should stay another day to scavenge for food," Reb argues.

Pepi disagrees. "It is better to keep moving. We slept too long. Besides, we will not find much here."

"I am hungry." Reb is stubborn.

Pepi dismisses him. "Hunger will not kill you. I have known men to go over twenty-one days without food. Our bigger problem is that we are low on liquid."

"I thought you said we would have enough?" Reb gives Pepi a look.

Paser shakes the waterskin. "There's just under half left."

I hold up the jar, wanting to smooth the rising tension. "At least we still have the honey." Praises to Ra, it did not appeal to the hyena.

"With careful conservation we *should* have enough." Pepi narrows his eyes at Reb, a subtle insinuation that he may not be capable of properly rationing the drink. "But we need to leave now," Pepi says. "Every minute without adequate liquid brings us closer to the underworld. We must use every minute of night available."

Nefer brays her agreement.

I sigh. "At least it will not take us long to pack."

17

THERE IS NO SINGING THAT NIGHT. Unless you count our stomachs, which grumble together in a disharmonious chant of hunger. We share the honey before leaving the oasis. Each of us sticks a finger into the jar and scoops out a small portion. With our consent, Pepi also offers Nefer a fingerful, which she licks from his hand. I savour the sweet substance as if it is my last bit of food. It may very well be.

Pepi offers me Nefer's back, which I refuse at first. But after we've walked on the rocky sand for several pyramid lengths, my pride yields to the soles of my bare feet. Pepi hoists me on top of Nefer, who does not seem to mind much. I am wary at first. It feels strange lurching along in such a manner, but my body soon grows accustomed to the odd rhythm and settles into its new gait. I sit on the folded linen at an angle, legs to one side. The bundle of sticks strapped to the donkey rests horizontally behind me and I hold on to it every now and then for support.

Reb and Paser walk ahead, speaking in low tones. Pepi walks beside Nefer and me. The donkey and her owner seem very fond of one another.

Trying to distract myself from my thirst, I look up at the dark skies. I get Pepi to teach me the names of some of the lesser-known patterns shining above. There are a countless number. Many lights streak across the sky, going about their lives, bright tails streaming behind them.

"Where do you think the gods go when they dart across the sky in such a great hurry?" I ask, thinking of Merat, the reason we push on despite one blow after another. She would have a creative answer. Her Highness is a poet with a romantic streak as bright as the stars above. Perhaps she is looking up at the sky this very moment, composing poems for Paser. The thought chafes, like the sand between my toes. Not wanting to examine it too closely, I focus on what Pepi is saying.

"Perhaps the lights come down to be with us for a time," Pepi says. "Making their lives among us, as friends and family."

"Do you have any family?" I ask, shifting my weight on Nefer, who walks at a plodding pace.

"I do," he says, but does not elaborate. Extracting information from Pepi is like squeezing water from a stone.

"What of the chieftain Merat was given to?" I ask. "Do you think he knew where you were?"

"Perhaps." Pepi's tone is evasive.

"Then why did he not free you?"

"I can think of many reasons. Bargaining for the princess's hand would have kept him occupied. If indeed he did know, I could have been a casualty of the negotiation." He keeps his head straight, his tone difficult to interpret. "Or maybe he believes that a spy who fails in his duties no longer has any value."

"What about your value as a man?" I ask. "Our king thinks your people are preparing for a battle. Does an army not need all its soldiers?"

"Why does the king think there will be an attack?" Pepi asks. "We have ruled from the North since our ancestors settled there years ago, without any major conflicts."

"Perhaps he thinks the rulers of foreign lands wish to expand their territory." If there is indeed famine throughout the land, resources will be scarce. I think of Queen Anat's words about giving away her priceless treasures as tribute. Maybe the Hyksos will also protest if the stream of riches coming from the palace stops.

"We have brought many good things to this land," Pepi says. "When is one allowed to call a place their home? My family came here generations ago. How long must we wait?"

I do not know how to answer. My family has been in Thebes for many years as well, and yet, according to those who rule it, it is no longer open to me, no longer my home.

"How are your feet, young scribe?" Pepi asks.

"Fine," I say. "How is your hand?" I forgot to look at it at the oasis, the devastation of losing our food overriding everything else, even my duties. My own finger, hastily bound in a linen strip, still throbs from the cut of the blade.

"Fair enough," Pepi remarks. "You have much skill as a physician. Perhaps the Hyksos will not kill you three after all."

"Would they really harm us?" Children and young people are revered in Thebes, as many do not make it to adulthood. During the moon Ky and I spent on the streets, a few strangers inquired about our well-being, but we avoided them, unsure whom to trust.

"I cannot answer for them," Pepi says. "Did your own queen really intend to have you entombed alive?"

"I believe that was her plan," I admit. Perhaps not everyone in Thebes reveres youth.

He shrugs. "You will be no worse off with the Hyksos tribe. You said your father was the physician to the royal family. How does he feel about his queen attempting to do away with his offspring?"

With difficulty, I swallow the anger and pain, forcing the emotions down, a lumpy, bitter brew. "She did away with him before he had a chance to object."

"Ah," Pepi says, voice quiet. "And have you no other family?"

"My mother is gone," I say, voice as sad as the scraggly grasses Nefer was chewing on this morning. I do not feel her with me anymore. I hope she is with Ky. "Many of our family perished in the plague some years back. Mother and Father did not have any surviving brothers and sisters." Plague, intermittent famine, the great line of kings fracturing and splintering — our land and its people have suffered much of late. "My brother remains at the palace."

"With the queen?"

"He is young Prince Tutan's closest confidant and friend. The queen loves the prince and would not wish to make him unhappy. She will not let any harm come to his companion." I hope her threat was only bluster. "He is treated as one of the royal sons."

"I recall seeing the pair running around together during my brief time in the palace, as a … messenger."

"Is that your official occupation?"

"One of them," Pepi says.

A realization is growing on me, like a warty lesion needing removal. "I do not think Queen Anat will harm my brother," I say slowly. "But she might use him in her schemes. I can only pray that she does not bother to concern herself with a young boy." And that Ahmes and Bebi will help protect him.

"I, too, will pray for your brother's safety." Pepi pats Nefer on her side. "And that the queen does not use him like a pawn in a game of Senet."

I look at him, startled at his generous words. He gives me a half-smile. "Are you more surprised by my prayers or by my familiarity with the game of Senet? I happen to be an excellent player, you know."

"Perhaps when we arrive at the camp, we can have a match," I say, no longer wishing to think about Queen Anat's potential schemes. "I beat my father a few times." I smile at Pepi. "He did not let me win, if that is what you are thinking."

"I was thinking no such thing." Pepi's voice is solemn. "To survive the deaths of your parents, the complexities of palace life, and now a perilous journey up the Nile and into the desert?" He holds up his bandaged hand. "All this, in addition to your skills as a healer, leaves little doubt of your brilliance."

I look down at Nefer's back, flushing at his words. "Or of your courage," he adds, voice soft.

"Tell me of your strategies for Senet," I say, suppressing my confusion. "Since you will not tell me anything else about yourself."

"The best strategy," Pepi begins, smiling, "is to make someone think you are not a threat. Until it is too late." He shares a few of his favourite moves, and I try not to think about why he gives them up so easily — I did challenge him to a match when we reach camp, after all. Despite my best efforts, a bleak thought crystallizes. *Maybe it is because he thinks we will never have the opportunity to play the game.*

Speaking of Senet, we continue our trek through a desert with no end in sight.

18

THE SUN IS RISING AND THERE IS NO SIGN of shade. While the temperature is still mildly tolerable, it will not be long before it becomes unbearable.

Pepi gauges the clear sky. "We should stop."

"Here?" Reb looks around. "There is no shelter. The barley drink is almost gone. We have no food."

"It is best if you forget about food, young scribe," Pepi says. "It only increases the need for water." He picks up a small rock and licks the dewy bottom of it. "There is moisture to be found. Take what you can. Then we must dig."

"Dig what?" Paser says through cracked lips. My mouth feels like the desert itself, dry and full of sand. I am no longer hungry. Water is all I can think of.

Pepi scans the sands. "There." He points to a depression between two dunes. "We will dig a trench and pile the sand high along the sides, which will block the worst of the rays. Hurry." He picks up another rock and licks the bottom. "Ra is coming."

After licking more rocks than one should have to in their lifetime, we start digging. The fiery orange ball ascends higher in the sky. Paser and I dig while Reb and Pepi pile the sand high on three sides, leaving one open for airflow. Sand is everywhere: under my fingernails, on my tongue, up my nose, in my eyes. But we keep digging, racing against the unstoppable morning. Ra's relentless pursuit feels almost personal. Maybe Reb is right and the gods are angry at us for desecrating the tombs of our ancestors, for betraying the royal family, their representatives.

Pepi unties the bundle of sticks and unfolds the sheet from Nefer's back. "Sesha, your blade," he says, and I hand it to him. Making four small slits in each corner, he hands me back the knife, then offers each of us an end of the sheet. We pull the fabric taut over the long hole. Pepi stabs a stick through one of the corner slits in the sheet and spears it deep into the ground. Reb, Paser, and I each grab a stick and do the same. It strikes me, with his calm and sure movements, that Pepi has done this before and survived. This gives me hope. We work in silence, too parched to talk, burrowing the sticks as far into the sand as we can, our efforts causing us to lose precious moisture through our sweat.

Pepi picks up a few of the licked rocks and piles them around the base of the sticks for support. He turns and gestures for us to do the same. His hands then mimic the winds, which can blow strong in the desert, and our shelter flying away. We pile rocks where necessary to reinforce our makeshift tent.

The sun climbs even higher. Our quick work will have to do; it is time to get out of the heat. Pepi clicks his tongue at Nefer and she lies down on the sand at the entrance to our shelter. He begins to bury her. The shelter is not big enough for her body, but she will stick her head inside, as she did our first day in the desert. We help him cover her with sand. She grunts, then licks the salty sweat from my face. Her tongue feels as dry and scratchy as mine.

Paser and Reb manoeuvre around Nefer into the shelter. I follow them, feeling the immediate relief of the shade. It is cooler under the linen sheet, but still roasting hot. We have many hours to go until evening. It is too hot to sleep and too hot to talk, so we lie side by side, cooking like sausages, and wait for night.

We make it to dusk.

Barely.

My lips are split and it feels as if sand fills my head and insides, like the salt the priests stuff into bodies to preserve the dead. I cannot move. All I can think of is water, water, water. I would give anything to be in the cool depths of the Nile right at this very moment …

"Sesha," Paser croaks. "We must be on our way."

Pepi, already outside the shelter, scans for the first stars. "We must get to water." His voice, too, is raspy. "The camp is not far. Now that it is night, they may send a scout to patrol the borders."

"Who would approach your borders?" Reb's voice is a hoarse whisper. "Why would anyone enter these hostile lands?"

"It's not as bad when you are prepared," Pepi says. "We did not have that opportunity."

I roll over onto my side, groaning. "Leave me," I say. I am done. Done with this desert. *Forgive me, Merat.*

"Get up." Paser walks over to me and offers his hand. I do not take it. He bends down and grabs my arm, pulling me to my feet. He hands me the water-skin, and we each take a too-short drink before passing it to Reb and Pepi. It is almost empty.

"Yes, young physician," Pepi says, passing me the warm drink again. I tilt it back against my mouth and one final drop lands on my parched tongue. "We have come far. You cannot give up now." He yanks the sticks out of their holes. Paser and Reb grab the ends of the sheet and walk them together, folding it in half as neatly as palace handmaidens.

I sigh, swaying. Pepi is right. Besides, I would rather die on my feet than in a pool of sand. Though I may not have much choice in the matter.

Nefer also gets to her feet. She blinks at me but seems otherwise all right from being baked by the sun. Her thick hair and the sand provided an effective layer of protection from the worst of the rays. Pepi puts the sheet over her back again and brings his hands together for me to place my foot in, to hoist me up.

"Someone else should take a turn," I croak, desperately wanting to climb onto Nefer's back but feeling guilty for riding her the previous night.

"We still have our sandals," Paser points out.

I nod, too tired to argue. Placing one foot in Pepi's hands, I climb up onto the donkey, who I now regard as an unequivocal beauty. He then passes me the bundle of sticks and we reposition them behind me. We set off: bellies empty, mouths dry, heads and hearts downcast.

As the sky grows darker, the stars grow brighter.

"Are we almost there?" Reb ventures.

"We are close," Pepi says. "We should reach the camp by mid-morning if all goes well. A good thing, as I do not like to push Nefer for more than three days without water, though she has gone longer."

"I do not think I will mind much if the Hyksos decide to put me out of my misery," Reb says, voicing my own thoughts.

"Merat will not let them do that," I whisper.

"Your skills as physicians may be welcome," Pepi says, despite his previous assertion that they would be as liable to kill us all.

"You will speak for us, then?" Paser asks Pepi. A welcome breeze picks up, reviving us somewhat.

"I will. Do you have any other talents that might persuade the tribe to adopt you?"

"As scribes, we can read and write and teach others to do the same," Paser says.

"The Hyksos are mighty warriors," Pepi says. "While your skills as scribes might have been useful had we gone to Avaris, I am not sure a camp full of soldiers will appreciate them."

"I can fight," Paser says, the wind ruffling his hair. "My grandfather was one of the pharaoh's best soldiers and trained me well."

"And Sesha can charm snakes," Reb offers feebly.

"I am not worried about Sesha. She can charm

more than just snakes," Pepi says. "A young woman will be a welcome addition to the Hyksos."

"What are you saying?" Pepi's words bring me out of my thirsty delirium.

"One of the warriors will likely want you for a wife," Pepi says simply.

Paser stops so abruptly that Reb almost walks into him. "I will say she is spoken for," Paser says, turning to face us.

"Then they will definitely kill you." Pepi sounds amused.

"What am I to do?" I feel sick, but there is nothing in my stomach to come up.

"It is obvious." Reb looks up at the sky. "Pepi will have to say you are his."

"I am no one's," I say. My heels kick Nefer's side in emphatic protest of this suggestion and she grunts. I give her an apologetic pat.

"Reb is right." Paser looks at Pepi. "You must have known this from the beginning."

"It occurred to me," Pepi agrees. "I did not want to speak of it, as the odds were against us making it this far. There was no point in adding to the burden you carry."

"You think we will reach the oasis, then?" Reb, who does not seem bothered by my unexpected betrothal, is hopeful. Pepi does not respond and we fall silent, as talking dries our throats almost beyond bearing.

"It does not have to be real," Pepi whispers to me. "Only appear so. Like the way the desert sun makes the air shimmer, tricking those who view it into seeing something that is not there."

I shake my head, unable to answer.

"If you say that your friends are your brothers, and therefore my family as well, no harm will come to them." Pepi looks at me. I glance back and forth between him and them, seeing the truth in Pepi's eyes of what would happen should I not offer that protection to Reb and Paser.

"*If* we survive the desert I will abide by this plan." Licking my cracked lips, I lift my head to look at the sands before me, stretching as far as my eyes can see. "But at this moment, that feels like a very big *if*."

I JERK AWAKE, HEAD SNAPPING UP. Nefer's rhythmic gait has lulled me into sleep, but now she missteps, and I almost fall off. We stop.

"Peace." Pepi soothes her, but at the same time scans the horizon, searching for what her unease tells him. I feel it, too; her body is restless, she moves from foot to foot. The breeze has turned into gusts, ruffling her coarse mane.

"What is it?" I ask.

"There." He points ahead and just off to the left. Reb and Paser stop to look. The sky is black.

"I see nothing," I say, wondering if what Pepi's been looking for has finally caught up to us. Will we have to stand and face Queen Anat's soldiers? A ravenous lion?

"Precisely," Pepi responds, voice terse. "The stars vanish, one by one."

"How can that be?" Reb asks.

"Sandstorm."

Alarm joins the thirst and fatigue in my body. A sandstorm we cannot fight. "Is it moving this way?"

"It appears so." Pepi mutters a curse under his breath.

"How far off?" Paser asks.

"Not far." A huge gust almost blows me off Nefer. I cannot see the dust rising in the air, but I can feel it.

"Tie your headscarves around your faces," Pepi shouts. He leads Nefer down a dune. I hold on to her, half falling off when we reach the bottom. She brays loudly, eyes rolling in her head. The wind whips at us like a ferocious beast.

"It is Set," Reb says, naming the desert god of chaos. "He is coming for us."

Pepi quickly removes the linen from Nefer's back. "The sticks will not work here. We will need to sit under the sheet, facing in, heads together and backs to the storm. Each of you tuck a corner underneath yourself."

"We will suffocate under there," Reb argues, his voice panicked.

"It is better than being blinded and choking to death on sand and rock," Pepi says. "There are invisible holes in the fabric where the air will come through."

The dust storm is moving closer. In the dark of the night, it is difficult to see. But the sky grows even dimmer as the light of the stars — and then the moon — is blocked out. There are tales of entire villages and caravans being swallowed by the sands. Are we about to join them? I can hear the storm now, whirling and howling, the massive cloud growing in strength and size the closer it gets.

Reb, Paser, and I each take a corner, pulling the sheet over our heads. A sudden gust catches the linen, tearing it from our hands. Only Paser manages to hold on. Nefer rears loudly, sending a high-pitched scream into the air, and bolts.

Pepi yells at Paser. "Do not let go!" Then he chases after the frightened donkey.

The wind whips the fabric like a sail. Reb and I try to catch it, but only succeed in banging heads. Paser, ever calm under dire circumstances, gathers the linen to his chest in a ball. The storm is almost upon us and we are exposed to the elements. We choke and cough, eyes watering.

"Do not let go." Paser rasps Pepi's command, and we each grab a corner of the sheet, managing to get it over our heads. We sit on the sand forming a tight triangle, backs facing outwards. With our heads together, mine still smarting from smacking Reb's, we shift the sheet underneath our bottoms until we sit solidly upon it, pulling the edges up between our legs. I feel Paser and Reb's breath on my cheeks, as they must feel mine. It is even darker under the linen.

"What about Pepi?" I say, frantic. Why did he go after Nefer?

"He will be all right, Sesha," Paser says. I cannot see his face well, but I hear the doubt in his voice. He grabs my hand and Reb's and the three of us sit there, gripping one another tightly. Then the storm is upon us, howling and raging and dancing on our backs. Set flings sands and rocks in every direction, and despite the dark, I close my eyes.

I do not know if it has been hours or days, but at last the roar of the wind fades. I cannot stay one second longer under the suffocating fabric, so I come out, breathing in a lungful of dusty air. Immediately, I begin coughing and duck back under the sheet, which has become untucked. I feel dizzy and thirsty beyond anything I have ever known. Our last sip of the barley drink feels like hours ago.

"How is it?" Reb asks after I gain control of myself. Eyes watering, I shake my head, indicating he should wait a few more minutes before venturing out from under the linen. Pepi has not come back. He is gone, along with any remaining hope that we will make it out of the desert alive.

"Could you tell if it is still night?" Paser asks, tongue going to his split bottom lip.

"It must be morning," Reb says. "The dust will settle just in time for the sun to boil us alive."

"There is an equally good chance we will suffocate under here." I cough. My body feels sore and bruised after being relentlessly pelted by sand and small rocks.

"We are forsaken." Reb closes his eyes. "I wish I never left Thebes."

Paser and I remain silent, though part of me agrees with Reb.

Whoosh!

The worn sheet is ripped off us. Another storm? I cannot bear it. We blink into the sandy air, which seems clearer than when I poked my head out.

Pepi stands over us, head wrapped up, only his dark eyes showing. Nefer stands behind him. An unfamiliar face looms beside the donkey. Pepi nods back over his shoulder, and though his voice is muffled by the wrappings around his head, his words are sweeter than fresh honey: "We are here."

20

"I THOUGHT HE SAID WE WERE HERE," Reb mutters
under his breath a little while later. Pepi and
the stranger walk ahead, talking in low voices.
I ride Nefer, who, like us, seems to have a few lives to
spare. Paser and Reb walk on either side of the donkey.

"How did he survive the storm?" I say, sandstruck.

"Probably stuck his head up Nefer's bum," Reb
grumbles. Paser bursts out laughing, sounding like a
frog croaking to death. Pepi and the man, who we gather is a scout for the tribe, look over their shoulders as
the three of us dissolve into staccato giggles, a trio of
deranged hyenas.

The man shakes his head and says something to
Pepi I don't quite catch. If I were to wager, I would say
it is along the lines of, *The desert has taken their minds.*

Snorting and huffing, we manage to get ourselves under control, though our near encounter with death leaves us easily amused. Nefer farts loudly, which sends us into more hysterics, and I hold my stomach, which is cramping from too little food and water, as well as from the vigorous workout it's getting.

"Look," Paser says between gasps of laughter. He points at a shimmer on the horizon, and I wonder if it is another of the desert's tricks.

But as we get closer, the shape of the oasis solidifies. Green bursts out of the sands, birds fly overhead, the smell of fresh water is in the air — it is the most beautiful sight.

"Just in time." Paser shields his eyes from the sun, which is high in the sky.

The man walking with Pepi hands him his own waterskin, and the spy takes a healthy drink, throat moving as he swallows. I long to run over and rip the container from Pepi's hands, guzzling till I burst. The drink the man gave us right after the sandstorm did not do much to quench my thirst.

Pepi stops and holds out the waterskin to Paser, who is closest. Paser takes the skin and turns, offering it to me.

I shake my head. "You first." I know he has had less than his share on the journey, leaving more for Reb and me. Paser puts the water to his lips. He hands it to me when he is done, and I pass it to Reb.

"Here. You are likely thirstier than I." I grin at him, feeling my lip split open, tasting the coppery warmth of blood. "Seeing as how you never shut up."

Gratitude flashes in Reb's eyes as he takes the container and drinks. At last it is my turn. I pour the liquid into my mouth, feeling it slide down my throat in a blissful river, as life-giving as the Nile itself.

"Not too much at once," Pepi warns. Forcing myself to take a breath, I give the container back to Paser and we pass it around in a circle a few more times. Too soon, Pepi takes it from us and gives it back to the man, who stares at us in curiosity.

Now that I am somewhat hydrated, I have more attention for the Hyksos scout. He is tall and sinewy, tendons and muscles visible under weathered skin. Dressed in a short linen skirt and worn sandals, his chest is partially covered by the hide of some animal. My eyes focus on the dagger strapped at his waist. My own blade rests at nearly the same spot, wrapped and secured on my person with linen strips. I notice Paser also looking at the scout's dagger. My friend is wary of the stranger. We all are.

"Come," says Pepi. "There will be food for us."

With my burning thirst slightly abated, there is something I must know. "Is Merat here?"

The scout looks at Pepi and says something under his breath. An unreadable expression crosses Pepi's face.

"What did he say?" I demand.

"The princess is here," Pepi says, turning to face us. "It seems we have arrived just in time for her wedding celebration."

People stare openly as we make our way in from the edge of the oasis.

"Remember," Pepi whispers to us. "Sesha and I are to be married. Let me do the speaking."

There are many people in the camp going about the daily tasks one sees in any small village: preparing food, doing the washing, making beer. A few children run around, playing. There are more men than women. I feel their interested stares, even though I must look like a sand-crusted carcass the lioness dragged in. Perhaps Pepi's plan is a good one after all.

Tall date palms tower over us, providing protection from the sun. Other grasses and plants grow everywhere, in every direction. The oasis is lush, fragrant, and blooming. After seeing nothing but beige for days, I am struck by the colours: not only the numerous shades of green, but the deep purple of the dates dripping from the palms, the brilliant yellows of the flowers from the acacia trees, and off in the distance, the sparkling blue of a giant lake rising from the desert floor. Several goats run up to us, *meh*-ing and sniffing our hands. We are tattered, filthy, and half-starved. But we are alive. The oasis seems to stretch out all around us. There are huts and tents everywhere; it is a proper, bustling camp.

"I wonder where they are keeping Merat." I glance around, excitement rising, trying to catch a glimpse of my friend.

"Do you think they will believe Pepi about your engagement?" Reb whispers, looking uneasy.

"Let us hope so," I whisper back.

"I wonder who he is to these people," Paser says in a low voice. "He is one of them, but in what way?" He eyes the back of the spy, who is laughing and greeting people around us. "And why is he helping us? He said once we arrived, we would be on our own."

Paser is right. I swallow, remembering Pepi's words when we first freed him and asked him to take us to the Hyksos: *It is likely they will kill you.*

I shake my head, thinking of the quicksand, the bonds forged by the sands. "He saved our lives by leading us this far, and he came back for us after the storm." I am not sure if I am trying to convince Paser and Reb or myself that it will be all right. "He could have left us for dead."

Pepi stops outside a hut that is slightly larger than the others and turns to us. "Wait here," he says, then walks into the building. It is decorated with flowers and is the most important-looking dwelling we have seen so far.

"That must be the chieftain's residence," I whisper to Paser and Reb as I dismount Nefer.

A few men standing guard outside watch the three of us with suspicion. We stand there trying to look harmless, which is fairly easy given our present condition.

A loud shout comes from the hut, and the guards rush toward the door. My hand goes to the obsidian blade, but luckily the guards do not notice. Pepi emerges, an enormous man beside him. The pair are in high spirits, clapping each other on the back. Relief floods my body as I recognize the large man as the chieftain I saw storming out of the palace. He was furious then. Now he looks happy, relaxed. A crowd is gathering, a message passing unspoken between members of the tribe that something out of the ordinary is happening.

"It is time for much celebration!" the Hyksos chieftain calls, his thundering voice loud and clear. "My cousin is safely returned from the land of the jackals!"

Reb, Paser, and I look at each other. Cousin?

"He brings with him a bride. A feisty jackal, like my own princess."

My friends and I exchange another look. I think he speaks of me.

"We will teach her to be a lioness!" He raises a fist in the air and Pepi shrugs, resigned.

"It is a great sign from the gods that you return this day," the giant Hyksos says to Pepi. "You and your betrothed will marry beside my bride and me tonight. Two daughters of Thebes and two members of our tribe joining together!"

Wait. My mouth drops open. *Does he mean —*

"The weddings begin at sundown!"

21

"ONE MOMENT HE LEAVES HIS COUSIN in a pit in the 'land of the jackals,' the next he wishes to share his wedding day with him?" Reb, chomping down on a piece of bread, is back to his skeptical self.

"It would seem the chieftain did not know about Pepi's predicament," Paser muses. "Or else he is putting on a good show."

"Never mind that," I say, panic rising up in my chest. "The pricklier of the plants here is that I am to be married!" The words sound strange coming out of my mouth, and I wonder if this is an extended hallucination caused by the desert heat.

"Sesha!" a voice cries, and my heart leaps like an antelope across the plains.

Merat.

I turn and she races toward me, almost knocking me over with her embrace. I hold her tightly, sharing in her joy, tears coming to my eyes.

"What are you doing here? You came for me?" As questions tumble out of her, she pats my body, as if making sure she herself is not seeing things. It has only been days, but she looks different somehow, sharper and more defined, if that is possible.

Reb stands and swallows his bread. "Princess, we hope you are well."

"Have you been treated fairly?" Paser asks. Both are happy to see her but do not embrace her, remaining formal with their princess despite the fact that we journeyed an unmeasurable distance, risking our lives to be here.

She turns to them and inclines her head graciously. "I am well. Despite being given away like a prized cow by my father and mother." She waves an impervious hand. "Have they changed their minds and sent you to bring me home?"

A shadow must have crossed my face at her mention of the queen, because she seizes upon it. "What is it? What of my mother?"

"We will speak of it later," I say, wanting to avoid any discomfort at our reunion.

Reb has no such qualms. "She tried to have us

killed," he says, quite cheerful now that his belly is full and there is no immediate danger of dying.

"What?" Merat looks shocked. "That cannot be true."

"She claimed she was protecting her kingdom," I say, wondering why I defend Queen Anat.

Reb goes on. "She did not want your father squandering away her treasures to pay for his campaigns. She also thinks that caring for the people during famine is not her concern." I want to kick Reb, but that would only bruise my already-aching feet.

Paser interrupts. "We hear you are to be married."

Merat still looks stunned, but the thought of her impending marriage captures her attention, seeming to bring as much distress to her as mine does to me.

"Tonight." Her tone is bleak. "Unless … maybe you and I can say we are to be married?" She looks up at Paser, eyes wide.

"We thought of that already," says Reb. "Pepi thinks that will just make them kill us. It is why he told the chieftain he is marrying Sesha himself."

"Pepi?" Merat blinks at us. "Who is Pepi?"

"The Hyksos spy and cousin to the chieftain," Paser says.

"To your betrothed," Reb adds, ever helpful.

Merat looks at me. "You are marrying a Hyksos spy named Pepi?"

I offer a weak smile. "Apparently we are going to share a wedding day."

"We will be cousins?" Merat asks, uncertain.

"While that thought does not make me unhappy, I cannot accept this situation," I say.

"What if it is the gods' will?" Reb asks, then yawns. We have slept almost as poorly as we have eaten.

"It is not mine," I say, as stubborn as Nefer, who must possess much of this quality to survive sandstorms and frequent desert treks. I turn to Merat. "I have an idea, but I will need your help."

Her lips curve up in a delighted smile. "I am always happy to give it."

After gathering the items we need, Merat brings them to me and I prepare the concoction.

Paser sniffs at the potion. "That smells like a body that was not properly preserved."

We are in Merat's hut. As a courtesy to his bride, the chieftain provided her with her own private, but small, quarters. The Hyksos are letting us rest in the company of our fellow jackal princess after our gruelling journey through the sands. Pepi did try to convince the chieftain that I need a few days to recover from our trek, but the oasis's leader is insisting the ceremony will go on as planned.

Merat looks at the foul-smelling brew. "Can we not just fake our symptoms?"

"For them to postpone the wedding, we must appear seriously ill," I say. "Paser and Reb will also recommend they isolate us to prevent it spreading."

She sighs. "I do not enjoy expelling the contents of my stomach."

"Nor do I," I say, giving her shoulder a comforting pat. "But at least it is only temporary. Marriage is a more permanent condition."

Merat writhes on the ground, clutching her stomach. "Ohhh," she moans. "Maybe a wedding would not be so bad after all."

I vomit in response.

The boys, leaving us with water and in misery, go to inform Pepi and the chieftain of our sudden and alarming illness — which I am already regretting. Dehydrated and lacking food, my body is not happy with the continued punishment.

Pepi sticks his head in the hut. "Sesha, are you well? Paser and Reb say you have taken ill."

"Yes," I say, and do not need to exaggerate my groan. "The princess and I are suffering from a terrible illness. It may be catching."

Confusion crosses his face. "Both? I can see if you were sick on your own, but for you two to suffer so suddenly from the same thing ... did you even take a meal together?"

Again, I am reminded that Pepi's intelligence is not to be underestimated. His gaze falls on the small pot, and he walks over to sniff at the contents. He looks back at us, pale and sweating, and raises a brow.

"I will see you are taken to the pools until your condition improves. Your 'brothers' may attend you there." He stops at the exit to the tent, looking back over his shoulder. "A bold move, Sesha. Perhaps, when you feel better, we can have our game of Senet at last. Something tells me I will find you a formidable opponent."

22

"I NEED TO WASH," I CROAK, standing on wobbling feet. Paser and Reb snore away under the shade of a large fig tree, its branches offering ample shade.

"I will join you." Merat clutches at my arm. We make our way unsteadily down to the water's edge, holding on to each other for support.

My clothes are dirty and disintegrating. I strip down before wading into the water. Merat does the same, and we float side by side, staring up at the sky.

"Do you remember that day I brought you a clean robe in the baths at the palace?" she asks.

"I remember well," I say. "You were very kind to me."

"It was mostly because I wanted you to teach me to read and write," she says, honest as always. "Though I grew to like you for yourself, after only a short while in your company."

"And I grew to like you as well," I say, smiling up at the wisps of clouds floating by.

"Is it true what Reb says about my mother?"

I do not want to lie to my friend, even if the truth causes bad feelings between us. "Yes."

Merat is silent for a moment. "I used to think I knew her well, and that she would do anything for me."

"I am sure she would." Queen Anat said that her family would be just fine despite potential famine. She must believe the gods are on her side. Maybe they are.

"Then why did she give me away?" Merat's tone is bitter. "I know I must do my duty. But it is one thing to marry a noble that you half know, and quite another to be delivered into the hands of strangers who live in the desert."

"Perhaps she felt you'd be safer with the Hyksos." Again, I wonder why I defend the queen. But as someone who knows the pain of losing a mother, I do not want Merat to suffer. "They flourish in Avaris and the surrounding lands, growing in strength and wealth." Whereas the last few dynasties at Thebes have floundered, weakened by famine and plagues. As scribes tasked with recording the glories of our civilization, we do not like to admit this, but facts are difficult to ignore. And should the Hyksos prove successful in assuming control of the whole land, it will serve the queen well to have a daughter on the other side. "Likely she did not know they lived in the desert," I add. "She probably thought you'd be in the bustling city of Avaris." A place we might still very well end up fleeing to. My stomach twists. One dune at a time.

"Perhaps," Merat says, still sounding sad.

I change the direction of our conversation. "How are you feeling?"

"Not all that well," she admits. "But at least I am no longer considering drowning myself in this lake."

"The concoction is not lasting as long as I hoped," I say, treading water. In a way, I am relieved — or at least my insides are — but there must be continued symptoms if the chieftain inquires after his bride's wellbeing. Or checks on her himself.

A whistle comes from the shore and I look up to see Pepi, holding fresh linens aloft. "Clean garments," he calls.

I raise a weak hand to indicate he leave them there. With a nod, he places the clothes on the ground and walks past Paser and Reb, who are still sleeping.

Merat treads water beside me. Colour is coming back into her cheeks. She is clean and water dots her brow; her dark hair is slicked back, her beautiful eyes inquisitive.

"So that is the Hyksos spy," she remarks, eyes following Pepi. "He does not resemble his cousin much."

Though average height, Pepi does not compare in size to the chieftain, who is one of the largest men I have ever seen. "He seems kind enough."

"I do not know if we can trust him," I admit as Merat turns to face me. "There is more to him than what's on the surface. Yet we would not have made it here without his guidance."

"Then I have much to be grateful to him for." Merat looks at me intently. "When your life is turned upside down, it is everything to have friends by your side." Her gaze turns to the slumbering boys on the beach.

"It is." I agree with my whole heart.

"The spy, what is his name? Pepi? He must be fond of you." Merat pulls her wet hair to the side. "Especially if he proposed after only a few days."

"It is not like that." I give my head a small shake. "He said the only way to keep Reb, Paser, and me safe is to say that I am his intended and that they are my brothers, and so also his family."

"He is likely right. His cousin rules this clan and they respect and love him. No harm will come to you if you are part of his family. But ..." Her eyes search mine. "This seems like a most elaborate ruse on his part, just to keep you safe."

Though the water is cool, a flush spreads through my body. "We saved him. Perhaps he feels a sense of obligation. And the desert is a strange place." I try to keep my voice light. "It can make friends out of enemies."

"What about something more than friends?" She flutters her dark lashes.

"You tease me, Princess," I say.

It is her turn to change the subject. "Tell me, whose idea was it to come after me?" She looks over to the riverbank.

"We made the decision together," I say. "Reb was hesitant at first, but changed currents quickly enough." If she's disappointed by my response, she does not show it.

Two Hyksos women come into view and leave a small pile of food next to the clothes. They scurry off, not wanting to risk becoming ill. Though my stomach was just turned inside out, it rumbles at the sight of food.

"How are you feeling?" I ask as we make our way back to shore.

"A little better," she admits. "If anyone checks on us again, I do not think complaints of a few stomach pains will be enough to keep the weddings from happening."

"Then we are going to have to demonstrate more symptoms," I say as our feet touch bottom. My stomach lets out a loud gurgle of protest.

"That looks most uncomfortable," Reb says, peering at me.

"It *feels* most uncomfortable." I scratch my arms, which are red and splotchy. Unable to bear doing any further damage to my insides, I conferred with Paser and we concluded that an angry rash should be enough to put off talk of immediate wedding ceremonies. It will also buy us some time to figure out our next plan of action now that we have found the princess.

"Sesha, my skin feels like it is on fire!" Merat says, scratching her neck. She is covered in small red bumps, as am I. We rubbed the sap from the fig tree over our bodies; it causes irritation upon contact.

"Try not to scratch," Paser advises us.

I give him a dark look. "Many thanks, doctor." My voice is as dry as the desert. "I would never have guessed that."

"Easy for you to say," Merat says to him, using the palm of her hand, rather than her nails, to rub vigorously at her skin. "You do not look like you were stung by a thousand scorpions."

We hear a throat clear and we whirl around. Pepi stands there. His eyes widen as he takes in Merat's and my matching red bumps and miserable faces.

"The sickness is worsening," I say before he can speak. He rubs his chin with one hand, possibly to hide the smile tugging at the corners of his mouth.

"I see," he says. "I will have to inform my cousin that there will indeed be no ceremony tonight. He thought you two might be exaggerating your condition, given the princess's previous ... reluctance to be wed. But I told him no one would go through such lengths to avoid joining such a great and noble family."

I nod, wishing I could crawl out of my skin like a snake shedding its outer layer. "You should leave us now. The illness is very contagious."

"What of your friends?" Pepi tilts his head at Reb and Paser. "Are you not worried for their well-being?"

"Ahh, yes," I say. "They must leave as well. Will they be safe with you?"

"Safer than they are with you," Pepi murmurs, looking at poor Merat, who is scratching her back against the tree like a frenzied, yet still graceful, giraffe. "We will put them to work," Pepi adds. "They can attend to some of the minor physical ailments of the people."

Reb perks up. "You have no physician?"

"We do," Pepi says. "He went to Avaris for supplies. He is due back soon, but there are a few complaints that can be dealt with. And if you wish the tribe to adopt you, this is an opportunity to show your value."

This has me looking up from a particularly irritating welt to glance at Paser and Reb. Is that what we want? We need to discuss things soon.

"You and Merat should rest, Sesha," Pepi says. "Prayers to the gods that this terrible … illness will soon pass."

"Yes." I scratch my stomach. "Perhaps Paser and Reb can bring some salve back with them, if you have any." Giving the four of us a chance to talk.

"Of course," Pepi agrees. "I believe there is quite a selection. The physician is an avid brewer and collector of herbal remedies."

"Thank you," I say, meaning it. "And for the fresh clothes as well."

"It is my pleasure," he says. "Coming?" He looks at Paser and Reb, who follow him. Paser shrugs helplessly and I nod that we will be all right.

"Do not forget the salve," I call after them, unable to resist scratching another bump on my arm. "And maybe bring something to bind our hands together?" Merat looks over at me like I am joking, but I know it will be the only way to stop us from raking our skin off.

23

MERAT AND I GO FOR ANOTHER SWIM, the water providing some relief from our itching skin. I catch a glimpse of my reflection in the water and see a scrawny, sandblasted, blistered orphan. Perhaps I will not need to pretend I am Pepi's betrothed. I cannot imagine who'd want me in my current state: half-starved, spotted, and supposedly contagious.

When Paser and Reb return with the salve, we fall upon it gratefully, coating ourselves liberally from top to bottom.

"How long until the symptoms fade?" Merat asks. Her face is shiny from the balm, which appears to be a combination of almond oil, honey, bee pollen, and propolis. It is quite fresh; there must be a thriving hive somewhere in the oasis, which explains the variety of plants and trees.

"In a few days." I eye the strips Paser has faithfully brought us for bindings. "If we can manage not to infect our wounds, we should be fine."

"Would you like me to tie your hands, Princess?" Paser asks, unable to keep the grin off his face.

She sighs. "I think my vanity is enough to keep me from scratching too much. I do not want scars pitting my skin."

"Did you see any patients?" I ask Paser to distract myself from the itching. They tell us about a few cases, the most successful treatment of the day belonging to Reb, who pulled an infected tooth for one of the commanders in a showy spray of blood and saliva. It had been paining him for days, and the soldier was extremely grateful for the relief Reb's deft work provided him.

"Did you tend to the commander at the training grounds?" I ask.

"No, we were in the main village section," Paser says. "I get the feeling there is something over there they do not wish us to see. The path is guarded and the people are furtive, as if they are hiding something."

"We are strangers in their midst," Merat says. She takes some more of the nourishing balm and coats her dark strands of hair with it. "They do not trust us. If they are planning a military assault, they will not want us escaping and bringing their secrets back to Thebes."

Reb snorts. "They do not need to worry about that. There is no way I am going back through the Red Land."

Thankfully, the balm is beginning to work, and I am able at last to address the hippo in our midst. "You wish to stay, then?" I ask, stomach plummeting like a falcon. We will not be able to put off the marriages forever.

Reb looks down at the ground. I sigh. I cannot blame him for not wanting to go back into the desert so soon. Or at all.

"How was your own journey here?" Paser asks Merat.

"We came most of the way by boat along the Nile," she says. "The desert crossing was hot and uncomfortable, but we had several donkeys laden with supplies to bear the load."

"We also tried taking the river," Paser says, bringing to my mind arrows and crocodiles.

"It did not go all that well," Reb adds, one hand going to the fading bruise on his forehead.

"My journey was fairly uneventful, though most of it felt like a bad dream," Merat says, dark strands swinging as she shakes her head. "Being given so abruptly to the chieftain." A shadow crosses her face. "What was your plan once you arrived here?"

"It was not well thought out," I admit, looking at Paser.

"I have family in Avaris," he tells Merat. "After finding you, we thought we might go to them for help, then disappear in the city crowds or catch a ship somewhere."

"And how will we get to Avaris?" Reb asks.

"Pepi spoke of a caravan coming with the physician," Paser says. "As Merat said, donkeys and supplies will ease the journey. Perhaps we can persuade those among them to take us."

The princess and I share a look, knowing well that the odds of that happening are small. The boys might have a chance, but Merat and I are bound to the Hyksos, even if my commitment is only a ruse.

"We may need Pepi's help if we want any hope of doing that," I say at last. Our total dependence on the spy is not lost on me.

"Let us hold off until we are sure there are no other options," Paser says. "I still do not fully trust him."

Reb nods his agreement. "We should be on our way, before anyone feels we are spending too long in your company."

"Reb is right." Paser looks at us in apology. "They will not want us working on patients if there's a chance of us spreading your 'ailment.' If all of us are thought infectious, it might be easier for them to decide what to do with us."

"We are well," I assure him, and Merat nods. Now that the itching has lessened somewhat, I feel very tired, not having slept well, or often, since I was back at the palace. Like my time on the streets, that seems like someone else's life. I have had several in the course of my thirteen years.

Reb starts down the path, but Paser lingers. Merat looks at him in expectation.

"I will leave you then." Paser nods with a final glance at us both. "The chieftain says his bride may keep the balm."

I settle down under a tree to rest my eyes. Merat stares after Paser, a look of longing on her face. Being unchaperoned in the wild with the person who has her heart must seem most romantic to her.

"Take care of your face," I say, my voice soft. "Looking at him like that in front of the Hyksos, especially the chieftain, will get him killed."

She gives me a wry smile. "I do not have my mother's trick of hiding my thoughts."

"Then it is probably best if there are no thoughts to hide." I motion for her to come sit beside me. "I know how you feel about Paser, and it must seem terribly brave, his showing up here to rescue you. But —" I take her hand in mine "— you will need to put him out of your mind if you want to keep him safe. Our position here is precarious enough."

I hesitate, then decide to tell the truth. Though it might hurt her a little, it is necessary for Paser's continued existence. "It was not Paser's idea to come after you." I look into her eyes. "It was mine."

She nods as if she knew this all along — and maybe she has. "I will try my best to guard my thoughts. And my face."

I squeeze her hand, wanting to impress the urgency of the situation upon the princess, who has never had to fear for her life. "You must not try. You must do."

Merat and I wake from our nap to the faraway sound of cheering, laughter, and shouts. I feel like I've been to the underworld and back, so deep was my slumber. Our small fire burns low.

"What is that noise?" I say blearily, scratching my arms, which are beginning to itch again. Time for another application of balm.

"It sounds like a celebration," Merat says with the assurance of one who has attended countless parties of the royal court.

"What can they be celebrating? There are no weddings taking place."

She shrugs. "If I had to guess, men are fighting. Or someone has killed something large."

"Let us hope it is an animal." The cheering grows even more raucous. I think of our friends and worry for them, even though I did give Paser my father's blade to hold on to shortly after we arrived. "Do you think we should go and check on Paser and Reb?" It is dark, and if we move quietly perhaps no one will see us. With luck, the Hyksos are not turning on them after they tended the people all day.

"They are likely well enough." Merat scratches at her legs. She looks like she was bitten by a hundred insects. There is a loud cry and she glances up from her shins. "But perhaps we could take a quick look."

I pick up the balm. "I am sorry for all the discomfort I've caused you. At the most, it may only offer a few days' reprieve from your situation." Especially if we are forced to stay.

"Do you not mean *our* situation?" Her words are a cold splash of water in my face. Exhausted, I momentarily forgot my own engagement. Just because it is not real does not lessen the chance of a marriage actually happening. "Besides, a few days should be time enough for us to work out another plan." Her teeth flash in the night. "One that — by the gods — does not involve purging and boils."

We creep like animals being stalked in the dark. A glow in the distance hints of a large fire. A distinct smell permeates the air, one I encounter often in my profession.

The smell of blood.

A curdling scream sends a bolt down my spine, like one of Set's flaming spears shot down from the sky.

"Hurry," I whisper to Merat. We walk faster toward the fire, looking around for anyone who might spot us, but whatever is happening, everyone is there.

The fire is located past a large wall of bushes and trees, sending sparks up into the sky. We peer over the thick brush. At first, the bodies are indistinguishable, black shapes in the night, forming a circle around two people.

Pepi and Paser stand off, facing each other, crouched low and moving in circles, each watching the other intently. The Hyksos people cheer for Pepi. Reb, Paser's lone supporter, stands off to the side, shouting encouragement.

"It *is* a fight," Merat whispers in my ear, one hand over her chest.

"What do you think happens to the loser?" I say, thinking of the blood smell, which is much stronger here, closer to the fire.

"I do not know," Merat says. She clutches at my arm. Frozen, and unable to do anything else, we watch the match unfold.

24

PEPI LUNGES QUICK AS A COBRA. Paser only narrowly manages to avoid his swing. They continue circling, while everyone cheers and shouts their suggestions. I try to feel the mood of the crowd, which seems to be more merry than deadly. For the moment.

"Why are they fighting?" Merat asks. "Do you think Paser challenged Pepi for your honour?"

"He is supposed to be my brother," I whisper.

"There is nothing brotherly about the way Paser looks at you," Merat says, and I look at her in shock. She makes a face. "It is only your obliviousness that keeps me from being completely jealous."

"I told you before, Paser is a friend," I stammer.

"It never occurs that he would like to be more?"

The crowd lets out a shout and I turn my attention back to the fight, ignoring her question.

Pepi has years of experience and only the gods know what kind of training, but Paser holds his ground. He lunges at the spy; Pepi catches his arm and pulls him off balance, to the delight of his supporters. Paser stumbles but does not fall. He spins around, hands held high in a defensive posture. The crowd jeers and someone darts forward, pushing Paser from behind. Again Paser stumbles but does not fall.

Pepi turns to the crowd. "He is good on his feet, for a Theban." Several members vocalize their disagreement.

Why is Pepi doing this? He helped us, saved our lives, even.

"I think it will be all right," Merat says. "They are testing Paser's strength and skill as a fighter. Probably to see if he is worthy of joining them."

"Of course he is," I say. We clutch at each other in the darkness. I hope she's right and the fight is only sport, not something more sinister.

Pepi lunges again at Paser. Someone from the crowd sticks out a leg, and this time Paser goes sprawling backwards. Pepi lands on top of him. The audience cheers, but the fight is not over yet. Wrapping his legs high around Pepi's waist, Paser prevents the Hyksos from landing a solid blow on his upper body and head, his arms blocking Pepi's flying fists. Paser manages to catch hold of Pepi's arms and, like a crocodile in a death roll, he uses his body weight to flip the Hyksos onto his back, shoving his left arm tight under Pepi's throat. Reb lets out a loud, lone cheer.

Pepi's hands scramble back in the sands. He grabs a fistful of dirt and flings it into Paser's face. Coughing and choking, Paser's grip on Pepi weakens. The spy jumps to his feet while Paser wipes at his watering eyes.

"That's cheating!" I protest loudly. Merat shushes me.

"After all that time in the desert, you'd think you'd be accustomed to a little sand in the face." Pepi grins. The crowd laughs, everyone apparently thinking the tactic fair play.

"Paser had him," I say.

Pepi offers his hand to Paser, who is still on his knees. Paser accepts it and Pepi pulls him to his feet.

"Still, you are a brave fighter," Pepi says. "Our troops welcome you to their ranks."

The chieftain steps into the circle. "Not so fast, my cousin."

"He's so big." I do not realize I speak aloud.

"Tell me something I do not know, Sesha," Merat mutters beside me.

"Though this young one fights well, how are we to know that when the time comes, he will be able to face his own people?"

My heart stops. The chieftain makes a fair point. If, for some reason, we are unable to escape the tribe, Paser would never truly be able to fight against his fellow Egyptians. Hopefully, it will never come to that.

Pepi does not look concerned despite the unspoken threat. "His people rejected him. His queen tried to end his life. He owes them nothing."

Paser nods at Pepi's claim, seeming to sense the immediate danger in not gaining the chieftain's trust. He measures his own words carefully. "What your cousin says is true. I am honoured to fight alongside you and your men, if you will have me."

"What do your people know of honour?" The chieftain crosses his arms, firelight gleaming off his bare chest. A collar of smooth animal bones sits around his neck, impressive as any necklace of precious stones. A rhino horn hangs at its centre, a protective charm. "Your rulers enter into treaties with our people, then break them when it suits their purpose."

"They are no longer my rulers," Paser insists. He is doing a good job, though I am not convinced he could pick up a weapon against Pharaoh or the sons and grandsons of his grandsire's friends. The chieftain does not look convinced, either. Pepi, as if expecting this, nods at someone in the crowd and a stony-faced man comes forward, holding up a large bucket.

Pepi lifts his arms wide. "Let us wash away his Egyptian blood then, so he may be reborn as one of us."

From here I can see Reb's swallow, but he moves into the firelight. "And mine as well," he calls out, voice cracking only slightly.

Pepi nods and another bucket is brought to him.

"The spy seems well prepared." Merat echoes my thoughts. I realize the fight, probably this whole ceremony, was planned by Pepi.

An older man in a leopard skin joins them; he must be the village priest or wise man or whatever the Hyksos call those who perform these types of magical rites and incantations. He holds up his hands like Pepi had, fire glinting off the copper cuffs encircling his wrists. His voice rings out in the night, entering directly into my bones. The drums start then, and the people slowly circle Reb and Paser. They chant along with the priest, whose voice rises in strength and volume. Faster and faster the drums beat. Louder and louder the chanting gets. It makes me want to squirm out of my skin. I look over at Merat, whose spotted face is white in the moonlight.

The priest says something loudly in a language that I do not understand, but his meaning is clear enough. He brings his hands down in a cutting gesture and the crowd immediately falls silent. The buckets are held high over Paser's and Reb's heads. When the buckets are dumped over the boys, I expect water, but a thick black liquid spills out, coating them completely. The smell that first caught my attention before I was distracted by the excitement of the fight is back, and much stronger.

Blood.

"Do you think ... that is from a person?" I gulp. The blood runs in rivulets down their half-clothed bodies, claiming them as the tribe's own.

"I pray not," Merat says, holding my hand tightly.

The crowd cheers as Paser and Reb wipe the dark, sticky stuff from their eyes, their faces streaked black-red.

"There may not be a wedding tonight," Pepi shouts, "but there will be a celebration! We have two new members of our tribe." He looks Paser and Reb up and down. "And while they may not be as comely as my cousin's bride-to-be and my own —" the crowd laughs; Pepi has the way of a born entertainer about him "— we welcome them into our midst!"

The chieftain crosses his arms and nods. The crowd roars in approval. The drums resume and the festivities begin. A few women, perhaps wives of the soldiers, start dancing. They ululate, twirl, and swirl around the fire like the sands during a storm. The body of a giant lion, hanging from a large branch, is carried into the firelight by several men. I feel a pang for the noble creature but am relieved the blood did not come from humans.

"Come," I whisper to Merat. "We should get back before we are seen."

"Yes. It will do us no good to be caught sneaking around in the dark."

We slink back the way we came, careful to remain unseen. It takes time for our eyes to adjust after the light of the fire and we stumble blindly along a half-worn path.

We are almost back to our quarantine area when a low growl stops us in mid-step.

"What is that?" Merat asks, the lion likely still fresh in her mind. Perhaps his mate has come looking for him. But I recognize the sound, having heard it many times before. It is the sound of a woman about to give birth.

25

"**T**HIS WAY." I PULL MERAT ALONG. We find the woman on all fours, panting. I drop to my knees by her side. She looks at me, terror in her eyes.

"Get away from me!" she says. "You are diseased!"

"Never mind that," I say. "How long have you been labouring?"

"The pains came on quickly." She grits her teeth as another contraction grips her body. Arching her back, she groans, and the ferocity of it causes Merat to take a step back. "I was overcome with thirst and going to get more water."

"You have nothing to fear." I keep my voice soothing. "Will you allow us to help you?"

"You will make the baby and me sick," she says,

eyes wide with fear, perhaps not only of an infectious stranger, but also with the anxiety that comes with delivering a child. Fear that it will not end well. Another contraction hits her and she closes her eyes.

"Do not hold your air. Breathe." When the worst of the contraction passes, I ask, "Is this your first?" and place one hand on her lower back to massage it. She looks only a few years older than Merat.

"Yes," she pants. "Please, do not touch me."

"I am not contagious," I say firmly. "It was a ploy to delay the wedding." There's no help for it now — I need her to let me assist. I look over at the princess to confirm my words. "Tell her, Merat." Merat stands frozen, a look of horror on her face. "What is it?" I glance around, expecting to see a wild animal about to attack, but we are alone.

And then I remember.

Merat's sister Nefertiri died in childbirth at seventeen. The two princesses were inseparable. Sisters not only of blood, but of the heart. They were together always, laughing and playing, unconcerned with serious matters, as is the privilege of young princesses.

"It will be all right," I say to her. But she does not see me, as she is lost in memories. "Merat!" I sharpen my tone. "Go find some water." The pregnant girl was on her way back from the lake, and her container lies spilled on the ground. Merat will not be of any help to me in her present state anyway.

She stumbles off into the darkness. I do not know if she will return, but I turn my thoughts to the patient beside me.

"What is your name?" I ask the girl.

"Amara."

"Amara, will you let me help you?"

Reluctantly, she nods. She does not have much choice in the matter, as I am the only one here. I feel her abdomen, the outline of the child. Bastet and Taweret, goddesses of birth and mothers, are with us. The baby is in the proper position.

"It's not supposed to be my time," Amara says. "The baby comes early."

"Perhaps she has a mind of her own. A good quality. Or maybe she is just eager to meet you," I say. A flicker of a smile crosses her face. It is replaced by a grimace of pain as she is struck by another contraction. It will not be long now. I help her off the path.

"Try squatting," I urge. "Many women find that a beneficial position."

"You have done this before?" she pants through the next wave of pain. Her dark hair is matted with sweat and I smooth it back from her brow, wishing for my bag, some herbs, something more to help her. But all I have are my words, and so I encourage her to push, find a stick for her to bite on, and massage her between the quick and hard contractions.

"I see the head," I say excitedly, after what feels like hours, but is probably no time at all.

She grunts in response.

"Push," I urge. She grips my hand, squeezing my fingers, and with a howl to summon the dead, she pushes with all her strength.

The baby's head emerges. "Again!" I command. Amara closes her eyes tight and bears down. The shoulders are next and I let her do her job, instinctive and as old as the time of Isis, the Mother Goddess who gave birth to Horus. As I gently manipulate and murmur, the baby slowly emerges into this world. Amara gives a final grunt, and the baby comes out in a plop of fluids.

The infant, a girl, lets out a startled cry as I wipe her with my clean robes, making sure her mouth and nostrils are clear. Her eyes are wide open and she seems fairly calm, despite the hurried exit from her mother, who lies beside me.

"Here." Merat is back, with water and linens. She lets out a shaky breath. "Are they all right?"

"They are well," I say, securely swaddling the babe to keep her warm and lessen her distress at being abruptly expelled from the cozy quarters she occupied these past nine moons. Amara lies on her back, one hand over her brow, eyes closed in exhaustion.

"You have a beautiful daughter," I say, beaming. *Beautiful* may be a slight exaggeration to describe the baby in her present state, but a good wash will take care of that. This has been a messy evening.

Amara props herself up on her elbows, tears streaming down her face. Merat helps her to a seated position and I place the babe in her arms. "Thanks be to the gods, and to you …"

"Sesha."

"Sesha." She smiles. Amara puts the baby to her breast, and she begins to suckle, hungry from the difficult task of being born.

"Will you stay with her?" I ask Merat. "I need to find something to cut the cord with." My father's obsidian blade will do nicely. But first I must get it from Paser.

"Yes, I will stay," Merat says, watching the tender scene of mother and newborn before her.

I touch Merat's shoulder. "Thank you for coming back with the linens and water." Princesses are not used to being told what to do by their lessers. But Merat is not your average princess. "Give her some water. She will need it for her milk."

My friend nods and I make my way along the path, back to the continued merriment of the Hyksos. The celebrations sound fully underway. I suppose the villagers were looking forward to a party, one way or another. I am reminded of my last night at the palace, of another celebration, of finding the scroll and of Ky's surgery. That night ended in the physical loss of my home, and the even more devastating loss of my brother.

Keeping my eye out for either Reb or Paser, I walk closer to where the fire is, but I don't see either of them. The smell of blood has been replaced by the aroma of cooked meat, and my stomach rumbles. I hope the Hyksos gave proper thanks to the lion-headed goddess, Sekhmet, for the life of one of her own. The goddess of protection and healing, she is also one of vengeance, and if proper appreciation is not shown for her sacrifice, she may be angered. It is said her breath formed the desert, and having had recent experience with *that* place, I would not wish for her wrath to come down on me. Or on the people I currently reside with.

"Sesha." A figure wobbles toward me. It is Paser. I wonder if the power of my thoughts summoned him.

"Paser," I whisper. "I need my father's blade. Do you have it?"

"Yes," Paser says. He seems a little unsteady on his feet, body still stained with blood.

"Have you been drinking?" I say, thinking of an oasis vineyard Merat mentioned during one of our swims. This may take longer than I want.

"Not by my choice. But I am well enough." He pulls the blade from the belt around his waist and places it in my hands. "Are you feeling better?" He peers closely at my face, and I feel the warmth of the fire coming from his clothes, his skin.

Now that he asks, I am quite itchy again. "I will be fine." I wave a hand. "Are you?" I ask, with a pointed look at the scuff on his cheek.

"You witnessed that?" he says, looking slightly abashed. "It was the spy's idea," he says, confirming my guess that Pepi planned the whole thing.

Still exulted from the delivery, I rush to tell him. "I helped a mother birth her child tonight."

"That is wonderful," he exclaims. "The child will share my birth day."

"Your birth day?" I repeat, shocked. "Why did you not speak of this earlier?"

"There has been much happening." He smiles. "It is not important."

"Of course it is important. Every year alive is something to be celebrated." Especially in these perilous times and considering our recent journey.

"I did not say I have not been celebrating." His smile widens.

"I wish there was something I could give you, as a gift." I look down at my father's blade. He wraps his hands around mine, silently suggesting I do no such thing.

"Your friendship is enough," he insists. "And you give me one adventure after another. Remember I told you how much I enjoy them?"

"Likely more adventures than you bargained on." I smile, thinking of him helping me find the scroll and free the spy from the pits, and of our perilous crossing of the Red Land.

"Oh, listen to you." Reb stumbles up to us, also splattered with dried blood. It looks like he, too, has been enjoying the festivities. I do not begrudge them. After everything that has happened, they deserve a night to celebrate. "There *is* something you can give him."

Paser gives Reb a look that would silence anyone with more sense. But Reb is never one to shy away from saying exactly what he thinks. "A kiss."

26

A KISS?

"Pay him no attention." Paser shoots Reb another menacing look.

"The Hyksos's drink is quick in, quick out," Reb says, hurrying off into the bush to relieve himself.

"Sesha, I am sorry —" Paser starts to apologize, ever a man with honour. As it is his birth day, and he is now fifteen, he *is* a man, not only in age but also as evidenced by his behaviour and bravery.

Before I change my mind, I stand on the tips of my toes and brush my lips lightly to his warm cheek. "The happiest of birth days to you, Paser," I say softly. His hand comes to his cheek, but before he responds I am off, on my way back to my healer's duties.

What made me do that? Perhaps it was the celebratory mood of the camp, the thrill of a new life, and a thank you for seeing me safe. Paser has always made me feel safe. He and Merat, and even Reb, are my home now, as much as people can be.

I reach Merat and Amara. Both the mother and child are doing well.

"How is the baby eating?" I inquire. Early attempts at feeding can be as challenging as the birth itself.

"She is a greedy thing." Amara nuzzles her baby's nose. I cut the cord while they are both distracted, but it is no matter, as neither feels it.

"Do you wish me to find the father?" I ask, reluctant to go back to the party. It will be difficult to find a stranger in the dark. In addition, I do not wish to start a panic if someone sees me, infectious as Merat and I are assumed to be.

But Amara looks up at me, eagerness all over her face. "Yes, could you please?"

Merat squeezes my hand. "I will go. The people will not harm me, ill or not."

"What will you tell the chieftain?"

She shrugs. "That the dangerous time has passed."

"What if he thinks it is too soon?" The chieftain

does not strike me as someone who is easily fooled. I think of Pepi, trying to hide his smile at our obvious schemes. "Find Pepi," I ask, feeling certain. "He will assist you."

"What is your husband's name?" Merat asks Amara.

"Akin. He is the chieftain's man."

Merat nods and leaves.

"Are you able to walk?" I ask Amara. It is better if we go to a spot nearer the water. She will want to wash.

"I think so," she says, and I help her stand. She is strong and young, and as the birth was simple, she should recover well, by the grace of the gods. She wraps one arm around my shoulders, holding the baby tight to her chest with the other.

We awkwardly make our way to Merat's and my small fire, which is almost out. I blow on the ashes and add a few twigs, hoping to get it going again.

"Go wash." I nod at the water. "I will hold the baby."

At first she does not want to leave the child, even for a second, but she relents and makes her way down to the water's edge. Stripping and wading in, she scoops silt from the bottom of the lake and rubs her skin with it in a circular motion.

The moonlight is much brighter on the beach. "Let us have a look at you," I say to the baby, unswaddling and examining her closely. Like Reb and Paser, she is streaked with dried blood, but seems alert and healthy enough. I feel a sense of responsibility for this child, the first I have delivered entirely on my own.

Her lashes are long and dark, and she has more hair than most. She blinks at me sleepily, and I smile. "Would you like to bathe as well?" I take the child down to the water's edge and give her to her mother, who, now clean, begins to wash the baby. Surprised by the cool water, the baby lets out a cry, piercing in the night. Soothingly, in a low sweet voice, Amara begins to sing to the child.

The tune is hauntingly familiar, and I am stunned to recognize it. "Where did you learn that song?"

"My mother sang it to me." The baby whimpers at the interruption, then lets out a few more squawks of protest at her bath.

"As did mine," I say. How is that possible? We are from two different worlds.

"There are many similarities between our people," Amara says. "The Hyksos have lived in the delta for many years. We all speak your language, have assumed many of your ways, and shared our knowledge as well. Perhaps we are more alike than those at Thebes would allow you to believe." She continues singing, and after a few moments, I join in softly, our voices mingling together in the night. The baby's crying stops.

Merat and I remain in quarantine for the next few days as the self-inflicted rashes on our bodies begin to heal. We vehemently concur we do not want to marry and try to work out a way to leave the oasis. She agrees with the impossible suggestion of fleeing north to the Hyksos capital, as well as with the equally difficult tasks of finding Paser's estranged family once we reach the city, and convincing them to help us.

First, though, there's one small matter: how to depart the oasis. Or rather, not how to depart it, but how to survive the desert once we do. The caravan is a tenuous option, should it ever arrive, but it is doubtful we can join it undetected. Despite Paser and Reb's mistrust of Pepi, it is looking more and more like I will have to speak to him. Preferably before talks of weddings resume. Most fortunate for us, the celebration seems to have satisfied everyone for the moment. During one of his visits Paser reports that the extra stores of food and beer put aside for the wedding were consumed and, reassuringly, that it will take a few weeks to increase the stocks again.

He does not mention the brief kiss, and I wonder if he has forgotten, as there was much happening that night. Yet, something slight has shifted between us, like when the sun hits an object from a different angle, illuminating something previously unseen but always there. I do not mention the kiss to Merat, unsure if doing so will give it more meaning than I intended in giving it.

Aside from Amara, who visits once with the baby, both doing well, I am forbidden to see patients. She does not repeat what I told her of our fake illness, whether as a courtesy to me or because she is so wrapped up in her new infant.

Our other visitors, Paser and Reb, occasionally bring us food and more balm. We spend our time under the shade of thick palms thinking of ways to reach Avaris, only to dismiss this plan and the next as impossible, as futile as looking for tiny crystals in the desert sands. Frustrated by the morning's unproductive scheming, Merat and I take a break, and instead resume her study of hieratic scripts, which we began at the pharaoh's palace. We draw them over and over again in the sand.

She frowns at a particularly complex one now. Her red welts are almost gone, as her skin darkens in the sun, unused to so much time out of palace walls. "I cannot seem to write this one," she says, biting her lip. Merat has a quick mind and becomes frustrated when there is something she does not immediately grasp.

I draw it again. "You cross it here. Then up, down, and loop it around."

"Up, down, loop it around," she repeats under her breath, focusing on perfecting the script, which is already decent enough.

Loud voices have us looking up from the sand. The chieftain and Pepi come into view. Merat and I glance at each other. This is the tribe leader's first time visiting since our "sickness" began. I am not sure if Pepi deliberately kept him away or if he did not want to risk becoming ill. Either way, it looks like our temporary reprieve has come to an end.

27

"**T**HERE IS MY BRIDE!" the chieftain calls as he gets closer, examining us carefully. I get the feeling that, like his cousin, he does not miss much. "You are looking much healthier, dear one."

Merat nods, acknowledging his compliment. "Many thanks. I seem to be recovering well."

"It helps when you have your own personal physician attending you," Pepi says, eyes dancing mischievously.

"Yes," Merat says, with no trace of irony. "I am very lucky to have Sesha."

The chieftain's gaze falls to the ground, noticing the letters written in the sand. "What is this?" He kicks at the inscriptions.

"Nothing," Merat answers quickly. "Just something to pass the time."

"If you are well, you both should be helping the other women," the chieftain admonishes us. "Not scribbling in the sand. All hands are needed here. No one rests in the desert, not even princesses."

"As to that, we come to ask what duties might interest you," Pepi interjects smoothly. He is more diplomatic than the chieftain, who is obviously accustomed to his commands being followed without question. "You may choose how you will assist the tribe."

I look at Pepi, feeling slighted, even if it is irrational. Though we do not plan to stay permanently with the Hyksos, he does not know that. He *does* know about my experience as a physician and, thus, where I would prefer to be: tending patients alongside Paser, Reb, and the other physician, yet to arrive with the sandblasted caravan. I am unable to resist asking, "Am I not to doctor the people, then?"

"We have enough physicians." The chieftain waves a hand. "Your brothers and the tribe's healer are more than able to care for the villagers. One of our scouts says the caravan will arrive today, and the doctor with it." Merat stiffens beside me. "Besides, a young woman is better used in other areas, like preparing the food and washing the linens." His eyes narrow at me. "Which you seem to go through a lot of."

"Ah …" I look at Pepi, wanting to protest.

He gives his head a slight shake in warning. Future family member or not, I am not to question the chieftain's commands. "Is there something else that interests you, Sesha?" Pepi asks. My mind tries to come up with another task, but for me there is nothing but helping those who medically need it. I despise cooking, hate laundering, and have no talent for making things clean and tidy.

"Perhaps the gardens?" Merat suggests, sensing my distress. "She can help prepare the medicines. I am afraid we have gone through all of the balm." She holds up the empty tub.

"Very well," says the chieftain gruffly. "And you, Merat?" She startles at the use of her name. It sounds strange coming from his full lips, spoken with care, respect.

"What about helping with the children … Yanassi?" she says tentatively, calling him by his own name in return. It is the first time I have heard her do so. "Sesha has taught me enough that I can pass on some knowledge of writing. Or at least keep them occupied so their mothers may give full attention to their own tasks?"

"The children can already make shapes in the sand."

Not ones that mean anything.

Merat bites her lip. I do not think the princess wants to be cooking and cleaning either. The chieftain puts a hand under her chin. "Very well," he says, tilting her face up to look at him. "You may care for the little ones. It will give you knowledge for when we have our own. When the time comes, I wish to have many sons and daughters." Merat blinks and he lets go of her, turning to Pepi. "Come, let us see what the caravan brings us."

"Helping in the gardens? I'd rather be sewing up wounds and setting bones!" Merat and I walk toward the main village camp, having been given the official pardon to rejoin the people. "Not that I do not appreciate your quick thinking," I say to Merat, sighing. It *is* better than laundering or cooking and a small thing when compared to the enormity of our plight. Perhaps that is why it's easy to be upset about it.

"We do not plan to be here long," Merat reminds me again. "Will it be so bad, preparing medicines? An effective poultice or brewed concoction can do much to help the wounded or ill. And you will have access to valuable items should we need them for our journey."

"This is true," I admit. "It is only my pride taking issue with stirring pots and grinding up herbs instead of being the one to administer them with instructions and care."

"At least your main job in life is not to give a giant many babies," Merat says darkly. I look at her with sympathy, knowing her fear of childbirth and remembering her courage in facing it by coming back with water and linens for Amara.

"As you said, we will not be here long enough for that to happen." It is my turn to remind her.

We reach the village. I did not take detailed notice of it upon our arrival, in the condition I was in then. I look at it now, spreading out before us. There are several huts in addition to the chieftain's, doubtless for some of his higher-ranking men. The rest of the accommodation consists of tents. Skins and linens are stretched out as far as the eye can see, under the shade of numerous palms and other plants.

"The oasis is truly a gift of the gods." I can't help but admire its size and organization, as well as its lush abundance.

"I am glad you like your new home," Pepi says, suddenly behind us. "For now, you two will share one of the huts."

Merat and I look at each other in relief. For our people, a woman is considered married when she moves her belongings into her husband's house and there is a celebration to mark the occasion. Now that

I think upon it, as I have so little to my name, I wonder if the arrangement can even take place?

Pepi laughs at the expression on our faces. "We are not so bad," he says, spreading his hands, presumably to encompass his cousin and his people. "We will provide for you and keep you safe."

I owe Pepi much, including the lives of my friends, not to mention my own, so I smile, though I can feel that it does not quite reach my eyes. He seems to think we are staying. Unless we can come up with a brilliant scheme, that may very well be our fate.

I point at the thickest part of the oasis, far off in the distance. "What is over there?" I ask, though I have a fair idea.

"The training grounds," he says.

"Why do you come all the way to the desert to train?" Merat asks. "Would it not be easier to remain at Avaris?"

"It would," Pepi agrees. "But part of winning battles is the element of surprise. There are many eyes and ears in the city, and the Nile is a great communicator of gossip and news." He clasps his hands behind his back. "The king there is my uncle and the King of all Foreign Rulers. Yanassi persuaded him that some of our training should be done in secret, in the chance war becomes necessary. There are many soldiers in Avaris, of course, but here there is a more … specialized regiment."

Wait. Pepi's uncle is the King of all Foreign Rulers at Avaris? A Hyksos king?

The Hyksos king?

That makes the chieftain ... a ... a prince?

MERAT LOOKS AS STUNNED AS I FEEL. The chieftain is son to the most powerful man in the Nile Delta? Who is also Pepi's uncle? Maybe Pharaoh and the queen did not do as poorly by their daughter as she feels. Rather than marry the princess off to one of the lesser nobles, they have engaged her to the son of the king at Avaris.

"What kind of regiment is it?" I ask, trying to take in the revelations of the chieftain's and Pepi's lineage, as well as the fact that Yanassi has encouraged those at Avaris to make secret war preparations.

"You will see soon." Pepi's smile is full of mystery. "But for now, I must go greet the caravan."

His words snap us out of our dazed shock. The caravan.

"It is really arriving, then?" Merat says, hope in her voice.

"As we speak," Pepi says. "The oasis is an important stop on our trading route with the Nubians. Fresh supplies and goods come through here regularly." He looks at us, thoughtful. "Would you like to accompany me?"

We nod, eager to set eyes upon a possible method of escape at last. Some visual stimulation after days of nothing but sand and palm trees would not go amiss either. Following Pepi through one of the paths that cuts through the oasis, we walk around a roving group of ducks, and people going about their daily tasks. Everyone greets Pepi with respect, though they are much less formal than one would be in Thebes for a member of the royal family. The Hyksos people are friendly and good humoured, trading jokes and winks when they see us walking behind him.

I hear someone call my name. Amara approaches, the babe on her front in a cozy sling. Her husband, a fierce-looking warrior, walks beside her. We met him the other night when Merat came back with him to meet his offspring. Though he gave us several suspicious looks over his shoulder, he was tender and loving toward his woman and child, seemingly awed by the new life they'd created. Amara's husband and Pepi greet each other and begin speaking, voices low. The two men seem to know each other well, yet I sense a slight tension between them, in the way they stand, the tilt of their heads, and the tone of their voices.

"How do you fare?" I ask Amara warmly.

"Very well, thanks to you." She smiles.

"May I?" Merat says, with a quick nod at the baby. Amara brings out the sleeping babe. Her mouth is pursed in a small pucker; her brow is furrowed as if she is thinking about a complex problem; all that wild dark hair she was born with is gone, shaved clean so it will grow in evenly while remaining free of sand fleas and lice.

Merat coos over the baby, who awakes, blinks at us, and immediately begins to squawk. Hastily, we hand her back to her mother. She expertly manoeuvres the little one back into the sling and motions to her husband that they should be going.

"I did not know you were fond of babies," I say to Merat. Pepi walks on ahead as we pass a few goats grazing on the grasses.

"I think they are very sweet," she admits. "It is how they arrive that I am not overly fond of."

"It is not always difficult." Amara's birth was fairly straightforward. "I attended many where all went well."

"I neglect Taweret," Merat admits, naming the goddess of childbirth and fertility. "I have ignored her since Nefertiri died. I was so angry with her." She hesitates. "Perhaps she will take revenge for my disrespect when my own time comes."

I touch her shoulder lightly. "If that time comes, I will be there as well."

Chaos greets our ears as we reach a clearing. A large crowd is shouting as they help unload items from donkeys and give water and food to tired and thirsty travellers.

We inspect the caravan, looking for someone who might be bribed, or for a place to conceal ourselves on departure, but nothing readily makes itself known. My heart sinks like a heavy stone to the bottom of the Nile.

I scan for the healer, who the chieftain said was arriving with the supplies, and my attention is drawn to a great deal of fuss being made over several large baskets brought off the backs of many donkeys. I wonder if any are relatives of Nefer. Pepi strides toward the caravan to help. A few of the men cast furtive looks in our direction as they unpack.

"They do not wish us to see what they have," Merat murmurs.

"If it is such a secret, why did Pepi bring us here?" I say.

"He probably thinks the more we know, the more bound to them we will be."

And the less likely they will be to let us go.

"Sesha!" Pepi raises his hand and beckons us over. "Would you like to meet the healer?" We walk in his direction.

There. My eyes immediately pick the physician out of the group.

It is nothing obvious that gives him away. He is elderly, maybe in his forties. But he smiles at someone offering him a drink, showing teeth that are mostly accounted for and in good condition. He and Reb will get along well. A satchel, similar to the one the hyena made off with, hangs at his side, bulging. As we get closer, I see his fingernails are stained green, as mine will soon be, with the herbs and plants he prepares for medicines. There is also something indefinable about him, an air of authority and calm despite the commotion around him. I trust my instincts that this is a man who helps others.

"May I present Min," Pepi says. Min raps his chest twice and nods. "Min, this is Sesha and Merat. Two daughters of Thebes who have come to be with us."

"You look Egyptian," Merat blurts out.

Min smiles, showing his impressive teeth. "My mother was Egyptian. My father was Hyksos," he says. "I trained in one of the Houses of Life in Thebes years ago, when things were slightly less ... delicate between our peoples."

"Did you know my father?" I ask, unable to stop myself.

Min squints at me. "Who was your father?"

"Ay, Chief Physician to the pharaoh."

Min looks surprised. "Yes, I know Ay. He is a talented and extremely capable healer. How does he fare?"

My throat is tight again. "He is no longer of this world."

"I am sorry for your loss," Min says sincerely. "May he know much happiness in the Field of Reeds."

I nod.

"Sesha is a talented physician, like her father," Merat says with a toss of her braids. "She is extremely competent and capable."

"Is that so?" Min squints his eyes at me. "I cannot say I am surprised. Ay would have trained his offspring well."

"Sesha will assist in the gardens," Pepi says to the healer. "Please let her know if you need any help brewing your medicines and potions."

"Would you mind bringing some of my things to my hut, then?" Min asks. Intrigued by the physician, I obey as he points at various bags and baskets. If I prove myself useful, Min might be persuaded to let me tend some patients. He might also be induced to tell me more about my father. Pepi goes to check on some of the other items that have arrived, while Merat and I grab what we can and follow the healer back to the village.

29

MERAT AND I REPORT TO PASER AND REB that the odds of leaving undiscovered with the caravan are slim. They take the news in stride; we expected as much. Reb even looks relieved at not having to go back into the desert so soon. We agree that we will have to devise another plan, and again I bring up the possibility of speaking with Pepi, which they still shake their heads at. Especially when they hear he is nephew to the king at Avaris.

Over the next few days, I ponder our escape as I work in the gardens. Situated not far from the lake, the plants and herbs growing here are thriving and extensive. I learn that this oasis has been in operation for hundreds of years and it flourishes. Paser and Reb come for various herbal remedies, sharing their assessments of patients and their diagnoses, consulting with Min on what he thinks best. They ask my opinion as well, which prevents too much sand from rubbing into the wound of not being allowed to heal. When Min is not listening, we continue to discuss and discard our extremely limited options in leaving the oasis. Merat and I try not to think too much about weddings.

Also preventing much chafing is Min himself, who prepares his concoctions in his tidy hut by the gardens. This is where the seriously ill or hurt are kept. He instructs me on many herbal remedies, and I share the ones I know with him, though his knowledge is far greater than mine due to his age and experience. I am still gathering up my courage to ask him to tell me about my father.

Despite my original hope for an opportunity to assist Min, the population at the oasis is healthy, and there is little left over for me to do in terms of tending patients. Instead I am responsible mainly for the back-breaking work of watering, removing weeds, and keeping a vigilant eye out for small pests that come to feast on the plants in the garden.

Up with the sun today, I till the soil, obsessing about our prospects of escape. An idea has been brewing at the back of my mind, like one of Min's many potions.

Pepi asked if there was anything that appeals to me aside from tending patients. More and more, I am coming to realize that there *is* another occupation that captures my interest: the very one held by Pepi himself.

That of a spy.

After all, I've done it before, when Pharaoh enlisted me to find the scroll. Spies can go places others cannot, make themselves invisible, gain access to private information, and use that information to influence others. My mind churns with the dirt. Perhaps if I can convince Pepi to train me, my friends and I might better devise a way to get to Avaris. With the knowledge I learn, whether about the city itself or about the higher powers who operate there, we will be more equipped to survive. Knowing what I do now of Pepi's family, these are very likely the "interests" he represents, which he mentioned during our trek.

Speaking of family, *did* the chieftain know that his cousin was in a pit? Paser thought not, but what if he did?

Gripping my gardening tools, I think back to my conversations with the spy, trying to remember our desert talks. Like Merat said, it seems a fading dream, one enshrouded by delirious hunger and thirst and fear of pursuit by the queen. Closing my eyes, I slowly breathe in and out, bringing myself back to the sands.

"What of the chieftain Merat was given to? Do you think he knew where you were?"

"Perhaps."

"Then why did he not free you?"

"I can think of many reasons. Bargaining for the princess's hand would have kept him occupied ... I could have been a casualty of the negotiation ... Or maybe he believes that a spy who fails in his duties no longer has any value."

If Pepi *did* think the chieftain knew he was in the pits, he might be angry with Yanassi for abandoning him and more inclined to help us. Maybe their camaraderie is all an act. Then again, Paser could be right that the chieftain was unaware of Pepi's predicament. After all, why would he leave his cousin in a pit?

I spot Amara walking toward me, interrupting my thoughts. I raise a hand in greeting.

"How are you this day, Sesha?"

"How did you do this with a babe in your belly?" I straighten from my crouching position, placing my hands on my lower back. A small pile of weeds lies to my left. I've learned that it is Amara's position I am filling, while she spends time with her baby.

"You sound like an old woman. Do not worry, you will become used to it." She smiles, but I see her face is strained, brow furrowed, and my instincts have me looking down at the child.

"How is the little one?"

"She does not seem to want to eat or drink."

"Min is away at the moment, but I can take a look."

Sighing with relief, she takes the baby out of her wrappings, cooing and kissing her forehead, and then passes her to me. The baby feels warm, but that could be from being pressed against her mother's body. She regards me sleepily, her eyes unable to focus. She does not appear all that ill, but the instincts of a mother are strong, and if the child will not eat or drink, this is a problem. "How many times a day do you change her linens?" I say, examining the tiny being in my hands.

"Not often these past few days. She is rarely soiled." The furrow between Amara's brow deepens.

"Does she show no interest in eating at all?"

"At times she seems frantic and starving, but then she fusses and stops after only a few moments."

An idea occurs to me. "Show me how you feed her." Amara does so, wincing, and the baby tries her best, but gives up after a few moments of frustrated struggle.

"Open wide, little one," I say, sticking a finger into the baby's mouth. She sucks automatically, but the pull is weak. Removing my finger, I peer into the tiny pink cavern, gently lifting the tongue. It is as I suspected. The thin band attaching the tongue to the mouth is too short, making it difficult for the child to feed properly.

"This is an ailment that I will treat." I smile reassuringly at Amara. Ky had the same trouble with nursing and my father said he was able to fix the problem with a little snip.

I hurry back to the hut, looking for Min's scissors, which I've been eyeing covetously. They lie, gleaming in the sunlight, on a shelf along with a few of the healer's other tools. Though they are made of a dull yellow-gold metal, they are sharp to the touch. Hurrying back to Amara and her baby, I say a brief incantation before quickly snipping the little band. The baby cries and immediately Amara brings her to her chest, where she begins to suckle. Amara's face contorts with pain as the milk first comes through, but then clears as the baby begins to take long, healthy swallows. The relief in the new mother's face makes me smile again.

"Gods be praised, Sesha."

"Feed her regularly. This will keep the tongue moving so it does not reattach." Amara's milk will also heal the baby's mouth and keep it clean. A mother's elixir is liquid magic and can treat everything from skin conditions to eye maladies. I parcel her out some honey, another wondrous elixir, to mix into her own drink and send her on her way, brushing off her profuse thanks. I hope Min does not mind; new mothers should have extra nourishment.

After she leaves, I clean and return the scissors to their home, pleased to have been of use. I am just putting the honey away when there is a shout in the distance. A young man runs toward Min's hut, panting, his face pale despite his exertions. "Help! Where is the healer? There's been an accident!"

"What's happened?" I say, still holding the jar.

"The chieftain's second-in-command is badly injured," he says, panic all over his face. "We must find the healer."

"I am a healer," I say, my blood still dancing from helping Amara and her baby. "Take me to him."

"You?" he says, in disbelief. "You are a young girl."

"And?" I demand, hand on my hip, resisting the urge to stomp my foot. I do not think it will help my cause. "Does that automatically render me incompetent?"

The soldier starts to protest. "Let us go now," I cut him off, striving for calm. "The time you spend arguing only delays your friend's treatment." The soldier balks at how I speak to him but turns and starts back in the direction he came. I learned from Father that talking in a commanding voice works wonders when people are rattled from injury or sudden illness.

I follow him with nothing but the honey in my hands and an incantation on my lips.

30

"WHAT IS THE NATURE OF THE INJURY?" I hurry to keep pace with the soldier's long strides. We are nearing the restricted part of the oasis where the training takes place.

"A fall." The soldier swallows.

A fall? "From a tree?" It seems unusual, but maybe the soldiers' drills involve leaping from palms onto unsuspecting enemies.

"No," he says shortly as we make our way into the clearing. "From one of those."

I gape at the creatures before me. Beautiful four-legged animals with long manes, graceful necks, and swishing tails. They resemble Nefer but are taller, more majestic, lean and muscled, with coats of russet, black, and tan gleaming in the sun.

"What are they?" I say, marvelling at their beauty.

"Horses." The soldier cannot keep the pride from his voice.

A cry of pain interrupts my admiration of the otherworldly animals. The men are attempting to move the fallen soldier. I hurry over, my reluctant escort leading the way.

"Back away, please," I say in that same firm and controlled voice my father used. Surprisingly, it works, and they make space for me at the wounded man's side.

My eyes widen at the sight of his leg. It is a gruesome break, the bone jutting this way, then that, like one of Set's jagged bolts of light from the sky. The soldier is dazed and pale, his skin feels cold to the touch, and his breath comes quickly. I recognize him. It is Amara's husband, Akin.

"This is an ailment with which I will contend," I say in what I hope is a reassuring manner. I turn my gaze to the soldier who came to fetch Min. "You will need to hold him." His lip curls at being told what to do by someone younger, but he doesn't protest. "What is your name?"

"Sham," he says.

"Sit astride his body at his waist but put no weight on him," I say. "You —" I nod at another soldier, who murmurs encouragement to his fallen friend "— find me two long sticks and a shorter one. And you, there."

I look at the man beside him. "Is there anything on hand to drink?"

Both men nod and run off to complete their assigned tasks. Tearing a strip of linen from the bottom of my dress, I turn to Akin, who is starting to shiver, even though the air is warm. "Listen carefully to my words." I put a hand on his clammy brow. "I am going to speak a powerful charm. All will be well."

He manages a quick nod, eyes clenched tight. I shut my own eyes briefly, summoning *Heka*, the divine force and universal healing energy. Opening them, I begin to recite an incantation for healing, making my voice soothing and calm, murmuring the words over and over, easing the injured soldier's mind and giving him something to focus on other than his pain. The break is below the knee, which is fortunate. A jagged end pokes out of the skin, but praises to Shai, there is not much blood.

The soldiers hurry back with beer and sticks of varying shapes and sizes, which they drop on the ground beside me. I take the shorter stick and give it to Akin to bite on, then pour beer over the wound, rinsing away the sand and dirt. Sham looks over his shoulder at me, waiting for his signal, and I nod, indicating he should hold Akin's upper body immobile if necessary.

Still murmuring the incantation and with *Heka* flowing through me, I take firm hold of the foot. Akin makes a brief strangled noise, clenching his comrades' hands. I pull the leg straight until it reaches the length of the other leg. The bone slips back beneath the skin. A few more heartbeats and I get the bone back into place as best I can, smear honey on the wound, then bind it with the linen strips.

Still chanting, I hold up two fingers to the soldier who brought the sticks, then hold my hands apart indicating the size I need. He passes me two longer ones and I break them over my knee, a good length for a splint. One will go along the man's inner leg, the other along the outside. I realize I have nothing left to bind them without losing a significant portion of my dress, and I cast my eyes about. One of the soldiers gripping his friend's hand, the one who retrieved the beer, anticipates my need and removes his skirt, ripping it into strips. All this time I utter the incantation in a hypnotic manner. Along with the restorative magic it lends, it seems to be having a calming effect; everyone is following my instructions, without need for explanations. The man donating his skirt, who was fortunately wearing a loincloth beneath it, hands me four sections of cloth. I use two of them to bind the leg to the splints, not too tight, not too loose. I tie the remaining swathes of cloth around the ankle, and it is done. I nod at Sham to move and he obliges. He did not need to restrain the man; Amara's husband is very brave. I finish intoning the incantation and look into Akin's eyes, which are unfocused, pupils large and black with pain and shock.

"My friend," I say softly, willing him to believe my words. "You will heal well." He licks his dry lips, and I bring the remaining beer to his mouth. "Move him out of the sun," I say to the soldiers who assisted with the proceedings. "Take care, now."

The three of them are settling Akin under a large tree when several people come into view: Pepi and the chieftain, Min, Paser, and Reb, led by another soldier who must have gone for the tribe's leader.

I watch Paser's and Reb's faces as they take in the incredible creatures across the way. They look as if they do not quite believe what they are seeing. Reb blinks, rubbing his eyes like he is having a lingering desert vision. Min and the chieftain, who seems extremely concerned about his soldier, examine the patient.

Pepi heads straight for me. "What happened?" he asks.

"He broke his leg."

"How?"

Sham interrupts. "He fell. I wanted to wait for Min."

Pepi walks over to confer with Min and Yanassi. The chieftain stands, concern turning to anger that his second-in-command is now out of commission. I did the best I could with what I had available, but it is too early to say if his gait will be altered or if other complications might arise. He most definitely will not be riding anything for some time.

The chieftain's arms are crossed, and his voice is loud. His narrowed gaze falls on me, and suddenly he strides in my direction. For a few heartbeats I think he is going to strike me. After all, I am not supposed to be here, or tending patients.

He towers over my small frame. I force myself not to step back, and I raise my chin to look at him directly. Out of the corner of my eye, I see Pepi take a few steps closer to us.

"You have my thanks," the chieftain says, looking down his bold nose. I blink. "Min says he could not have done better." His next words have me blinking again. "You may assist the healer in his work, in addition to preparing medicines." He turns to Sham, who straightens considerably at his approach. "You will take Akin's place."

Sham nods.

The chieftain looks over at Paser and Reb, who are ogling the horses, sizing each of them in turn. "Young Paser," he says, and Paser looks over. "You will join our ranks. Every man is needed." He looks at Reb, who cannot tear his eyes from the horses. "You, too, tooth puller." Reb glances at him, startled.

The chieftain looks back at his fallen man. "Tend him well," he commands Min, who instructs a few of the other soldiers to assist with bringing Akin back to the main part of the camp.

The chieftain stalks off, Pepi at his side, the cousins talking in low tones. The rest of the soldiers disperse as the sun reaches its highest point, getting out of the blazing heat to rest. A few men round the horses up into a large pen under the trees, then head to the village, the day's training done.

Paser and Reb stand by me and we watch the creatures in silence. There are a few dozen in all, varying in size and colour.

"Congratulations on your promotion, Sesha," Paser says quietly after a few moments. It is always jarring how a life can crack open in an instant. Healers know this especially well.

"I don't know whether to congratulate you on yours," I say faintly.

"I suppose that will depend on how permanent it is," Paser murmurs. "I do not mind training, but let us hope it goes no further. Despite having my Egyptian blood washed away the other night, I do not want to face my countrymen in battle."

I shiver. Battle wounds would make the soldier's broken leg seem like a papyrus cut in comparison.

Paser and Reb take a closer look at the horses. I watch them marvel at the creatures. After surviving the brutal desert, the relative sanctuary of the oasis made thoughts of war seem distant. As did recovering from the gruelling trek, being preoccupied with impending marriage, and plotting our escape.

But now, seeing the training grounds first-hand and up close, as well as the injuries that come with the territory, brings back the realities of combat, fierce and fresh. I do not know if Thebes still contemplates battle with the Hyksos. With the threat of famine, they may have more pressing concerns. But it seems the Hyksos at the camp are indeed preparing. Standing in the middle of an empty meadow as dusk approaches, I am struck hard by the potential peril to the people I care for.

Ky's face appears suddenly in my mind and my heart contracts, painfully. I try not to think of him too often; it causes only sorrow. Yet, in this moment, I can think of nothing *but* my brother and those I left behind in Thebes: Ahmes, Bebi, even prickly Kewat. And, on the other side, the people here at the oasis: Paser and Reb, now soldiers, Merat, Amara and her babe, even Pepi. Heart pounding, blood roaring, I feel the earth spin out from under me.

Sitting down hard, I force myself to breathe in and out. Father always said not to underestimate the power of a simple breath. I see his smiling face, his intelligent eyes. *After all, it is the only thing that separates life from death, Sesha.*

Reb reaches out a hand to one of the horses, murmuring soothing words to calm the skittish creature, which rears back at his approach. A few more words and the horse stills, allowing Reb to stroke its long hair as it flutters in the wind.

Maybe, in addition to getting us to Avaris, there is something I can do to help calm the tensions between the tribes, as Reb's words soothe the horse's ruffled nerves. Something that can help prevent injuries, loss of life, and the devastation that comes with fighting. My earlier notion to ask Pepi to train me in his line of work crystallizes into a sharp point, like the tip of my father's obsidian dagger — a way to cut two strands of rope with one blade. I must speak with Pepi at once.

After all, who understands diplomatic relations better than a spy?

31

EARLY THE NEXT MORNING, I seek Pepi out. I slept little last night, telling no one of my idea. I wanted to sit with it for a bit, turning things over in my mind, considering the enormity of what I am asking. Paser and Reb are still wary of the spy, and Merat will be most distressed to hear that plans of escape may be on hold for a while. As I make my way quietly through the oasis, the sky begins to lighten around me. Dark blue fades into light blue, melting into a soft orange glow. I recall our journey through the desert, how Pepi liked to watch Ra come up.

I find him at last, tending the horses. Nefer is there, lazily chewing her food, looking unimpressed by the competition. The sun rises slowly and peacefully from the underworld. There is no one else about but the birds, chirping their good mornings, everyone else still taking their morning meal.

"Pepi."

He turns at my call and blinks, perhaps at my determined face. "Sesha. You are up with Ra this morning. I take it you wish something of me?"

"Yes." I decide not to dance around the palm and instead come straight out with it. "I want you to teach me to be a spy."

He does not look as shocked at my outrageous request as I am expecting. "Why?"

"For several reasons." The faces of all the people I love appear in my head. "But ultimately, I am of the same mind as you. I wish to ease things between our peoples and, if possible, avoid war." *And get my friends to Avaris*, I remind myself.

Folding his arms, he examines me, his sharp gaze equal parts amusement and challenge. "What makes you think I do not want war?"

"A feeling." I hesitate. "Am I wrong?"

I expect him to deny my request, to tell me I am mistaken, to go back and eat my morning meal. Instead, he lets out a snort, sounding like one of the strange creatures behind him. "Good instincts will serve you well in the profession."

A thrill shoots through my body. "You will do it, then?"

"The idea is actually not the most ludicrous thing I have heard," he admits, rubbing his chin. "But do you and your friends not have plans of your own, perhaps other places you want to be?" I try to keep my face impassive. He's known the whole time. Of course he has. He continues. "Being a spy is exceptionally dangerous. You are often in peril and the life is not always a comfortable one."

"I am not afraid of discomfort." I scratch my arms reflexively, the remnants of a rash almost faded.

"While boils are never fun, neither is lying at the bottom of a pit awaiting death or dismemberment," he reminds me, and I look up at him, swallowing. "I only want you to be aware of what you are asking." Unlike his words, his tone is gentle.

I think of Ky. Of Paser and Reb, who will have to fight in battle. "If I can do anything to make the lives of those I care for safer, I am at peace with that."

"Very well." He studies me for a moment longer. "Meet me here at dusk and we will begin your training."

"May I ask a question?"

"You may. Though I reserve the right not to answer it."

"Though I know the reasons I wish to avoid war, I am curious about yours," I say in a rush. "Your thoughts do not seem aligned with your cousin's." Maybe that was why the chieftain left him in a pit?

This is something I intend to inquire further about in the future, but one thing at a time. "Does it have anything to do with the other interests you represent? The ones you mentioned on our journey here?"

Pepi looks off into the distance at something I am unable to see and is quiet. "I have seen enough people die," he says finally, and I sense there is more than he is telling me. "Though I feel otherwise, Yanassi wants those at Thebes to acknowledge us as rulers, not only in the North but throughout the whole land. He is ambitious and wishes to extend our reach. He thinks the recent dynasties at Thebes grow weak and sees an opportunity. He also sees the treasures that come from there, the tribute previous rulers paid to our people. He seeks not only recognition, but his share of the wealth."

I have seen the treasures for myself. A huge cache hidden beneath the temple catacombs. Too many to count, and there may well be more rooms like that one.

"You have no desire for riches or recognition yourself?"

Pepi must hear the doubt in my voice, because he looks at me intently. "I have no use for material things. Or titles," he says, his look full of meaning. "Give me the earth beneath my feet, the sun on my face, water and food in my belly, music in my ears, and people who love me. That is enough."

"Do you have people who love you?"

"I did once." His face closes and I know the conversation is over. "You are good at getting people to talk, Sesha, a useful skill in our profession." Pepi is back to business. "It goes hand in hand with the first rule of a spy: protecting your information. Knowledge is currency. It is learning that makes us truly rich, not things."

"My father felt the same," I say, inwardly cheering that he said *our profession*. "He and my mother taught me many things." Not only about medicine, but about how to love and what it means to be a good friend, a family.

"Your parents made you rich indeed, Sesha," Pepi says, his voice soft again. It occurs to me that I am learning to read him.

I arch a brow. "And now you are going to make me richer?"

He smiles, his white teeth flashing in the sun. "I can make you the wealthiest woman in all of the lands."

The rest of the morning passes agonizingly slowly. Anxious for my training to start, I cannot keep my mind focused on the gardening tasks. Min senses my distraction and sends me on my way with a poultice for Akin, dismissing me for the day.

I run into Amara on my way to the village. "Sesha!" she exclaims, eyeing the poultice in my hands. "Is that for Akin?"

"Yes. How is he doing?"

She looks back at the hut. "He is managing. I can take it to him," she offers, one hand on the baby strapped to her.

"Are you sure?" I say. "I am happy to do it."

"I know how to apply a poultice, Sesha," she says with a smile. "Besides, he prefers me to tend him. I do not think he likes others seeing him in pain."

"Very well." I hand her the poultice, familiar with soldiers and their pride. "But let us know if anything changes in his condition, or if he needs more medicine for his discomfort."

"I will," she promises. "You have been most helpful to us of late."

"It is my privilege to attend you," I say, then peer at the cozy bundle on her chest. "How is the little one doing after yesterday's snip?"

"It does not seem to bother her much," she says, expression lightening.

"Wonderful." I beam. We exchange a few more words and then, with another reminder to seek Min out should Akin need his attention, we part ways, she to her husband, me to grab a quick meal before heading to my other, more clandestine, duties.

"One of the key tasks of being a spy," Pepi says, "is to remain unseen in plain sight." We are back at the training grounds. Ra is on his way down, his setting rays casting the oasis in a dusky glow, as beautiful as the one this morning. Pepi frowns at me. "You may find this difficult."

"I did this for an entire moon after my parents' death," I point out.

"You are a wanted woman now," Pepi points out. "At least in Thebes. And your looks will make it difficult for you to go unnoticed."

My cheeks redden, one hand going to my hair. "Then I will change them."

"You possess a certain … quality that shines from the inside. Cutting off your hair will not alter that." Pepi's voice is matter-of-fact. "So you must become invisible as best you can, with the language of your body, your voice and mannerisms, skill at disguise. Watch Namu, the storyteller, closely at the fire tonight. Learn how he embodies animals and people, how he captures their essence."

"I will study his magic," I promise.

"The second thing, and just as important as blending in, if not more so, is the ability to think clearly in the midst of chaos. You must analyze situations quickly and logically. You cannot let emotion get the better of you, or all will be lost."

I think of Akin's broken leg and my other experiences with medical emergencies. "I can remain calm in tense situations."

"Maybe when tending patients," Pepi agrees. "But all of us have weak areas. We must find yours, expose them, and make them strong."

"How?" I say, slightly nervous.

"I am going to give you a series of tests. If you fail too many, your training will end."

"But —"

Pepi interrupts me. "You have many of the qualities it takes to be a good spy. You are extremely intelligent, a quick thinker, and brave and honourable. I would not be doing this if I did not think you would be good at it." I blush at his compliment, though he says it objectively. "You are also young and have lived mostly a privileged life. You might see much that will affect you. We must train you not to react during fraught situations."

I think of the fire that took my parents' lives, of surviving the streets of Thebes, of Queen Anat and Crooked Nose's treachery, of murderous fruit vendors who wanted Ky and me to pay with our lives for merely trying to survive. Then there was the desert crossing, severe dehydration, starvation, sandstorms. I feel I can handle most things.

Pepi's next words are like punches in my gut. "You no longer have a family. Your parents are dead, your brother lost to you. This will limit your weaknesses."

Firmly shoving my distress aside for the moment, I look up at Pepi. "When do we begin the tests?"

He puts two fingers in his mouth and whistles loudly. A horse whinnies in response. "Now."

32

"I HAVE NOT HAD TIME TO STUDY," I protest.

"The tests are based on intuition and skills you must already possess," Pepi calls over his shoulder, walking to the horses. I follow at a slower pace, apprehensive of the mysterious creatures. Particularly after witnessing what can happen as a result of getting too close. Unfortunately, Pepi has decided that if anyone is curious about our activities, we will say he is teaching me to ride. Thank Shai we encountered only Paser and Reb, who were on their way back to the village. As new additions, they are the last to leave the training grounds, responsible for cleanup. Both gave us a curious look as we greeted them but made no comment, presumably starving after a long day and in a hurry to go eat.

"Abilities can be cultivated, but the seeds of them must already be there, or no amount of water will make them grow."

"Very well," I say, feeling my stomach twist as we approach the horses, my heart beating faster. "What am I to do?"

He nods at the four-legged animals. "Your first task is to get on one of those."

"What?" I gape at him. So Pepi teaching me to ride was not a pretense after all. "I just mended a man's leg snapped in two by one of those beasts."

"His was an unlucky accident. Besides," he points out, "it is no different from riding Nefer, which you did in the desert."

"Nefer *is* different." I eye the horses. They are much faster and not as solid as the donkey, whose gait is best described as plodding.

"As this is your first task, I will give you some assistance." A few of the horses paw the ground as we approach, tossing their heads like the ladies at court, manes flying out behind them. "Which one do you want?"

I scan the herd. My eyes lock with a russet-haired creature. It appears calmer than most, chewing placidly at tufts of grass.

"That one." I lick my lips, nodding at the horse. "Are you sure this is safe?"

"No." His teeth flash in a brief smile. "But it will not be the most dangerous thing you will have to do as a spy."

I exhale loudly. "How do I approach her?"

"Hold your hand out." Pepi takes something from his pocket and places it in my palm. "It is good manners to bring an offering when approaching someone you wish something of."

Holding the pomegranate in my hand, I walk forward slowly, giving myself some inner encouragement. *Come, Sesha, if you can tame venomous snakes, you can handle a horse.*

The creature looks up as I draw nearer, nostrils flaring. "Greetings," I say to it. "I am Sesha." It snorts. "May I ride you?" It gives a toss of its long mane. I am not sure if this is a yes or a no. It turns its head. A brush-off, then. "Has it been ridden before?" I ask Pepi uncertainly.

"That is why these ones are here," he says from behind me. "They are being trained."

"Who is their trainer?"

"Akin was. I will be assisting for now."

"Nefer is not jealous?"

"You are stalling, Sesha."

I take the few remaining steps toward the creature. It does not back away. Holding my hand as far from my body as I can, I console myself that if the horse

213

bites me, I will probably not die — one advantage over Apep, the snake I worked with. The horse sniffs, nostrils flaring wide again. It noses my hand, then its long pink tongue reaches out and takes the fruit from my palm with such surprising delicacy that Merat herself would be impressed by its manners.

"It tickles," I say, feeling the smile bloom on my face.

"And now that you are acquainted, it is best to get on with it. Hesitation will only make both of you more nervous." He grips his hands together, making a place for my foot, as he did when helping me onto Nefer. With my hands on the horse's back and a boost from the Hyksos, I swing my left leg over the horse. It shifts under my weight, and my heart flutters as I try to keep my balance.

"Peace, brown one." My voice is soothing, as if addressing a patient. The horse sidesteps and I clutch on to its neck. It gives a whinny of protest at the pulling of its hair. Forcing myself to release its tresses, I sit up straight, balancing awkwardly. "Now what?" I ask Pepi.

"Ride her."

"Is that not what I am doing?" I retort.

Pepi brings his hand up to his mouth to hide a smile. "You are not moving."

"I am," I say, wobbling slightly, trying to keep steady but failing. "It's the horse that's not moving."

Pepi presses on. "Horse riding is not a skill many in this land have. It will give you a great advantage of speed. And a convenient method of escape."

"If people do not ride them, what are the soldiers doing with them?" I squeeze my stomach muscles tight so that my weight stays centred on the warm back.

"You will learn that soon enough," he says. "For now, focus on the task at hand."

I grit my teeth, hands resting lightly on the base of the horse's neck. "How am I to make her go forward?"

"Nudge her with a squeeze of your legs," Pepi says.

I apply some pressure to the horse. She doesn't budge.

"Harder," he says encouragingly. I do as he says. The horse huffs and takes a few steps over to a patch of grass that has caught her attention.

"It's not working," I say.

"Do not give up so easily. If one way does not produce results, try another."

I slide off the horse's back and give Pepi a look. "This is not me giving up," I say, walking around to the horse's front. She lifts her head and looks at me, chewing the grass in languid chomps.

Looking into her eyes, I will the horse to see my thoughts and my heart. Like the snake, she must sense my *Ba*, my very essence, if there is any hope of connecting. I stand there for several minutes, gazing at the horse, letting all sounds fade away. Her eyes are old. Wise. She has seen my kind before, even if hers is new to me.

You have nothing to fear.

The horse blinks. This time I place both my hands on her back and clamber on without Pepi's assistance. There is no elegance in the manoeuvre, but the horse lets me haul myself up, and though I still wobble slightly, I keep my balance a little more easily this time.

"Go!" I nudge her forward with pressure from my thighs. Nothing. Sighing, I turn to look at Pepi. "I think she is feeling lazy to—"

With no warning, the horse rears up and I tumble off in a tangle of limbs, ending up flat on my back. Pepi is laughing and both my pride and my bottom feel the beginnings of a bruise. It will be purple and blue, like the sky I stare up at. Pepi offers his hand. I take it and he hefts me to my feet as I force air back into my lungs.

"Does that mean I fail?" I wince, rubbing my backside. My training is not off to a good start.

"You will not know if you pass or fail until I say so," he says, with a glance at the darkening sky. We should be getting back to the main camp. There are animals that come to the oasis at night to drink and to feed on the smaller prey. Pepi echoes my thoughts. "It is always good to get back on the horse, but for now, let us go get our dinner before something decides to make us theirs."

33

MERAT, REB, PASER, AND I SIT BY THE FIRE, up later than usual that evening. Namu, the storyteller, tells a tale of one of Akin's many exploits, in honour of the fallen soldier. Weaving his words around the crowd, Namu entrances the people of the village, who often gather after the sun goes down to share adventures of the day and exchange stories, music, and dance.

Despite the adventure Namu enacts, it's difficult to pay attention. Although excited by my plan, I am unsure what my friends' reactions will be, given the boys' mistrust of Pepi and Merat's desire to escape the oasis. My gaze wanders around those at the fire. We are the only ones of similar age in the community; everyone else is a few years older, like Amara, or much younger, like her baby. At last the tale is done and the conversation is dying, along with the flames. People begin to leave the fire, one at a time, then in twos and threes, shaking their heads at Akin's misfortune and discussing the outcome for recovery as they retire for the evening. Soon Paser, Merat, Reb, and I are alone at the embers, chatting quietly among ourselves. The time has come.

Glancing at their three firelit faces, I send a prayer up with the smoke. "I need to tell you something."

"You have come up with a way to get to Avaris!" Merat exclaims in a happy whisper, clapping her hands together.

"Perhaps." I keep my voice low.

"Is it to do with Pepi?" Paser asks.

"Yes," I say, taking a deep breath. "He is training me to be a spy."

Paser's eyebrows disappear into his hairline. "A spy?"

Reb also looks doubtful. "A spy for whom? The Hyksos?"

I am not sure how to answer this, as I do not quite know myself. "It is not much different from soldiering," I reason. "Besides, there is no way we can get to Avaris without his help."

Reb gives his head a shake. "How did we come to be here?" He poses his question to no one in particular. "Soldiers and spies against our own people?"

"Things are not always so black and red. This might be our best chance of leaving the oasis," I say, urging them to understand. "And it is better than doing nothing. I also do not wish to see things escalate between our peoples. Perhaps there is something I can learn or do to keep a battle from happening."

"You? Stop a war?" Reb snorts, looking into the embers. "You always did think highly of yourself."

Merat comes to my defence, her voice cool. "Sesha is right. Fighting is not the answer." I give her a grateful smile.

"Not all the Hyksos want war," I say, bolstered by Merat's support. "There are those who wish to resolve conflict, rather than provoke it."

"Like Pepi?" Paser says, an edge in his voice.

"Yes, like Pepi," I say.

"You are quick to believe the words of someone you've known only a short time," Paser remarks. "Do not forget the man *is* a spy, Sesha. He is skilled in making people believe he is on their side. He could be using you."

"He brought us through the desert and saved our lives. We never would have found Merat without his help," I say. "What reason would he have for manipulating me?"

"I can think of several," Paser says. "Perhaps he thinks you'll be able to extract valuable information out of Thebes." He throws the stone he has been palming into the fire. "Or maybe it is as simple as wanting an excuse to spend time with you."

"He doesn't need an excuse for that," Merat says, "Sesha is his betrothed." Her words are like a bucket on the fire.

"As you are the chieftain's." Paser stands, brushing himself off.

"That is not our fault," I say, voice quiet.

"You are right." Paser's expression is bleak, and I notice a bruise high on his arm, a token of the day's drills. It pains me to see my friend so wretched. "We must rise early for training," he says to Reb, then nods at us. "Good night."

Reb stands to follow his friend, bidding good night to Merat and me, leaving us among the dying coals. That did not go as well as I hoped.

Emotions tumbling, like a desert weed caught in a strong gust of wind, I turn to Merat. "Why is everything getting so complicated?"

"This is the time in our lives when it becomes so," she says, standing as well. "Good night, Sesha." Her voice is strained.

"Merat," I call after her. "Wait."

She stops and turns.

"Are you upset with me?"

"You are only doing what you think is best for all

of us," she says, not meeting my eye. "I cannot fault you for acting in accordance with your conscience."

"We will get to Avaris," I promise.

"No, Sesha. *You* will get to Avaris." She looks at me then, pulling her hair back from her face. "But perhaps it is time I stop avoiding my fate and begin to act like a princess."

34

THE NEXT MORNING MERAT IS CIVIL ENOUGH, but I sense some lingering tension as we part ways after our morning meal, she to tend the children, I to the gardens. It seems odd going about these daily tasks while other plans are in motion, but I suppose we are surviving the best way we know how: moment to moment. Slicing up some eye-watering herbs, I am wondering how to smooth things over with my friends when Amara appears in the distance. I lift a hand in greeting.

"How is everything this day?" I ask when she gets closer, wiping my hands on my robes.

"The little one is eating well." I glance down at the babe, who does look better, cheeks tinted a rosy colour. "She's soiled herself three times in the past hours."

There is as much pride in Amara's voice, as if the new-born had swum the length of the Nile.

"Praises!" I say, returning her smile, which, despite this good news, still seems tinged with sadness. Akin's mangled leg appears in my mind. "How is your man?" I ask.

"Not as well," she admits, and I see the dark circles under her eyes that come from tending a new baby and an injured husband. "I think he's in pain, but he says nothing."

I feel bad for the young mother and put a hand on her arm. She's been struck a few blows this moon.

"Sesha, Amara." Min, who was at the other end of the garden, walks over and greets us. "How is Akin? I was planning to come by today with a fresh poultice."

"His spirits are low," Amara confesses. "They seem to have taken a turn for the worse."

"We will bring him something to ease his discomfort," Min assures her. "Come, Sesha, let's go check on our patient."

"You have my thanks." Amara's eyes shine with grateful tears.

"Why don't you and the babe go and bathe?" I say, smelling sour milk on the exhausted mother, who likely has not taken a minute for herself. "We will go to Akin at once." She nods obediently, too tired to resist my gentle insistence. "Be well, Amara." I kiss the baby on the forehead. "May you have the appetite of the caterpillars who mow their way through the leaves of our garden," I whisper. Min's been cursing the creatures all morning for devouring some of the rarer herbs.

Amara starts for the lake, her step a little lighter, while the physician and I walk toward the village. I carry his bag for him, full of medicines and instruments.

"Amara told me how you helped her and the baby." Min gives me a sidelong look. "That was a smart thing, clipping the tongue."

I incline my head at his compliment. "Your impressive tools made it easy," I say, with an admiring glance down at the bag at my side. "What is that metal called?"

"Bronze. It is a combination of metals, much stronger than copper alone. Our people use it to make many of our devices."

"You said you knew my father," I say in a rush, looking at the ground. Min has been gracious about letting me work with him, continuing my training while respecting my own knowledge. I take that as a sign he respected my father.

"Yes, he came and trained some of our physicians in the delta."

I look at him in surprise. "He did?"

"Some years ago. You would not have been on this earth yet."

We reach the hut where Akin and Amara are residing. "Do you think we might speak more of him later?" I say, shy but determined.

"We will need a fresh batch of pain medicine. You can ask me your questions later, while we grind up the herbs."

I follow him into the hut and turn in a circle, amazed. It appears to be the main storage facility for the entire village. Crowded with odds and ends, it looks as if all the caravan goods were brought here.

Among all the items is a body. Akin lies on a blanket in the only clear space in the room. A cup and plate of food rest beside him, untouched.

"Hello, friend. How are you this day?" Min asks. I focus on the patient.

The soldier nods his head, but his expression is bleak. "Well enough."

"Let's take a look," Min says, kneeling.

I stand back and the soldier's eyes meet mine as Min unwraps his leg. He starts speaking, probably in effort to distract himself from being poked at. "You have my thanks for attending my wife at the birth of my child. As well as treating my injury."

"I was happy to help them. Amara is very brave, like her husband." It's true — Akin barely winced when I set the bone. I do not wish to imagine what that felt like.

226

"A captain of the chieftain's army must be brave, if not foolish," he says, with a disgusted wave at his leg.

"You would not be in charge if you were foolish," Min says mildly, running a finger down the swollen limb, which sports an impressive assortment of colours. Blues, greens, and purples bloom proudly in varying shades of intensity.

"Maybe not foolish then, but definitely clumsy." The soldier's voice is bitter. Min presses down on the bone, but Akin does not flinch.

Surprised, I look at Min, but he is intent on his patient, prodding and pinching his way up and down Akin's legs. There is no reaction from Amara's husband.

A creeping coldness makes its way into my chest.

Just then, the chieftain comes into the hut, bending low. "I will not have you demean my best man that way," he says in his gruff voice, offsetting the mild scolding of his second-in-command with an affectionate smile. "How are you, my brother?"

"A scratch," Akin says, propping himself up on his elbows. "I will be up and about in no time."

My heart hurts for the soldier. I do not think this is true. I curse myself for not coming in to change the dressing myself yesterday. Though there is little I could've done, regardless.

"You will do no such thing." Min looks sternly at him. "You must not bear any weight for some time."

"How long?" the chieftain asks.

"One moon at least," Min says, lying through his decent teeth.

"This will delay our plans significantly." Akin nods at the chieftain in apology. "I am sorry, my chief."

"Just focus on getting well," the chieftain says, gripping his man's hand, but he looks grim. "I need you." He bows his head low to his friend and the men speak in lowered voices. There is a strong bond between them.

Min pulls items from his bag and applies the new poultice before rewrapping the leg with fresh bandages. He is administering some medicines when Amara returns with the baby, an expression of cautious hope on her face. "How are you, my husband?"

"Come, let us leave them to one another." Min motions to the chieftain to follow him out of the crowded hut. Grabbing Min's bag, I start to follow, wondering how the chieftain will react when Min delivers his news.

"Sesha," Amara calls, and I stop and turn. "We want you to know … we will be naming the baby for you."

I am shocked. "Me?" It does not escape me how the villagers here feel about Thebans. From what I understand, the people at the oasis are leaders in the conflict against my city; a rebel faction that Avaris does not appear to fully support. Yet.

"Yes." Amara smiles as if I am simple. "You've done much for our family."

"I am honoured," I say past the lump in my throat.

The child lets out a tiny grunt and an odour fills the air, as pungent as the poultice. Amara exclaims over the bowel movement, which demonstrates that my namesake is indeed getting adequate nourishment. "If she grows up as clever and kind as you, she will be very blessed," Amara says, patting the baby on the back. She goes to change her linens, and I wave good night to the family, leaving them to one another, my chest still aching.

35

THE AIR IS COOL AND FRESH after the stuffiness of the hut, the smell of the medicines, the unmistakeable stench of despair and bodily fluids.

It could have happened when he fell, or perhaps moving him to the hut shifted something in his spine. No matter the cause, the results are the same. Akin likely will not walk again. Desperate to help Amara's husband, I rack my brain for anything that can be done. Injuries to the head, neck, and spine are delicate and complicated, often ending in permanent lameness, or even death.

This is why the scroll was such an important discovery. Not only because of its value as a precious ancient artifact, but because it contained the wisdom and knowledge of how to deal with exactly these types of injuries. There's little chance Ahmes could have performed the surgery on Ky without it. The document and the physician's skills saved my brother's life.

I stop walking, as if the papyrus itself has struck me hard across the face.

The scroll.

Up ahead, Min and the chieftain confer in low voices. The chieftain buries his head in his hands as Min puts a sympathetic hand on his burly arm. "Likely nothing can be done," Min is saying quietly, just as Pepi rounds a bend in the path.

"No." The chieftain lifts his head, shaking it in furious denial. "I will not have it."

Pepi pauses, taking in the scene. "How goes it, my cousin?" Spotting me, he nods.

"Akin is lame," Min says to both of them, but mostly to the chieftain, I think. "Even if he does not want to admit it to you, or to his family, or even to himself."

"There is nothing you can do?" Anger and despair compete with stubborn hope in the chieftain's voice, and I recognize the desperate need to do something, anything, to help someone you love. "I do not care how poor the odds. If you, or another, can do even the smallest thing to aid him, I will give you whatever you ask for."

Min shakes his head. "This is an injury with which I cannot contend."

Still feeling the sting of the scroll across my cheek, I step forward, clearing my throat. "There may be something." My voice squeaks, like a mouse. The chieftain turns to examine me, hawk eyes red, ready to pounce, to rip me apart.

"Tell me," he demands, his expression becoming even more fierce, if that is possible.

I lick my lips. "There is a scroll." Min looks at me attentively and I force myself to continue. "A rare manual on surgery. There might be something in it that can help Akin."

"A scroll?" The chieftain's voice goes deadly soft. "What kind of scroll?"

I swallow. "An ancient medical document, believed to be written by Egypt's most renowned physician, Imhotep. Its authorship, and the information it contains, make it invaluable, one of our kingdom's greatest treasures." In my mind, at least. I think of the higher powers who sought it out. Maybe in their minds as well.

"You have seen this scroll and witnessed its effects first-hand?" Pepi asks. His voice, too, is curiously sharp.

"I transcribed parts of it myself," I say. "The scripts in it are old and take some work to decipher, but my brother was healed because of it. The knowledge it holds saved his life."

"Where is this scroll?" The chieftain clenches his hands at his sides as he takes a step toward me. I step back, my natural reflexes taking over.

"In Thebes." I blink up at them. "It resides with the pharaoh at the palace." Its brother with Queen Anat. Where my own brother also resides.

"Can you procure this document?" The chieftain's voice rasps with emotion, with need.

"I cannot go back to Thebes," I say, not having to feign my fear. "The queen wants me dead."

The chieftain crosses his arms. "Did you not hear what I said to Min? If you do this thing for me, for Akin, I will give you whatever you wish for. What does your heart desire, young scribe?"

I contemplate his offer a brief moment, though my outrageous request has been formulating since he first entreated Min. Lifting my chin, I look him directly in the eyes. "Merat and I wish to be married in Avaris. My brothers and I have family there, and the princess would like a proper celebration, befitting a queen." It is the best thing I can think of to get us all to the Hyksos capital. With luck, it will buy us more time, and it has the added benefit of concealing our desire to go free. Still holding the chieftain's gaze, I appeal to his pride, a quality I also know well. It occurs to me that Yanassi and I have more in common than I am entirely comfortable with. "You are the Hyksos prince. Do you not think your bride worthy of a royal welcome by your people and your own family there?"

The chieftain cocks his head, considering my words, as I hold my breath, praying to the gods that his desperation to see Akin healed, his affection for Merat, and his own self-regard are enough to make him agree to my proposal. He glances at Pepi, who shrugs — but not before giving me his own look. "Very well," the chieftain says curtly, drawing himself to his full height and glowering down his nose. "You will retrieve the scroll and bring it back to me. *If* you succeed in this task, I will *consider* your request." He turns to Min. "Do you think you can perform such a surgery?"

Min bows his head. "I will do what I can."

The chieftain turns back to me. "You will assist Min with the operation."

I nod, then clear my throat, trying again. "If I am to do this, I need more than your consideration that the wedding will take place in the capital. I would like your word." I pray we are the same in this respect as well.

Pepi walks between us. "An interesting proposition, Sesha. What say you, cousin?"

The chieftain huffs, a noise I take for agreement. Then, as if this compromise is more than he can bear, he turns on his heel and marches off, Min scurrying

234

beside him. I hear them begin talking about the logistics of performing such a risky operation and let out a giant exhale.

"Congratulations," Pepi murmurs, as we watch the pair walk off. "You just received your first assignment."

36

"I DID NOT KNOW MERAT so eagerly desired such a lavish ceremony or to be acquainted with her new family," Pepi says dryly, the moment we are alone. His eyes narrow at me. "Why did you not mention this scroll before?"

I blink at him. "I was not aware the document would be of any consequence." And yet, it had been of *great* consequence to several people in Thebes. To me and my family, to the powers who rule there.

Pepi echoes my thoughts. "An invaluable item like that is always of consequence," he says.

I know this too well. I think of Queen Anat and shiver. Am I really going back to Thebes? On one hand, if I can covertly retrieve the scroll and Akin's procedure is a success, the chieftain might actually take us to Avaris. On the other, Queen Anat and her faithful thug, Crooked Nose, would love nothing better than to see me dead should I return to the palace. Yet there is another stone that weighs heavy on my decision, heavier than all the gold in Nubia.

My brother.

The protective walls I built around Ky in my mind crumble, and I see my little brother, shorn head, cheerful smile, looking at me with love and trust, as he always has. How does he fare? Is he recovering well? Is he safe? I am struck by an overwhelming need to know.

"How am I to accomplish this mission?" I ask, anxiousness filling my chest at the magnitude of the task. "I've only had one test as a spy, and I failed it!"

"Who says you failed?" Pepi counters.

"I fell off the horse," I remind him.

"You also got on it. You obeyed my instructions without question, in spite of your fear. If you like, we can do a second test now."

"What test?"

"The hut. Did you notice anything about it?"

"Other than the fact that it was crammed floor to roof with items of every shape and size?"

"Precisely," Pepi says. "How many items can you recall?"

I stare at him blankly.

"Tell me about each of the objects you saw in the room," he says, moving to sit on a rock, as if this might take a while.

"I was giving my full attention to the patient," I protest. "Then Amara came in with the baby. There were many things happening at once."

"That does not matter." Pepi picks a piece of grass. "You must be able to observe the details of your surroundings. Even ones you think unimportant. Being aware of your environment is an essential skill for a spy. You do not know what might be crucial or relevant to your mission. Now, concentrate. And tell me what you see."

I close my eyes and take a breath, imagining myself back in the room. "There were crates," I begin slowly.

"And?"

"And … jars, a pile of weapons, bows, knives, some furs."

"What did the furs look like?" he asks.

"Yellow, spotted with black — leopard skins."

"And the weapons?"

"There looked to be some type of bow, but different, longer. Others, like the axes, seemed to be forged from a strange metal." The same as Min's scissors. The word comes to my tongue. "Bronze."

"Anything else?" Pepi says.

Biting my lip, I open my eyes. It feels like I'm failing him yet again. "I'll do better next time." I hate failing tests.

"I am sure you will." Pepi has the grass between his teeth and chews it thoughtfully. "We must speed up your training. My cousin is not known for his patience and will want us off to Thebes as soon as it is possible."

"Us?" Relief that I will not be expected to go alone floods my body. That Pepi will be there to help me. I sit down next to him, legs shaky.

"Yes, I will be going with you. I just have to inform Yanassi first."

"What about my friends?" Paser will not want to be left out of this adventure.

"What about them?" His gaze sharpens. "Have you told them of your training?"

Eye of Ra. "Ah, I might have mentioned something."

Pepi shakes his head. "Perhaps I did not impress upon you the importance of this. Discretion as a spy is no less valuable than the information you carry." His voice is serious. "You must tell no one about your mission. Consider this your third task, Sesha."

I stay quiet, and I suppose he takes my silence for acceptance, because he continues. "Guard your emotions and keep your thoughts hidden, like our friend the crocodile lies invisible beneath the water's surface. The element of surprise is a great asset." He reaches out and takes my hand. "Being a spy can be lonely, but you are not alone. You must trust me with your life as I will be trusting you with mine."

"I will do as you say." My voice comes out strange, like it is not me speaking but someone else. Perhaps I am becoming someone new.

"Good, because doing so will keep you and me alive." Pepi stands and offers his other hand to help me up. "I must go and speak with my cousin now. Meet me tomorrow after your duties, where the beekeeper tends his bees. I will have a better idea of things then."

I nod, unsure how I'm going to focus on pestles and mortars when I will soon be departing into the perilous sands. And having to keep it secret from my friends.

He bids his farewell and leaves me alone in the path. Ra's final rays shine through the trees, casting everything in dappled sunlight. This time of day at the oasis is peaceful, and I take a moment to breathe it in. When misfortune strikes others, it reminds us of our blessings. Blessings like the simple act of walking unencumbered and free from pain. Poor Akin. And though I have my own motivations in all of this, I am relieved there is something I can do for him after all.

Life is curious. I thought I'd learn something as a spy that would help my friends and me get to Avaris, and now it turns out I'm going to use these very skills to spy on my own people, steal back the scroll, and, with luck, be escorted directly to Avaris by the very person I thought we'd have to sneak away from. The gods have quite a sense of humour.

Involved in my thoughts, I almost bump into someone as I turn a corner in the path. Looking up to offer my apologies, I see it is Paser.

Like the night of the ceremony, he is dripping blood.

This time it is his own.

37

"W HAT'S HAPPENED?" I SAY, ALARMED.
His head is tilted back and the blood runs freely from his nose.

"Nothing." His voice is muffled. "Training."

"Let me look at it." I open the bag at my side and pull out some strips of linen. I think he is about to refuse, but he relents with a sigh, letting his hand fall away. The blood drips to the ground in slow, even splats. There is a cut on the bridge of his nose and his left eye is darkening at its inner corner.

I tear off two small pieces of linen and wad them into balls. "Insert these. What is it about the Hyksos's training?" I shake my head. "You would think they'd want their men in good health, not broken and bleeding."

"It is nothing." Paser deftly stuffs a wadded ball up each nostril. His voice sounds even odder with his nose plugged.

"Sesha," he begins, and I suspect he is about to apologize for his uncharacteristic brooding the other night. I touch his arm, letting him see in my eyes that there's nothing to apologize for. There is something endearing about him standing here before me, battered yet trying to make things better between us. I do not deserve his affections, even as much as I want to return them. Pepi insinuated that the fewer ties I have to the people around me, the safer they will be.

Paser must see something in my expression, because he sighs and changes the subject. "I've seen their weapons," he says finally, and I relax, though there is nothing calming about the Hyksos armoury.

"I have as well," I say, recalling the stacked piles in the storage hut.

"Their bow is incredible," Paser says, awe in his voice. "Its shape and size, and the power it has! The arrows fly so much farther, their aim true."

"Are they training you to use it?" I ask. An archer is a good position for a soldier, back from the enemy and safer than hand-to-hand combat. I shiver, thinking of their wicked-looking axes. Hopefully it will not come to that.

He nods. "Sesha, with these weapons ... the Hyksos are even more formidable than Thebes knows. If the chieftain is planning on battle …" His words trail off, but he does not need to finish them. Paser and I are quite adept at reading each other's thoughts. Days surviving in the desert with not much more than the strength of one's spirit will do that.

"It will not come to battle," I say, touching his arm again. His hand comes up to mine, covering it.

"Let us pray to the gods it does not." He is quiet. "Maybe you are right to do this thing with Pepi. To become a spy, to try to prevent conflict."

I long with every bone in my body to tell him about the mission to go back to our city, but Pepi's warning for discretion is still fresh in my mind. I bite my lip.

"What is it, Sesha?" he says, apparently sensing my own internal war. And despite my misgivings at angering Pepi and falling short of another task, I cannot keep something like this from my best friend.

The words come out of their own accord. "I am to return to Thebes, with Pepi."

He stares at me. "What?"

"Yanassi's second-in-command is direly hurt. I convinced the chieftain that there may be something in the scroll that can help heal his man."

"You are going to get the scroll?" he says in disbelief, hand falling away from mine. "Why would you do such a thing?"

"Many reasons," I say. "I am obligated to help my patient in whatever way I can. Akin is husband to a friend and father to a child I helped bring into this world. And" — I reach my hand toward him again — "if I succeed, the chieftain said he will take us to Avaris. I convinced him that Merat and I wish to marry in their capital. Once we get there, we can escape. We can find your family and perhaps, with their help, leave for another place. You and Reb will not have to fight, and Merat will not have to marry Yanassi. And in Thebes I will get to see Ky."

He shakes off my hand. "Do you think you are the only one who thinks of duty and obligation, Sesha? You make these elaborate plans without consulting any of us, as if only you know what is best."

Bewildered, I look at him. "I did not mean —"

But, like the chieftain, he spins round on his heel and marches off into the twilight, leaving me standing there alone.

That night after the evening meal, I go in search of my friends, determined to clear any lingering dust from the air. It was not my intention to be high-handed; things just happened so quickly that there was no time to consult with them. I hope Paser will understand. Perhaps it is only the stress of his training and what he witnessed there that made him snap at me. He seemed truly worried for Pharaoh and our kingdom. The weapons must be impressive in action. As grandson to one of the best generals in recent times, my friend knows what he's about when it comes to weapons and battle. Though Pepi and I go to Thebes for the scroll, and I also go for Ky, I think of my other reason for becoming a spy: doing what I can to help calm things between our peoples. At the least, someone needs to warn Pharaoh of the Hyksos's weapons. But who will he listen to?

Wujat.

I have not thought about the vizier, Pharaoh's constant companion and adviser, as I did not want to analyze too closely his role in my father's death. Does he know all that the queen has done? And what is the nature of his relationship with her? Does he love her, as we guessed that night she confronted us at the mastaba? A night that seems so long ago, when it's been just under a full moon's worth of days. Time is strange in the desert.

Putting my thoughts aside, I reach the clearing and spot my friends. Paser and Reb acknowledge my presence by moving over to make room for me at the fire, yet Paser's shoulders remain stiff. Merat was not at dinner. It was announced that she and the children would be giving a performance that night in honour of the chieftain and his second-in-command, that he may be restored to good health.

The children re-enact the story of the great hunt, the one told by Namu the other night. Judging by their ferocious roars, it was Yanassi and Akin who caught the lion. Next, they sing a tune Merat taught them, which I recognize. The audience doesn't seem to mind that they perform a Theban song; they clap and cheer for the children, their voices rise along with the flames into the night sky. It is unexplainable, but each song sung or tale performed stitches the audience closer together, sewing my friends and I along with everyone else into the skin of the community, helping to bind wounds that come from leaving home and loved ones behind. I even see the tension in Paser's shoulders melt away, such is the magic of music and stories.

When the little ones are done, they bow, with everyone heaping their generous praises. Laughing, the children pull Merat into the firelight, her cheeks flushed. One of the older ones begs her to dance and she demurs, still laughing. But another picks up the chant and they cry for her to dance. Soon everyone in the crowd calls her name — "Merat, Merat!" — and she puts up her hands in surrender.

Nodding at the drummers, who provide a steady beat, she assumes the beginning pose. A hush settles over the people as she begins to dance. Her hands move through the air, graceful as birds. Her hips sway, her feet step, and her hair swings, all in different directions yet all at the same time, in perfect rhythm with the beat. Her body weaves another type of magic upon the crowd as we watch, unable to tear our eyes away. The drums reach a frenzied pitch and I feel them in my own blood and head. My heart bursts with pride and a curious envy; Merat's beauty radiates from her very soul for all to witness as she moves.

The drums stop and she is still, except for her breath, which comes fast, firelight flashing in her eyes. There is an instant of silence, and then everyone erupts in cheers for their queen, for an Egyptian princess who has enchanted them, as she enchants me.

Her eyes find mine, and then her gaze moves past me, to Paser, and my heart cracks a little, as her eyes are all for him, yet his are for me. And then the chieftain steps forward and beckons Merat to him and she obliges, and I am reminded that there is a chance none of us will get what we want and that it is better not to want things at all, as their lack only brings heartache.

38

MERAT'S DANCE BRINGS THE NIGHT to a close, as there is nothing that can follow, and the crowds begin to leave the fire. People walk by her, complimenting the performance and her work with the children. As Paser and Reb stand, I notice one of the young women shooting subtle glances in Reb's direction. He feels her gaze on him as well; his shoulders go back and his head tilts to the side as he teases Paser about his black eye, which does not look so bad in the cover of night.

Merat finds us, breathless and buzzing like one of the bees I will see tomorrow during my training with Pepi. The chieftain shares a drink with his men, and I see his eyes follow her to us. Will he really be able to wait until we get to Avaris to claim her as his bride? I do not know if Merat was only being contrary the other night because she was angry, or if she truly means to accept her fate. Either way, I plan on talking her out of *that* notion.

"Well done, My Queen," I say to her with a slight bow of my head. "You are a most talented dancer."

"The High Priestesses who trained me would be glad to hear you say so," she says, colour still high in her cheeks, before turning boldly to Paser. "And you, friend? What did you think of the performance?"

"Most admirable, Your Highness." Paser smiles. "You have done wonders with the children."

Merat's own smile fades slightly, but Paser is smart not to heap too many praises on Merat's dancing. I still feel the chieftain's attention on us. On Merat. And on Paser.

"Shall we retire?" I suggest to Merat, wanting to get away from the chieftain's sharp gaze, as well as to share all that has happened.

"Let us walk you to your hut," Paser offers, and I know he, too, wishes to discuss recent developments.

The four of us start up the path.

"Paser tells me the Hyksos weapons are formidable," I begin, hesitantly.

"And so you are justified in wanting to become a spy and save the kingdom?" Merat inquires archly. I flush, but Paser and Reb laugh. Although it's directed at me, I do not mind too much, as it dissipates the tension in the air around us.

"Sesha was also involved in some inspired negotiations this day," Paser says. Reb and Merat look at me in surprise. "Tell them of your plans."

Relieved that Paser sounds more resigned than angry, I glance around and lower my voice. "Despite the wonderful performance tonight, no amount of beseeching the gods will have Akin walking again. The only thing that might help him is information contained in the scroll."

"Not that sandblasted papyrus again?" Reb says in disbelief. "Let it go, Sesha. That thing is cursed."

"Cursed? It saved my brother's life!"

"And ruined ours." Reb gestures at Paser and himself.

"The queen did that." I keep my voice even as I stop walking and turn to face my friends. "If I return with the scroll and it helps Akin, the chieftain has promised to take us all to Avaris." My words linger in the night air, shimmering with possibilities.

Reb and Merat both look stunned. "How ever did you manage that one, Sesha?" the princess asks.

"She told him that you both wished to be wed in the capital," Paser cuts in. "Not a bad plan, all in all." He gives me an acknowledging smile, which I return in gratitude.

I turn to Merat and Reb, hoping they, too, will understand. "I explained that my brothers and I have family in the capital and that the princess would like to be introduced to the royal powers and their subjects, in a ceremony befitting a queen."

Merat stares at me blankly. "You what?"

"It was the only thing I could think of," I say, anxiously examining her face, which — thankfully — does not seem angry.

Reb snorts, whether in disdain or admiration, I'm not sure. It is always hard to tell with him. "You appealed to his pride."

"At the least, it buys us some time," I say, bracing for a comment about how it takes one proud creature to recognize another. It doesn't come.

"But if the Hyksos do intend battle, will we be any safer in their city?" he says instead.

We continue walking and I let out the breath I'm holding. All three of them seem to be in agreement with this plan.

"We can find Paser's family and persuade them to help us vanish into the city, or escape on a ship and sail to a distant shore."

"The latter is probably a smarter option," Paser says, his voice quiet. "I can see the chieftain turning the city upside down for his bride."

"And leave our lands and the people we know, forever?" Merat looks uncertain. "I am thinking it is not so easy to run from our destiny."

Merat and Paser seem as conflicted as I feel. The oasis casts its spell on us all. Caught in the middle, they seem no more able to abandon either side than I am.

"Will you go and face the queen alone?" Reb asks finally. He looks worried for me, and I am touched at his concern.

"With any luck, I will not face her at all." I will do my best to stay out of Queen Anat's sights.

"She will not be alone," Paser adds as we reach our hut. "She will have Pepi."

Merat stands in the doorway. "And we will stay here, while Sesha goes to get the scroll with the spy?"

"We will not be gone long," I say. "Once I am back, Min and I will do our best to help Akin. If all goes well, then the four of us will soon be on our way to the Hyksos capital."

Paser shakes his head. "I still do not fully trust the spy. There is something he is not telling us."

I think of Pepi warning me not to tell my friends too much, saying it could endanger them, that discretion keeps us safer. "Maybe he has good reason," I say, feeling slightly guilty at having revealed our mission. I have a better appreciation for the fine line in the sand the spy must walk. On one side lies loyalty and honesty, on the other, keeping those you care for safe.

"Thank you for escorting us," Merat says to the boys. Her eyes linger on Paser.

"It is our honour, Princess," he says, and they walk off into the night to their own quarters.

I watch them walk away, then follow Her Highness into the hut. Merat combs out her hair in the near dark. She is unusually quiet.

"May we talk?" I say, wanting to make sure things are well between us.

"Always," is her reply, but there is something in her tone.

"I thought you would be happier about the delayed weddings."

She bites her lower lip. "I appreciate all you do for me, Sesha, truly."

"Then why do you seem upset?"

"Maybe I am a little." She sighs. "But not for the reasons you think. Your plan to get the scroll is a bold one. Better than anything the rest of us have come up with to leave the oasis."

"Even if Paser still does not trust Pepi?" It is the wrong thing to say.

She whirls around. "Paser is jealous of Pepi!" she bursts out. "Can you not see that? For someone so smart about some things, you can be vastly ignorant about others." Her words sting, and tears come to my eyes.

"I have done nothing to encourage —"

Merat cuts me off. "You do not need to. You only have to walk by for him to look at you, to speak for him to listen." Her hands fly up in exasperation. "He crossed a desert for you."

"That is true," I say, heading for the exit, needing to escape her hot resentment, the accusation on her face. Pushing back the skin covering the entrance to the hut, I look over my shoulder. "But we crossed it for you as well."

39

MERAT'S IRE SEARS MY HEART.

Paser's feelings are not my fault! I stalk along the path, no real destination in mind.

And yet, I would be lying if I said I felt nothing at all in return.

The moon provides only a little illumination, but my eyes have no problem adjusting. Everyone is settled in for the night. A baby cries, my namesake. Amara and her husband likely know the full extent of Akin's condition by now. They must. Passing the chieftain's hut, I notice the light of a torch flickering inside. I make out the chieftain's low guttural tones and Pepi's more subdued ones. A sharp increase in volume has me pausing outside the hut, one word in particular catching my attention.

"And the scroll she speaks of? Do you really think it is the one you were seeking?" the chieftain asks urgently. "The one from the prophecy?"

Whoosh.

All the breath is knocked out of me. Like I've fallen off the horse again, flat onto my back.

"It may be ..." I move closer, straining to hear Pepi's words. A branch cracks underfoot and I freeze.

"Good." The chieftain's voice is grim. "If what the oracle says is true, we will need it for battle, as well as for Akin."

"You are still planning on war, then?" Pepi's voice sounds resigned.

"Those at Thebes leave me little choice. It is we who bring riches to these lands, garnering and encouraging trade from across the seas." The chieftain's voice rises. "We bring skilled craftsmen, innovative ideas, and new weapons to the delta. The region flourishes because of us! Our grandfathers' fathers settled there, married, had children of their own. Is it not our home as well?"

"You are not wrong, cousin." Pepi says in a pacifying tone. "But our dynasty has managed to coexist with Thebes for many years — if not always smoothly, at least without significant bloodshed."

"For how long?" the chieftain growls. "They give us their daughters as tokens to bide their time, but they do not want us here in Egypt. They think we are unworthy. That we are a lesser people, I am a lesser man, for no other reason than we are not them. The Thebans are scared. We threaten their sovereignty as no people have before. They will rise up against us if we do not rise first. I've spoken with the Kushites, and they are with us. As are the people along the Nile, as far as Cusae."

Pepi tries another tactic. "We are not ready. The soldiers are still training. We have not finished working with the horses. There is also Akin's injury. Besides, we have had no word from Avaris about whether they will support our cause."

"Then we will confer with them when we return for our weddings." Yanassi's voice is mocking. "Besides, those at Avaris grow fat and complacent. It is time to act now, while the Thebans are weakened by famine and drought." His voice drops and I strain to hear. "You know what the oracle foretold. I require that scroll."

"Sesha!" I jump. It is Merat. "What are you doing?"

"Ah, I came to speak with Pepi," I whisper, nodding at the hut. "What are you doing?"

"I wanted to apologize for losing my temper. It is not right to take my frustrations out on you, especially after all you have done for me —"

Just then Pepi pokes his head out. "Sesha, Merat." He greets both of us, though his eyes stay solely on me, as if to inquire how long I've been standing there. I keep my face impassive. "I thought I heard the harmonies of your voices. What are you doing out of bed?"

I think fast. "We could not sleep after the excitement of the performance. I thought I might check on Akin, and Merat offered to accompany me."

Pepi does not look like he believes me, but he lets it go. "Min just checked on Akin," he says. "Perhaps you should let the man rest for now."

"If you think that is best." I turn to follow Merat up the path.

"Sesha," Pepi calls to me.

I freeze, then turn back. "Yes?"

"Meet me at the bees first thing tomorrow instead of after your regular duties. We will spend the morning there." He cocks his head. "I believe we have much to discuss."

"Very well."

Yes, I believe we do.

Still reeling from what I have just heard, I walk with Merat back to our hut. I am quiet, and the princess does most of the talking.

"It is not that I do not appreciate you coming after me, or all that you have done since you arrived," she continues as we enter our small dwelling. "I do. It is just that I cannot seem to make my feelings for Paser go away, no matter how hard I try." I do not think she tries all that hard, but I keep my tongue in place as she gets into bed. "And though I know how he feels about you, there is a small part of me that refuses to give up hope."

I am not sure what to say. Or rather, I am tired of chirping on like a bird perched outside the window when one is trying to sleep. So I say nothing except a few sympathetic exclamations here and there to punctuate her speech; now that she has started, she cannot seem to stop.

Ready for slumber and suddenly exhausted by the events of the last few days, I crawl into my sleeping place, shivering, and pull up a skin for warmth.

"Sesha?" Merat speaks into the dark, after a few moments of silence. "Are you all right?"

No. No, I am not. I am getting caught up in a dangerous game, one partly of my own making. But I do not want to trouble my friend, who seems to be feeling better now that she has vented her frustrations, like smoke escaping from the ashes.

"I am fine," I say. "Only tired."

"Why did you say I was accompanying you to see Akin?"

"I did not want you to get in trouble for wandering around after dark without an escort." I briefly wonder if deception comes too easily to me.

"What were you wanting to ask Pepi?" she asks.

What do I *not* want to ask Pepi? "Hmm?" I say blearily, unable to keep my eyes open. My mind and body are shutting down, unable to cope with anything more this day.

"When I found you outside the hut, you said you wanted to speak to Pepi about something."

"Ah, I wanted to see when we will be on our way to get the scroll." A scroll that he's apparently been searching for since before we even met.

How is that even possible?

Is Paser right not to trust him?

What did the chieftain say? *"The one from the prophecy."* What prophecy? I shake my head, trying and failing to clear the hazy fatigue. Unfathomably, the scroll is somehow still at the centre of it all. I *will* get some answers from Pepi tomorrow.

And with that thought, I fall asleep.

40

SOMEHOW, EVERYTHING IS ALWAYS better in the morning. Even if only a fraction. Maybe it's because you are rested, better equipped to face your troubles and problems. Maybe it is as simple as seeing Ra come up in the sky to light another day. Another day where you get to walk around and try to sort out those troubles or problems, a fresh opportunity to live your life in this too-short time we are allotted in the land of the living.

A chance to ask certain spies about certain prophecies concerning certain scrolls.

I leave Merat sleeping and go to meet Pepi at the bees, taking only a piece of fruit for my quick morning meal. The fig is delicious, and I savour its sweet flavour as I make my way to where the hives are kept.

The oasis is awakening, beginning to buzz like the creatures I am on my way to see. They are located just around the far tip of the sparkling lake, where the trees grow thicker, close to the training grounds. At last, I reach the apiary and look around for Pepi. There is a simple hut and, farther back, several dried cylinders of mud lie stacked on top of each other. The scent of beeswax permeates the air along with a loud humming.

I do not see Pepi, but the keeper of bees comes out of his hut. Like Min, he is older, but unlike the healer, he does not have many teeth left.

"Sesha." He lifts his hand in greeting and gives me a gummy smile. "How are you this morning?"

"Very well," I say cautiously, glancing around for Pepi.

"I am Pentu. Pepi said you will be helping to extract the honeycomb from the hives today."

I stare dubiously at the droning insects flying around their priceless horde of sweet nectar. Me? "I've never handled bees before," I tell Pentu. Beekeeping is a time-honoured and important tradition, but after my recent bout with rash and blisters, it is not something I am eager to experience.

Pentu smiles. "We will teach you what you need to know."

"We?"

"One should always replace what they take, Sesha," Pepi says at my ear. I whirl to see him standing next to me. He grins. "As you and Merat were the ones to use up the propolis balm, it seems only fair that you help collect the honeycomb."

On the surface, Pepi is right. Honey is worth a lot in trade. Aside from sweetening foods, its most important uses are, in my opinion, medicinal. It keeps wounds clean and sealed, and there are hundreds of medical recipes that call for its healing powers. The wealthy also use it for cosmetic purposes, applying the wax to their hair and in beauty balms, like the one Merat and I slathered on our tormented skin.

But somehow I suspect this is less about obtaining the precious substance and more along the lines of another test.

"Does it hurt when they stab you?" I direct my question to Pentu while staring defiantly at the spy.

"It is no more than a pinch," the bee charmer says. He gives my arm one to demonstrate.

I do not break eye contact with Pepi. "What about when it is in the back?"

"They do not sting often, and only to protect themselves," Pepi says, giving me a look that says we will talk later. "Pentu is good at his job."

Pentu claps his hands together, oblivious to our unspoken communication. "I think there is a new queen in the hive. I am going to try calling her today."

"Pentu has a way with the bees," Pepi says. "He speaks to them, and they answer back."

"Can you tell them not to sting me?" I say to Pentu, finally tearing my narrowed gaze away from the spy.

Pentu laughs. "Just move slowly. Bees can sense agitation. If you are calm, they will be calm. Wait here — I will return in a few moments."

I turn to Pepi the instant we are alone. "What is this supposed to test? My ability to work alongside a traitor under absurd conditions?"

"If that is how you prefer to look at it," he says, not denying the accusation.

"You've been seeking the scroll the whole time?" I hiss. "Why did you not say anything?"

"My missions were none of your business," he says coolly.

"They are now!"

Pepi lifts an eyebrow. "I will tell you what you want to know after this test. Now, if I were you, I'd calm myself. As Pentu says, the bees can sense agitation."

"Why are you making me do this?" I say in a furious whisper.

"Remember what I said about staying calm in the midst of chaos? It is also a lesson in distraction."

"How does it work?" Putting aside my anger for the moment, I try to focus on the task at hand. Despite being mad enough to stick something in Pepi myself, I would like to do well on one of my assignments at least. There is the matter of my pride, something I have never been accused of having a shortage of. Especially by Reb.

"You and I will wave smoking fronds at the back of the hives. This distracts the bees and keeps them calm," Pepi says. "They will escape from the front. Pentu will break the seal and extract the honeycomb."

Pentu returns with sleeved shirts to put on as we prepare for the task. We wrap linen around our heads to protect us from the bees and from breathing in too much smoke. Pepi lights a bundle of fronds, sticks, and leaves, which produces curling grey wisps, and passes it to me. He then lights his own bundle and walks slowly toward the hives with Pentu. I reluctantly follow. The buzzing increases, as does the sweet smell.

Pepi begins to softly wave his bundle of burning sticks as we slowly approach the hive. My breath starts coming faster and my body tenses, preparing for an onslaught of painful stings. Pepi seems relaxed. I force myself to breathe deeply and copy his motions, waving the smoking fronds. Soon we are in the thick of the hive, bees buzzing everywhere.

Pentu moves with the grace of a dancer. He extracts the honeycomb with the practised expertise of a long-time keeper, letting out the occasional high-pitched noise as he communicates with the bees.

There is a piping call over the general hum: *Zoo-ah-zee-zee-zee-zee. Zoo-ah-zee-zee-zee-zee.*

Pepi leans over to me. "That is the call of the new queen bee. She is challenging the old queen. Listen."

Over the short, insistent whine of the young queen comes a steady quacking response, an unusual sound from a bee. The reigning monarch, I assume, warning the new queen off. Pentu makes another high-pitched sound and the queens respond. I wonder if he is encouraging them to resolve things in a peaceful manner, or whether he is merely confusing them so he can make off with their liquid gold. The keeper of bees works quickly, extracting as much honeycomb as he can, while we waft the smoke over the disoriented insects.

I feel a sharp sting on my arm and almost drop my fronds. Pepi motions me to step backwards, one cautious foot at a time.

When at last we are far enough away, he unwraps the cloth from around his head, dark eyes sparkling. "A new queen has emerged," he says as I rub at the sting. It hurts, but it's nothing I cannot bear.

"The old queen will probably leave the hive with her loyal subjects," Pentu says. He points at another area of mud cylinders. "That one is ready for them."

"Thank you for allowing us to assist you today," Pepi says. "Sesha is building up her collection of skills here at the oasis."

"You are most welcome," Pentu says. "I am going to wash the stickiness off. If you like, you can prepare the honey." He demonstrates how to crush the honeycomb, squeezing the sweet liquid into the container. "Leave it in the hot sun. The wax from the bees will float to the top and the honey will stay below." He waves his farewell and makes his way down to the lake.

Pepi and I work in silence, crushing the hard honeycomb in our hands; the viscous substance oozes between my fingers. Now that we are alone, it is time for some answers. I do not even know where to begin. "Tell me about this prophecy," I say at last. A few of the insects buzz around, curious about what we are doing with the spoils of their labours. "And the scroll." I look at him, challenging him to refuse me, to put me off, to avoid my question. But he only nods.

"As you wish. Then *you* can tell me why you want to get to Avaris so badly." He grins at me. "I do not think it's because it is a superior wedding locale. Though the views of the water are quite spectacular."

"Very well," I say through gritted teeth, pulverizing the piece of honeycomb in my hands.

"Let us begin, then," Pepi says, clearing his throat like one of the head scribes settling in for a long lecture. Unable to stop myself, I lean forward.

41

"**T**HERE IS A SCROLL," Pepi begins, without pausing, "that lies at the centre of a prophecy. As I am sure you overheard." He gives me a pointed look and I give him one back. I was only doing what he is training me to. "This document —"

"What makes you think my scroll is the same one from your prophecy?" I interrupt.

"The scroll was referred to as the 'healer's papyrus' by an oracle." He gives me another look. "May I continue?" I nod. "The prophecy says that this document holds the power of life over death, and that whoever holds it holds the power to rule over their people."

"Eye of Ra," I say faintly. I shake my head to clear the buzzing; I am not sure if it comes from within my skull or outside it. "The scroll has the power of life over death? Why? Because it can help mend horrible injuries and save lives?"

Pepi picks out a large piece of honeycomb from his bowl. "That may be part of it," he concedes, examining the comb.

My eyes narrow. "What is the other part?"

"You would likely know better than I." He discards the honeycomb. "You transcribed it, assuming your scroll is the same one."

"Only parts of it," I protest. "I did not have it in my possession for long."

"Did you notice anything unusual about the document?" he asks as we continue extracting and filtering the honey, receiving a few more stings for our efforts.

"Other than the fact that it was written over a thousand years ago by one of the most respected physicians of Egypt?" I retort. Imhotep had been vizier to the pharaoh, first architect of the pyramids, an astronomer, a healer, a scribe, a High Priest, a magician. "The scroll was a masterful work blending art, magic, *Heka*, and science. Aside from a few spells, it is remarkably methodical and rational in its approach." I stop. Pepi is staring at me. "What? The spells?"

"Tell me about these incantations," Pepi asks, voice quiet, as if not to startle the bees.

"I do not remember much about them," I say. "They were difficult to decipher. The language was old, and many of the scripts are no longer in use, being written so long ago." At the time I was copying the scroll, my attention was focused on the case studies dealing with injuries to the head, on saving my brother. "Is that why your cousin wants it? Because he thinks it will ensure his succession to the throne?"

"Essentially, yes. Though I am sure my brother would also like to save Akin," Pepi adds generously. "He is the chieftain's number-one man, and Yanassi needs him badly, should he manage to convince those at Avaris to support his … activities."

"Wait." I wonder if all the stings I've received are causing me to hear things. "What did you say? Your *brother*?"

"Yes," Pepi says calmly, carrying the honey over to a flat rock to leave it in the sun as Pentu instructed.

I follow him, wiping my forehead, leaving a sticky streak across it. "Your brother in the sense that you and the chieftain are members of the same tribe?"

"My brother in the sense that we share a father." Pepi sets the honey down, careful not to spill a single precious drop.

My mouth hangs open. He has the most casual way of imparting ground-shaking news.

"Careful, Sesha," he remarks mildly. "That is a good way to swallow a bee."

271

I shut my mouth. Then open it again. "You two are only pretending to be cousins?"

"I am not sure," Pepi says, looking at the hives, which are ready for their new monarch to take the throne. "Or rather, one of us is at least. In actuality, I do not think he knows the truth."

"You have not thought to speak with him about such a thing?" I cannot keep the disbelief from my voice.

"I have thought about it," he concedes, looking around for something to wipe his sticky hands on. "But it may not be the wisest course of action."

"Why not?"

"Yanassi is set to inherit the Hyksos king's throne when he dies. Many rulers, with such a prize in their grasp, do not do well with competition. As I am nephew to the king, and in line for the throne, our relationship is already precarious." Pepi finds a rag and wipes his hands on it, then passes it to me to do the same. "I do not know if my father even knows I am his son, though he may suspect it." He looks at me. "My mother was a spy, sister to the wife of the Hyksos king. She told no one of my paternity, for several reasons, but it does not escape me that many may consider me a usurper and threat to the throne. Yanassi's throne. Those who support him, and he himself, would have good reason to kill me." He falls silent at these words. The distinct

272

piping of the challenging queen bee echoes throughout the area.

There are so many questions I want to ask, so much more I need to know, but Pentu returns just then, clean and refreshed from his wash, and our conversation pauses for the moment. The bee charmer is carrying a few small items in his hands.

"Take this back to Min for his supplies," Pentu says, passing over a sealed jar of honey. I nod. "This is for you as well." He presents me with a small beeswax candle.

"Am I also to give this to Min?" I ask. It will be useful when tending someone in the dark.

"It is for you, Sesha." Pentu smiles. "In honour of your first time working with the bees."

"I cannot accept," I say, honoured by his generosity. A beeswax candle is highly valued for how brightly and cleanly it burns. The last gift I received was my scribe tools from Pharaoh. I feel a pang for the precious writing instruments, used to transcribe the very scroll that, while already of inestimable worth, has just become even more priceless.

"Think of it as compensation for your stings." The bee charmer's eyes dance as he glances at Pepi and me. "Or as an early wedding gift, if that makes you feel better."

It does not.

I open my mouth to object, but Pepi gives me a sharp elbow. He inclines his head graciously. "Thank you for your generous gift, Pentu."

Saying our goodbyes, we leave Pentu to his bees. I hear the piping of the new queen again, calling out the older one to defend her territory.

Struck silent with all that I have learned before even eating my midday meal, I walk along the path with Pepi, letting the birds carry the conversation.

"It is your turn," he says finally.

Blankly, I look at him. "My turn for what?"

"A secret for a secret," Pepi says, reminding me of our bargain. "Why do you wish to get to Avaris so desperately?"

I look at the candle in my hand. I am aware that Pepi told me his story as a sign of faith. "My friends and I wish to be free," I say. It is nothing he couldn't have guessed on his own, and not much of a revelation when compared to his own confession.

"So it is not for the majestic views? I am shocked," he says, sounding nothing of the sort. "Have you told your friends about returning to Thebes?" We are approaching the healer's hut.

I hesitate too long, and he shakes his head in dismay. "Keeping secrets is a critical task of a spy. I understand and admire your loyalty. But I need to know I can trust you."

"You can, as I can trust them," I say. It does not feel right keeping things from Paser, Reb, and Merat. "They would never betray me."

Pepi grabs my hand and whirls me to face him. "Even if the betrayal is accidental, it will not matter if you are dead. Do not put faith in anyone but yourself." His dark eyes examine me intently. "Remember this."

"Not even you?" I challenge, off balance from the spin, from everything he has told me.

He is silent for a moment. "Not even me. Can I trust you to keep my secret?"

"That you are really a Hyksos prince?" I say, still in shock over his birthright. Is he telling the truth? I only have his word to go on. And what is the word of a spy worth?

"I am a prince of nothing but sand and secrets, Sesha," he says quietly, his smile full of sorrow. It is this heartbroken smile, so full of devastating honesty, that convinces me. In it, I see Pepi has lost much. Like me.

Yet, despite the death of my parents and the loss of my brother, I am not broken. I have others whom I care for and who care for me. The fate of their lives, even Pepi's, rests on my shoulders now. Pepi implies that love for others makes us vulnerable, weak. This may be true, but I wonder if he knows it also makes us strong. Straightening my spine, I take a deep breath. "I will tell no one of your secret."

"Good," he says. "Now, let us get down to planning. We leave for Thebes tomorrow night."

42

PEPI LEAVES ME AT MIN'S HUT with instructions to fill my belly and get a good rest that night. I do not think either will be possible. It seems as unfathomable as the sands that I am going back into the desert. The thought terrifies and electrifies me all at the same time. I will have a chance to find the scroll, to see Ky, maybe even to prevent notions of war from escalating. But I will also be in grave danger, especially if Queen Anat or Crooked Nose should discover me. I could end up in the same pit as Pepi.

I manage to eat some honey with bread and some dates for my afternoon meal and am just finishing when Amara appears at the hut. Today she is alone. She looks odd without the usual bundle on her chest.

"Amara," I say, jumping to my feet. "Where is the baby?"

"She is well. I left her with the princess. I wanted to speak with you."

"How is Akin?"

"The same. Min is with him now." I see by her posture, the tension in her face, and the way she holds her limbs that she knows of his diagnosis. "I hear what you are going to do for us," she says softly. "That you are going back into the sands with Pepi, to find a scroll that might help heal Akin."

I wonder how much is safe to say. "Yes. This scroll … it is very special."

"Do you really believe it will help?" She is seeking assurance, hope. It feels like I have lived this moment before, when debating whether or not my brother should have the risky operation that Ahmes performed. It is an odd feeling.

I touch her arm. "It healed my brother." Hope is a powerful thing, and I want to give some to her. "There is a good chance it may do something for Akin."

And a better option than leaving him to rot in a puddle of his own waste, thinks the ruthless healer in the back of my mind.

"You have my gratitude for all lifetimes," she says, tears glistening. She wipes them away and offers me a watery smile. "I am here for another reason. Pepi asked me to help you with something."

He did not say anything to me this morning, but

perhaps this is another test to see how I handle the unexpected. Or maybe it is meant to distract Amara and give her a moment away from her nursing duties. "What is it?" I say, happy to be a diversion for my friend.

"Where does Min keep the henna?"

I look at her in bafflement. There is a faint star in her eye, twinkling, and I see a glimpse of her character as it was before her troubles. Then what she said slowly dawns on me, like Ra himself. "Oh, no." I shake my head. "No, no, no."

Amara laughs as she walks past me. Despite my misgivings, it is a lovely sound. "I will find it."

"You are not colouring my hair," I call after her. But she takes no heed. It was commanded by the chieftain's cousin after all — and I once offered to cut it myself. Besides, judging by the look in her eyes, Amara is very much looking forward to carrying out her instructions.

"That should be long enough," Amara says, satisfied. "Let's wash it out." We are by the lake. Having little choice but to let her have her way with my hair, I sat with my arms folded as she coated my strands with the herbal dye. Whether this is a test or a distraction, an altered appearance will not come amiss when I am back in Thebes. My month on the streets comes to me, as it does now and then. I kept Ky and myself away from the royal eye for a whole moon, and this time I will have the benefit of Pepi's knowledge on how to re-main hidden. A churlish part of me wonders if perhaps I should be giving *him* some advice. After all, he was not in the pits for the benefit of his health. With all I know now, I wonder again how he ended up in there. A conversation to save for our journey; there will be plenty of time to talk.

I walk into the cool water and dive under, scrub-bing my head to rinse the dye from my hair. When at last I feel no more residue, I exit the lake to where Amara waits with worn linens for me to dry off with.

"Look how it changes your appearance," she says, pointing to the calm water. I peer at my reflection.

"It does not look all that different." My tone is doubtful.

"Wait until it dries," Amara advises. "You will not recognize yourself."

"Let us hope others do not as well," I murmur, rub-bing my hair with the cloth. The fabric comes away a deep purple-red, the colour of Pharaoh's best wine. The chieftain was not wrong about how fast I go through linens.

"Will it be dangerous, retrieving this scroll?" Amara asks, hearing my comment.

"Yes," I admit. "The powers at Thebes are very ... protective of it."

"I confess I do not understand all the fuss over a simple papyrus." Amara scrubs at her hands in the lake. She glances up at me. "Unless it is the one from the prophecy?"

I freeze. Water drips from my hair onto the ground. I wind up my hair in another linen, tucking the towel in at the back, then stand to face her. "What do you know of a prophecy?" Something, if she speaks of it.

"Only what Akin tells me." Her eyes are wary. "Yanassi confides everything in him."

"And he in you?"

She ignores my question. "I married my husband for love."

"I see you two are very close."

"I will not see him die, and I will not see him wither away in despair," she says, holding her hands out for the linens. I pass them to her, and she dries off her hands. "You must get this scroll so Akin can be healed." She glances around. "I will tell you what you need to know to see you back safely."

I am careful to keep my face as calm as the water's surface. "What is it I need to know?" Pepi said the oracle claims that the papyrus has power of life over death, and that whoever holds it holds the power to rule. He did not mention if that was the entirety of the oracle's message or if there was more to it, which — knowing the spy — was likely intentional. Is Amara about to reveal something new?

Amara leans forward and whispers, though there is no one around, "Pepi may have his own private reasons for seeking the scroll."

I force myself to speak calmly. "What would those be?" Though Amara does not appear to know any additional details about the prophecy, her warning to be wary of Pepi's motives has my heart pounding all the same.

"Perhaps he thinks he can impress those at Avaris, in particular the king there, if he retrieves such a prize for him," she says, thoughtful. "Yanassi's father holds him in high regard, and this could increase his standing further."

"You think he wants the scroll to seek glory for himself?" It is a point. Though Pepi says he has no desire to be king, perhaps he seeks his "uncle's" approval all the same. Amara looks perplexed. I understand and share her confusion. It does not seem to fit with his character. Unless he has fooled us all.

"I am not sure," she admits. "I only know Akin does not fully trust him."

I touch Amara's arm. "Thank you for confiding in me."

"It is for selfish reasons," she says. "I want you to return with the scroll." Her eyes, now bright with unshed tears, implore me. "Vow to me, on your honour as a healer, on the child you helped bring into this world, that you will come back to us."

"I will do all that I can," I say. Her shoulders slump in relief and she lets out a shaky breath. Queen Anat's face appears in my vision. "But I will have to contend with others. People much bigger and more powerful than I am." I hear the doubt in my voice.

Amara hears it as well. "Is a scorpion's bite no less effective because it is small?" she says softly. "I must get back to the babe. She will be hungry."

"Go to your family," I say. "You have my thanks for assisting with my hair."

"The red becomes you." She leans over to kiss my cheek, as if she knows we are saying goodbye. "Be well, Sesha."

"Be well, Amara."

43

I GET TO THE FIRE LATE, EXHAUSTED, mind still digesting all it has had to swallow today. Despite Pepi telling me to get a good rest, this may be my last night with my friends for some time, and I want to spend it with them.

They are there, listening to a story. Merat sits beside Paser, and Reb sits with the young woman from the other night, Zina. Everyone pays rapt attention. Everyone except the chieftain, whose eyes are on Merat, who sits just a little too close to Paser. The chieftain will not wait until Avaris to make Merat his bride if this continues. He might also not hesitate to throw Paser out of the oasis, or even kill him outright, if he perceives him a real rival for Merat's attentions, soldier or not.

Something more must be done, but what? Merat is accustomed to getting whatever she wants, and though she promised to try and hide her feelings, her every glance in my friend's direction, under lowered lashes, hints at them. Even her body leans toward him, unconsciously or not, like the flower bends toward the sun.

My friends nod at me as I sit quietly beside them, but they turn back to the story, captured by Namu's words and animated impersonations. They do not know it is my last night with them. I sit there, basking in the glow of the warm fire and in their presence, thinking about how to keep them safe.

At last, the story reaches its dramatic conclusion. People clap and cheer and the drums beat in appreciation for the teller. Paser puts his fingers to his mouth and lets out a loud, approving whistle. I look at him.

"One of the soldiers taught me." He smiles, and my heart turns over in my chest. Maybe it is because I will not see it for a while, but suddenly I realize how much I have come to love his smile. How much he has got me through. I cannot let any harm come to him. He is my sun, too.

We make our way from the fire. Merat is talking to the girl standing with Reb. I seize my chance and lean over to whisper to Paser.

"Meet me later?" I ask quietly. "Come to my hut when the moon is at its peak."

He looks surprised, but nods.

People mingle as they say their good nights. Merat and I take our leave and walk in the direction of our dwelling.

"It is nice that Reb has someone who seems enamoured of him," she says, a little wistful.

"For his sake, let us hope another from the tribe is not interested in *her*." My voice is a little sharper than I intended, and she sighs at my not-so-subtle reprimand. I change the subject, not wanting our last conversation to be a lecture. "I coloured my hair." It was dark by the fire and my friends did not notice.

"I wish I could see." She peers at me and I remember something.

"I will meet you back at the hut," I say, turning and heading straight for the fire. Fumbling in my robes, I pull out the candle Pentu gave me this morning, which feels like days ago. Crouching low to reach the embers, I light the candle, then carefully make my way back to the hut, one hand over the flame, but the breath of the gods does not blow strongly tonight.

I enter the hut. "I have a gift for you." Merat looks up in surprise and I present her with the sweet-smelling beeswax candle.

286

"Sesha!" Merat's delight warms me like the candle. "How lovely!" She holds it up to my hair. "Who did it for you?" she asks, a hint of jealousy in her tone.

"Amara."

Picking up a lock, she examines it with the expert eye of one well versed in cosmetics. "She did a good job," she admits.

"Do you … do you think it changes my appearance much?" I ask. The candle lends a soft glow to the room, the light flickering over our skin, casting shadows.

She looks at me curiously. "Yes, now that I look at you. You seem different. Older?"

I must look relieved, because she adds, "You will leave for Thebes soon, then?"

"Yes." I do not elaborate.

"Where did you come by the candle?" she asks, admiring it.

"Pentu, the beekeeper, gave it to me."

"Should we not save it for something special?"

"It was meant as a wedding gift," I say, reminding us that though we have bought some time, her engagement, and my own fake betrothal, still looms, especially if we are not able to escape once in the city. My words cause even more shadows to settle on her face.

She sits down on the floor, carefully setting the flame in front of her, and places her chin on folded arms on top of knees, watching the candle burn. I sit down beside her.

"I am sorry, Merat." My voice is soft. "We came to rescue you, and though it seems all we have done is delay your fate, you must not give up. At the least you can be sure of our company, no matter what befalls us."

"And that is everything to me." She reaches out her hand and I take it. It is warm and soft, her palms still smooth despite the hardships of the last few weeks. The hands of a princess. My princess. If Paser is my sun, then Merat is my moon. "You are a true friend of the heart, Sesha. The gods gave me a great gift in you."

"And to me in you." I lean over and kiss my friend lightly on the cheek, heart burning bright as the candle. We sit there in the semi-dark, holding hands beside the beeswax flame. Her head dips to rest on my shoulder, and she falls asleep, while I force myself to stay awake. There is Paser yet to deal with.

The moon beams brighter, or maybe it's just the night growing darker, and I hear a noise outside. Stealing quietly from the hut, I go to save my friend's life, doubting that he, or anyone else, realizes the danger he's in.

The night air is cool and fresh. I glance around for Paser and make out a shape on one of the paths.

"Paser," I whisper, and he steps out into Khonsu's warm light.

"Sesha, what is it?" He's aware I would not ask to speak to him in private after all have gone to their beds unless it was urgent.

"Let us walk a bit," I say. He looks confused but starts down the path, and I walk beside him. Waiting will not make what I am about to do any easier.

"I leave for Thebes tomorrow night," I say, the words rushing out in one breath. He stops abruptly. "I will get the scroll, warn Pharaoh, and see Ky."

"Those who do not know you well might say you have lost your sense of reason," he finally says, looking up at the sky.

"Reb expressed a similar sentiment when I proposed we go into the desert to find the Hyksos and Merat." I gesture around me. "We made it here all right."

"Sesha, we almost perished during that journey. It was only by the gods' good graces that we made it out of the Red Land alive."

"The gods' *and* Pepi's," I say. "He will be with me, and this time we will be better prepared. Do not fear for me." I put a hand out to him and he turns to face me. "I will be safe, my friend."

He shakes his head. "I should be coming with you."

"I can think of no one else I would like more at my side, but you must stay here for the princess and for Reb." I smile, thinking of the young woman by the fire. "He may need your advice in matters of the heart."

"I do not think any advice of mine will help," Paser says quietly, looking down at the ground.

In a rush of courage, I stand on my toes, place my hands on his strong arms, and press my mouth to his. Pulling away, I try to sort the emotions flooding my body and mind.

Paser gets his breath back first. "What was that for?"

And this is it. The reason I asked him to come here tonight.

"A token," I say, my voice as soft and warm as the moonlight. "To keep close to your heart until my return."

He blinks. "Are you telling me to wait for you?"

"I have no right to ask such a thing." I say these words, but let my eyes say otherwise. My hope is that by giving *him* hope, for us, I will limit his susceptibility to Merat's charms and keep him safe from the chieftain's wrath. "I must go." It is time to rest.

Paser nods, still looking stunned.

"Good night, my friend," I say. "Sleep well." I turn and walk quickly back to my hut before he stops me, before he can ask what I mean by sneaking out to kiss him in the middle of the night under the shimmering light of the stars and a nearly full moon, whose effects likely have something to do with the whole scenario anyway. Slipping back in under the cover of Merat's soft snores, I feel pricks of guilt, sharp as the stings of the bees.

I must harden my heart. As the Hyksos make their bronze weapons stronger by thrusting the metal alloy into the flames, I, too, must walk the red-hot coals of calculated decisions if any of us are to survive. What I do is for Paser's *and* Merat's safety. If he thinks there's a chance for us, it might stop him from falling for her. Because if he does *that*, they are both doomed.

I hear Pepi's voice, wryly resigned. *You are becoming a spy, Sesha.*

"How wonderful," I mutter under my breath, to no one but the gods who can still stand the sight of me. "I wonder if I will lose all honour in the process?" Closing my eyes, I focus on slowing my breathing, forcing myself to sleep; there is no question I will need my rest for the exhausting journey ahead.

The voice comes back, fainter now, so faint I am not sure what it says until that instant before nothingness, when the words fall into place.

Keeping your honour will be the least of your worries …

44

I WAKE THE NEXT MORNING with Ra's first rays. Merat still sleeps, and I look over at my friend, golden light striking just above her head. She looks like she's glowing. I get dressed quietly and leave the hut, trying not to think whether this might be the last time I see her.

The village is slowly waking, and there are a few people out as I make my way along the worn paths, nodding back at those who greet me as if I am one of them. Birds twitter and call to one another, trilling over their breakfasts. I breathe in the fresh air and soak up the sounds and colours around me — the vibrant greens of the oasis plants and trees, the beautiful pinks and purples of the flowers, the blue of the sparkling lake in the distance — stowing their lush intensity for the time ahead when I will see nothing but sand for days on end.

Reaching Min's neat hut, I look for the healer. This is my last day at the oasis and I mean to speak with him more about my father. With more pressing matters occupying my time, I have not had the chance to ask my questions. I find the physician in the gardens, cursing the caterpillars again; they've made a nice meal of another of the rarer and more difficult-to-grow plants.

"It does not matter what I do." Min shakes his head. "The villains eat until they are fat and bloated."

"But they turn into such beautiful creatures." I look up at a few of the butterflies that flit overhead, their wings as golden as the sunlight above. "At least the plant is not going completely to waste."

"It does more good brewed," he grumbles. "When combined with a few others, this plant creates a powerful potion that can bring one back from the underworld." I examine the innocent-looking leaves of the plant. "Careful," Min warns. "The seeds are the most potent part. Come, I am preparing it today."

Collecting what we need, Min points out different uses for each plant and herb, one for every sickness and ailment imaginable. The gods provide us with such an amazing array of options for healing. There are no urgent medical requests this morning, so we spend it preparing medicines in the peaceful shade of Min's small hut.

"Can you tell me about my father?" I ask at last, during one quiet moment.

"You knew him better than I," Min says, amused. "We first met when he was young and I was supplementing my training in Thebes. We crossed paths again a few years later when he visited the delta. By then he was an accomplished physician, and he had come for a few moons to instruct, as well as to learn new techniques from the physicians in Avaris."

I almost spill the potion I'm mixing. My father was in Avaris? Min mentioned he was in the delta, but I did not know he was in the Hyksos capital. It fits him, though. I can see him being intrigued by the sights and sounds of the bustling port city, the mingling of diverse cultures and traditions.

"He was very gifted," Min offers, sensing my desperate need to bring him close. "The brightest among his peers. He was also very open-minded, for a Theban."

"How so?"

Min snorts. "Those at Thebes think Ra rises and sets on them alone. Your father did not share the same … prejudices that others from his background have. He believed in the equality of people and that our differences make us stronger. He was eager to learn from other tribes and share his own knowledge with us."

This makes me prouder of him than anything he did as a healer.

My stomach lets out a loud grumble and Min turns, but not before I see his smile. "I suppose we should stop for lunch?" he says.

Pepi did say to eat my fill. Min prepares us a hearty meal of fruit and bread, vegetables and meat. I eat until I feel full and sleepy, side effects of the tasty food and a late night.

"Go rest, Sesha," Min says kindly. The sun is directly overhead, and others will be taking a quick nap in the shade. I go out to the garden, find a quiet spot under a tree, and curl up in the dappled sunlight.

No one disturbs me and I sleep away the afternoon, waking chilled in the shade. I wonder if Pepi has taken his own advice to eat and rest as much as possible. It is hard to imagine him needing either — he seems tireless to me. He is probably busy preparing for our journey.

I wander into the hut, but Min is gone, likely to check on Akin. I pray the soldier stays strong while we are away. Min left behind a small bundle of prepared medicines in a satchel similar to my old one. Included among the items is the potion we brewed from the seeds of the caterpillars' beloved plant. There is a long piece of grass, curved into an S, marking them for me. I think of Min stuffing me to my gills and letting me rest, leaving me these herbs and medicines to take. He must know. Did Pepi tell him or did the healer figure it out on his own? Slinging the bag over my shoulder, I leave the hut, keeping an eye out for the spy. I walk past Pentu and his bees; he gives a friendly wave. Ra still shines overhead, but it will not be long before he begins his descent.

I find myself at the training grounds. Paser and Reb are practising with the Hyksos bows. They both do very well. Nearly all of Reb's arrows hit their marks, and Paser does not miss a single shot. He is right. Their bows are far superior to ours, not only in their appearance, but also in their obvious lightness and ease of use. The arrows have a much longer range, and I shiver at one of them finding their mark in Pharaoh.

I see Pepi, who is a ways off with the horses. Two of the creatures pull something behind them and I squint, holding up a hand to block Ra's rays. The horses are tethered to a sled-like object, not dissimilar to the Sun God's royal vessel that carries him across the sky.

Pepi jumps on the sled and urges the horses to move at a quick pace, swatting their behinds lightly with a switch. He keeps his balance admirably and pulls an arrow from the quiver on his back to load the bow he holds in his left hand. The other soldiers turn to watch as he shoots from the moving sled, a direct hit on one of the targets. A loud cheer rises among the men as a chilling realization thunders through me, like the hooves over the ground.

Hathor, help us. They are going to use the horses.

Pharaoh's army will have much more than elite bows and bronze weapons to worry about if Yanassi convinces those at Avaris that battle is necessary. The Hyksos will have the advantages of speed and endurance, as well as increased projectile force, not to mention sheer intimidation with the creatures and their unearthly cries bearing down on their enemies.

The importance of all I must do makes me feel slightly ill: retrieve the elusive scroll and heal Akin so my friends and I can get to Avaris, in addition to warning Thebes of the Hyksos's weapons and of Yanassi's ambitions. These are no small things.

Pepi jumps off the back of the sled, landing on the sandy ground, and raps his chest twice in acknowledgement of the soldiers' cheers. With the other hand he lifts the bow high in triumph. Catching my eye, he gestures subtly with his head to wait over by the clump of palms that shelters the other animals. His showy display signals an end to the day's activities, and the soldiers begin to pack up their weapons and return to the village for the evening meal.

Paser and Reb walk toward me, their gait and gestures animated, presumably from witnessing the horses in action. "Sesha," Reb calls. "Is it you?"

I remember my hair. "I think so," I say, reaching up to touch it. Though, in all honesty, I am not sure exactly who that is anymore.

"It suits you," Paser says, his hand lifts, as if he, too, wants to touch it.

"Sesha." Pepi walks up behind Paser and Reb and notices the bag. Paser's hand lowers back down. "Thank you for bringing me those items I requested from Min."

"You are welcome," I say, holding out the bag.

"Sesha told us you are training her to be a spy," Reb says after commenting on Pepi's horsemanship. I want to slap my forehead. Or his. Pepi does not need to be reminded of my slip.

"That's right," Pepi says, taking the bag from me. "She is a natural." I am not sure if this is a compliment.

"You will put her in danger." Paser crosses his arms. It's not a question.

"I will do my best not to," Pepi says, shouldering the satchel. "Sesha and I leave tonight for Thebes."

The three of us look at Pepi, surprised by his easy admission.

"You are going back into the desert so soon?" Reb says, doubtful.

"Only for a short period," Pepi says. "We will travel farther by boat this time. Can you help tend the horses while I am away, Reb?" Eagerness flashes across Reb's face, replacing the uncertainty. "Sham has a way with them." Pepi names the soldier who found me after Akin's accident. "But it is always good to have another set of hands. If you like, I will ask Yanassi if he can spare you on occasion."

Reb nods, looking pleased.

"For someone so new to archery, you are very good with the bow," I add, and Reb beams further.

"He has a gift for it." Paser hits him on the shoulder. "Soon he will be a better shot than I."

"We all have different strengths," I say, thinking of Reb's struggle with scripts. I am glad he has found his talent, in addition to pulling teeth, of course. For all that, my mother used to say our worth does not lie in our skills, but in our hearts. She would tell my brother and me that being a good person is a far greater achievement than any external success, despite what the rest of the world tells us. "I have terrible aim," I add.

"We will have to work on that," I hear Pepi mutter under his breath.

"Will you bring Ky back with you?" Paser asks, naming something I had not dared hope for.

"I do not know," I admit, heart beating faster at the thought of seeing my brother again. "We will assess the situation." Though I would love nothing better than to collect my brother, if he is content and safe in Thebes, I am not sure I should force him to give up his comfortable life there.

"What about Queen Anat?" Reb asks. "She will not want you escaping again."

"Sesha will have me to look out for her," Pepi responds with confidence. "As well as her own wits and cunning, which are considerable."

"Bring her home safely," Paser says, arms still folded. "Or do not come back at all."

Pepi pulls himself to his full height, slightly shorter than the scribe turned warrior. "Because I know you mean well, I will let that comment pass. Sesha has come to mean as much to me as she does to you," he says. Paser snorts as if he very much doubts this.

"I can also take care of myself," I interject, with more conviction than I feel.

Paser gives me an acknowledging smile, one of his old ones. "I know you can."

"Say goodbye to your friends, Sesha." Pepi glances at the sky, judging the time, then back at me. "We are leaving now." He turns and walks off, giving me a few minutes alone with them.

We stand there, looking at each other. Reb's stomach lets out a loud gurgle and we all laugh. For a minute it is like we are back in temple and no time has passed since our days scratching hieroglyphs in the sand. The three of us have been through much. Paser and Reb are not only my friends; they are my brothers.

"Let us go and get some food, Reb," Paser says, his eyes meeting mine. We said our goodbye last night. "I am as ravenous as a lion."

Reb nods. "Safe travels, Sesha." The boys turn.

I walk toward where Pepi is unhitching the horses from the sled. He, too, has become an ally, one helping me reclaim the scroll, although perhaps for his own reasons. With his help, I will also see Ky again, my other brother, one I swore never to forsake or abandon.

The time has come to keep my word.

45

"WHY DID YOU TELL MY FRIENDS we leave for Thebes after you told me not to say anything?" I ask Pepi as we walk to the caravan.

"How else would I know how you did on your test?" He glances at me "Paser seemed most unsurprised at the announcement. He would not make a good spy."

"No," I agree. "He is too honest and good for that. This sticky concoction of deceit leaves a bad taste in my mouth."

"Sometimes the foulest-tasting medicines have the most beneficial effects," Pepi says, sounding like Min. "If you do not believe in doing difficult things for the greater good, maybe we should discontinue your training when we are back from Thebes."

"Because I failed yet another task?" The caravan comes into view. They are finishing up the loading, giving the donkeys their final drink of water and something to eat. "Though I said nothing of your own secret."

"I appreciate that," Pepi says, then sighs. "If your instincts told you to confide in your friend and you believed it the right thing to do, then I must also have faith you know what you're doing." He gives me an acknowledging smile. "I am aware trust goes both ways, Sesha."

"Thank you," I say, blinking. "You remind me of my father." He, too, had believed that I, a young woman, could do great things, could make a difference, could save lives.

An odd expression crosses his face. "Your words honour me."

We speak no more as we reach the organized chaos of the caravan, about to depart. Nefer is there and I climb onto her back, this time without a hand from Pepi. In all the tumult of the past few days, I never did get back on that horse. I suppose it can wait until our return. For we *will* return.

"Here," he says, binding something around my leg. "A gift, to mark our first mission together." I look down to see a plain yet well-made sheath. "For your blade," he says. Wordlessly, I take my father's obsidian knife from the bag at my side and slide it into the leather scabbard. It is a perfect fit.

"Thank you," I say simply. Pepi's gaze passes over me as if assessing whether I am ready. I sit higher in my seat, my shoulders going back. He gives a nod and firmly pats Nefer twice in quick succession. The sturdy donkey lets out a reassuring bray.

As if this was a signal, the leader of the caravan lets out his own ululating cry and we set off, Pepi walking alongside the donkey.

The sky blazes pink and gold as dusk creeps over the desert in the distance. Having taken my leave since the moment the chieftain commanded I retrieve the scroll for him, I do not look over my shoulder as we start out into Deshret, the Red Land. There is no sense in looking behind me as we leave the vivid colours and protection of the oasis, in debating if I do the right thing. There is only this moment, and I will live each one I am given to the fullest.

We reach the outskirts of Thebes three days later, sunburned, bedraggled, hungry, and thirsty, with sand in every crack and crevice of our bodies. But Pepi was right: the crossing was less harrowing than our first.

We part ways with the caravan at the Nile. It heads north to Avaris, and we go south to Thebes. The men travelling with us were curious but respectful. Pepi told them he was taking his betrothed to visit her brother, who had been ill recently.

"The best lies are the ones that hold a degree of truth." He tells me what I am fast learning, trying to pack in as much as he can about the particulars of his, and now my, profession. We went over our plan during the crossing, and now we take our final meal before putting it into action. We fill our bellies, and Nefer's, with food provided to us by the villagers of a small farming community that lies just outside the city. The Festival of the Inundation is over, and people have more to share now that it does not all go to the palace, though sustenance is still sparse. The rains have also come, dampening some of the panic with regard to the harvest. Pharaoh and Queen Anat will have regained a little of their stability among the people, their godlike positions fortified by the apparent success of their festival.

"Did your mother train you as a spy?" I swallow some beer to rinse down the dry bread.

"Yes, it was a profession she passed along to me and my sister," Pepi says. "She was a lover of knowledge and believed the more one knows, the better equipped one is. She thought information the most powerful weapon of all, and that those who control it control the world. Though knowledge does not necessarily equal wisdom," he adds.

I blink. "You have a sister?"

"I did." He turns his face away.

"I am sorry," I say, and cannot prevent my next question from slipping out, though I am fairly certain of the answer. "And your mother?"

"Also gone." Pepi's tone is clipped.

"You have my sympathies," I say quietly, and we sit there for a moment, eating our food. "I understand your mother's love for learning. My father felt the same. He taught me everything he knew, and I learned much at temple and in my education."

"You are blessed to have had access to that," Pepi remarks in an offhand way.

His words make me defensive, and I wonder if he deliberately baits me. "I work hard."

"There is no doubt about that. But hard work does not always guarantee success. If so, all the farmers in the fields would be as rich as the pharaoh."

I know he means no offence, but feel slighted all the same. "Must I apologize for the circumstances of my birth?"

"No, but your father was physician to the pharaoh, and his father before that, and so you not only had the right to become a physician, but the means as well. We must be mindful of our privileges even if we did not ask for them. The circumstances of our birth come down to luck." He takes another bite and chews, then swallows. "And the whims of the gods."

"Who have smiled on you as well," I point out. "Whether son or nephew, you are kin to the Hyksos king."

"I am." Pepi's smile takes the sting out of his previous words. "I am aware of my privileges, but I, too, know education can level the sands some. If I were king, I would let anyone who wants to learn glyphs do so, regardless of their station. It is a gift I would love to give all my people."

His words make me think of Amara's warning, as I have so often these past few days. Focused on our plans to retrieve the scroll, Pepi and I spoke of little else during the crossing, and my questions come fast now, particularly the ones too sensitive to discuss in the caravan's company. "Is this why you want the scroll?" I say. "Do you see yourself as King of the North?"

He shakes his head. "Even if I could convince the king I am his son, Yanassi would immediately challenge me for the throne. Despite any assurances that I am not interested in the position, it would not end well for one of us. And though I do not deny a treasure like this would impress my father, I seek the scroll to keep it from falling into the wrong hands, and because of the prophecy itself."

"What does the prophecy say, exactly?" I say, eagerness causing my voice to rise in volume. Immediately I lower it, with a look around, but there is only us. "Will you not reveal the precise wording?"

"I have told you the gist of it," Pepi says. He takes a drink, then wipes his mouth with the back of his hand. "Information and knowledge are empowering, but they can also be dangerous. Besides, oracles are notorious for speaking in riddles."

"So, you are protecting me?" I gesture back at the desert, at the oasis out there somewhere, my movement encompassing everything we've been through since Reb, Paser, and I freed him. "Do you not think I've earned the right to know?"

He sighs, passing me the drink. "Perhaps you are not meant to know everything, young scribe."

"Says who?" I say, feeling my cheeks flush. "You?"

"Says the one who spoke the prophecy. The oracle."

"Does this oracle know everything?" Struggling to keep my temper, I gain a sudden insight into the frustrations of my friends and brother when I have kept something from them.

"Many things."

"Does it know why your cousin left you in a pit?" I say on a notion, then take my own sip, steeling myself for a sharp retort.

Instead Pepi laughs loud, long, and freely. I realize it is the first time I've heard him do so. It is a surprisingly uplifting sound, and I feel myself grinning back, anger dissipating.

"Perhaps," Pepi concedes finally, growing thoughtful. "Though when we arrived at the oasis, Yanassi assured me that he had believed me more than capable of finding a way out."

So the chieftain *had* known Pepi was in there! I wonder if he has any inkling that the spy is his brother? Pepi doesn't seem to think so, but it would explain much.

Pepi looks at me. "And I did escape, after all, thanks to you and your friends."

"What if we had not come?" I say, putting the stopper back in the water container, wondering again how he landed in the hole in the first place. Pepi is a very good spy. He said on our first crossing that someone might have betrayed him. I wonder if he has any idea who. I suppose we should save something to talk about on our return to the oasis.

"But you did come," Pepi counters. "And I would be careful of what-ifs, Sesha. They can drive a person mad. Now," he says, signalling the end of our question period, "let us go over the finer details of how we can best deliver our message to the pharaoh and find that scroll."

46

WE DRESS AS SERVANTS. Pepi managed to procure a razor from the caravan and shaves his face and head, drastically altering his appearance.

I find two empty baskets, which we carry on our shoulders, our heads down. My heart is pounding. I told Pepi about a semi-private route to Ahmes's chambers that usually does not see much foot traffic. My obsidian blade, which Pepi showed me briefly how to wield in combat during our crossing, is concealed. I hope there will be no reason to use it. Though I am confident when using it in a medical procedure, brandishing it about in an altercation carries a greater risk of me losing a finger than anything else.

We conclude that the original scroll will be the easier and the slightly less dangerous of the two copies to find; there is no way of knowing if the copy Queen Anat took from me even still exists. The fragile ancient papyrus will likely be stored safely in Pharaoh's or Wujat's chambers, though I'd put my silver on the vizier's. Both rooms will need to be checked.

Making our way onto the palace grounds, we act as if we belong here. People pay us no attention as everyone goes about their morning. They are too busy with their duties that keep the palace running smoothly, all buzzing along like Pentu's bees, working for the queen.

"This way," I whisper to Pepi. He follows close behind. I keep my eyes sharp for anyone that might recognize me: Bebi, Kewat, any of the handmaidens I knew, Ky. We enter the palace's cool interior without any challenges and navigate the halls until we reach the physician's chambers. Motioning for Pepi to stop behind me, I poke my head inside. Shai is on our side this day. Ahmes is there, preparing a concoction, and he is alone. I quickly step into the room, Pepi behind me.

"Ahmes," I say in a soft voice.

Startled, he looks up, grip tightening on the ceramic jar he is holding.

"Sesha? Is that you?" He blinks disbelievingly. Doubt crosses his face as he sees Pepi behind me. But he looks relieved, and I take this as a good sign. "What are you doing here?" He looks past us, as if there are soldiers at our back. "If the queen finds out —"

"My friend and I come to warn Pharaoh," I say urgently, leaving out that Pepi is the escaped Hyksos spy, as well as our plan to take the scroll. The less Ahmes knows, the safer he will be. "The Hyksos prepare for battle. Ahmes, their weapons …"

I swallow, thinking of the lethal bow and their bronze armaments, the battle-axes, the horses. As a physician, Ahmes understands better than most the injuries, death, and destruction that come with war. And the more advanced the technology, the higher the number of deaths. Though being killed in combat is considered an honour, healers are preservers of life. Watching people die up close and in large numbers is not something a soul can bear lightly.

"Can you help us?" I ask.

"What will you have me do?" he says, locking eyes with me, his brown ones as warm as I remember.

My request is ready. "Wujat advises Pharaoh on these issues, and the king listens to him above all others. Is there any way you can bring the vizier to us so we may speak with him?" I can appeal to Wujat alone, while Pepi searches his chambers.

Ahmes blinks but does not balk at my suggestion. He thinks for a second. "Wujat is meeting with the members of council today. He will be there."

I glance at Pepi to gauge his reaction. This might work as well.

"It is a big risk, Sesha." Pepi has been letting me speak for the both of us, but I can tell he sees what I am thinking. "If the queen sees you —"

"She won't," I say, swallowing my fear. "It is what we came to do."

"The council meets after the ceremony —" Ahmes stops and looks at me.

"What ceremony?" I say, his glance sparking my instincts, which are becoming remarkedly honed.

Ahmes hesitates, then continues. "The queen and Pharaoh are formally adopting Ky. They will announce his betrothal at sundown."

It feels like I have been hit in the face with a brick. "Betrothal to whom?" I say in disbelief.

His voice is quiet. "Little Tabira. They are to be married when she is of age."

I am shocked. Anxious that the queen might exact her revenge on Ky in some physical way, it never occurred to me she would make him a *son*. My mind races to connect the dots, like a pattern in the sky.

Queen Anatmoset has only one male heir, Tutan. One of her daughters is dead in childbed, another has been given to the Hyksos prince, and her youngest, Tabira, suffers from The Fever, which comes and goes intermittently, her health fragile. Should anything happen to Pharaoh, or Tutan, or even the little princess, it would not hurt to have a groomed replacement on hand. This reduces the risk that a lesser wife of the pharaoh and one of their sons would make a move for the coveted role of ruler of the land, as well as any of the other madness that comes with no clear successor to the throne. Pepi is right: kingdoms and their power struggles are a deadly business.

"She sets up her pawns as in a game of Senet," I murmur.

"At least Ky is safe," Ahmes offers. "The queen dotes on him, and even checked on him herself as he recovered from his surgery."

I am sure she had her own motives for that. "He is not safe if he is in line to be Pharaoh." I shake my head. "There will be eyes on his back that were not there before."

"To the matter at hand," Pepi interrupts. "Where is the council meeting?"

"In the room off the great hall, where the engagement ceremony will be held," Ahmes says. "You may stay hidden in my chambers until then. You do not want the queen to see you."

No, I do not. "Do others know of our ... desertion?" I say, wondering how careful we will need to be.

Ahmes shakes his head. "The affair was kept quiet."

"It would not do well for the queen to be seen as bested by a young girl," Pepi says.

He is right. The queen cares very much about appearances and being regarded as all powerful. She would not want it revealed that she was thwarted by three young scribes.

Ahmes picks up the medicine he was preparing before we interrupted. "I must bring this to a patient. I will come back here to get you before the ceremony." He turns to leave the room.

"Ahmes, one last thing," I call after him. "Where might I find my brother?"

"He will be with Tutan, of course. The pair are inseparable. They are likely being bathed and readied in honour of the ceremony this evening, but I am not sure of their exact whereabouts."

"How does his health fare?" I am desperate to know.

"He has had no attacks since the operation," Ahmes assures me.

Relief sweeps through my body. "Thank you for caring for him."

He nods. "I will return as soon as I can." He leaves, looking dazed at our appearance and brief interrogation. I, too, am trying to process information as calmly as I can. No easy feat, with my brother involved and our lives at risk.

My gaze falls to the desk where I once transcribed a precious document on the eve of a critical surgery. I know the scroll is the reason why we are here, but I feel the tug of my brother on my heart. Pulled in two different directions, I turn to Pepi, opening my mouth.

"Why don't you go find your brother and wish him well on his engagement?" Pepi says before I speak.

"Really?" I say, my heart quickening. "You do not mind?"

Pepi waves me off. "You got us into the palace and arranged for Ahmes to bring us to the council meeting. I will search Pharaoh's and Wujat's chambers while you go and speak to Ky. Just promise me you will do your best to remain unseen."

"What about you?"

"I am like the wind. Besides, even if I am seen, no one will recognize me." He grins, rubbing one hand over his shaven scalp. "I am just another scribe, here to record the event for posterity."

"Thank you." I slip out the door before he changes his mind about this side mission.

"Sesha."

"Yes?" I say, turning to the spy. Pepi's face is sober.

"Be careful."

47

I DART THROUGH THE HALLS OF THE PALACE, contemplating the whereabouts of both Ky *and* the scroll. If the document is not in Pharaoh's or Wujat's chambers, there is a chance it may be with one of them. I wonder about the copy Queen Anat took from me, the one my father and I transcribed. Would she really destroy it? Or only bury it away somewhere in another room of hidden treasures, lost for eternity?

I stop in my tracks. Is it possible that Queen Anat heard of this mysterious prophecy somehow? Can this be why she wanted the scroll so badly?

Forcing myself to resume moving, I make my way to the handmaidens' quarters, slipping around corners unseen, keeping my head down. I've learned not to take unnecessary risks; the necessary ones are more than enough.

I draw nearer to the handmaidens' wing. At this time of day, it will be mostly empty, but there may be one or two girls around whom I can ask about Ky's whereabouts. With luck, my friend Bebi might even be there herself. Poking my head in, I scan the room's occupants and offer up a brief prayer of thanks. Bebi is not there, but someone else I know is: Kewat.

She lies, slumbering, one hand on the small swell of her stomach. Creating new life takes a lot of energy. I walk over.

"Kewat," I say softly. Her eyes flutter open, bleary. Upon seeing me, she rubs them and sits up quickly.

"Sesha? What are you doing here? Where have you been all this time? Bebi said you left in secrecy!"

"Bebi." I seize on her cousin's name. "I need to find her. Do you know where she is?"

"She is attending little Tabira."

I look at her in surprise. "Her position has changed?"

"Yes, the little princess now has her own handmaidens in addition to her nurse. She is helping her get ready for the engagement announcement later today." This means Bebi, too, may be in the wing that houses the royal baths. "Is that why you are here?"

"Yes, I am happy to be here for my brother on this … momentous occasion." An occasion that involves Queen Anat drawing him further into her sticky web.

"How is your pregnancy?" I ask, wanting to hear how she's been doing, as well as to distract her from asking any more questions.

"All is well." She gives her stomach a contented pat.

"Your father is letting you choose, then?" Kewat's father originally had his own ideas for his daughter, hoping to make a good match for her with a lesser noble. But Kewat loves another and has plans of her own.

"Yes, I will move into his house nearer my time, after completing my duties at the palace."

I am happy things have worked out the way she wanted them to. At least they have for someone.

"May Bes bless you and your new family."

As I go to leave the quarters, she calls after me, a hint of uncertainty in her voice. "Will you be here for the baby's birth?"

I walk back to her, place a hand on her abdomen, and murmur a brief incantation for an easy delivery and a healthy child. "Likely not, but you and the baby will fare well," I say firmly, imploring her with my eyes to believe me. Our thoughts are powerful things. Kewat is with the person she loves on will alone, showing how powerful intentions can be. Belief is the first step in accomplishing what you want to do. It is important that I also remember this.

I will find Ky. I will find the scroll. I will find Ky. I will find the scroll. I will find Ky. I will find the scroll.

I will find Ky. I repeat the mantra over and over in my head so that it becomes a prayer to the universe, to any gods who might still be listening and not yet growing weary of accommodating my endless requests. I turn another corner in the palace, drawing nearer to the baths. Seeing some folded linens, I pick them up and carry them with me, a ready excuse for being there.

I cannot find anyone.

The baths are quiet. The children have come and gone. They are likely getting dressed and having their hair plaited, oiled, and accessorized for the announcement. I should go back and regroup with Pepi.

Something cold and wet touches my hand and I bite back a screech.

"Anubis!" I whisper, dropping the linens and crouching down to hug the dog, rubbing my face in his soft fur. "Can you take me to Ky?"

He whines and licks my hand, then takes off at a trot. I follow him down a corridor leading to the children's chambers. Up ahead is the turn to Merat's old room, and a thought strikes me. Merat's grand chambers are reserved for the eldest princess in the palace, who is now little Tabira. I wonder if she might have moved there with her nurse.

"Good boy," I say to Ky's dog.

I am almost at the door when I hear someone inside. Stepping back into a small alcove, I press my body up against the wall. Anubis trots ahead into the room.

"You are right. The other necklace will suit much better," a bright voice chirps, "shall I retrieve it?"

Gods be praised. Bebi.

Eagerly, I step forward to intercept my friend as she leaves the chamber, but another voice calls behind her. "Yes." Queen Anat's commanding tone rings out, freezing me. "It is in my quarters. Be quick about it. The ceremony starts soon."

"Yes, Your Highness," Bebi says as she exits the room.

Hathor, help me. No matter if Ky is in there or not, entering that room now would not end well. I'd prefer that my brother not see me arrested and killed on this day. My engagement gift to him.

Waiting till my friend passes by, I reach out and touch her arm lightly. "Bebi," I whisper.

She gives a squeak of surprise. "Sesha?" she exclaims, taking in my altered appearance. "Is it really you?" She throws her arms around me. "What are you doing here?"

"Looking for you." I smile and guide her down the hallway, walking us speedily away from Tabira's chambers, away from immediate danger. "I need your help, my friend."

"How are you?" she asks breathlessly. "Where have you been?"

"I will explain on the way. Did I hear you are to get a necklace from Queen Anat's chambers?" If I cannot see my brother, then at least I can search the queen's room for the scroll. I remind myself to leave a big offering for the gods after this fortunate happenstance.

"Yes, for the ceremony tonight. She wants Tabira to look perfect when they announce her engagement …" She hesitates, looking at me.

"To my brother," I finish. "I know. I will accompany you."

"It is so wonderful to see you!" She chatters on about Tabira and Ky's betrothal as we walk down the hall. I keep my head low, occasionally glancing from side to side. Though Queen Anat would not want him lurking around, Crooked Nose, her personal guard — and my parents' killer — cannot be far off.

48

WE REACH QUEEN ANAT'S QUARTERS without incident, Bebi pecking at me with question after question. "The last time I saw you, you were sneaking away under most mysterious circumstances. Where did you go?"

"Paser, Reb, and I went north … for some additional training." As with Ahmes, telling Bebi as little as possible will protect her.

We approach the queen's chambers. Two soldiers stand guard, but thankfully I do not know them, nor they me. They see two young girls, servants, and nod at Bebi in greeting. She inclines her head graciously at them.

"The Great Royal Wife has bid me to retrieve a necklace for Princess Tabira," she says sweetly, in her singsong voice. They move aside and let us enter.

The queen's private chambers are luxurious and large, treasures sparkling from every corner of the room: fine linens and downs, pillows, an elaborately carved headrest. I remember Pepi's lesson, cataloguing and storing everything in my mind, as I've been doing all day.

Bebi walks to a large wooden chest inscribed with ancient scripts. It looks hundreds of years old. She lifts the lid and purses her lips at the glittering assortment of jewels winking up at us. "She wanted the gold one with the falcon heads …"

"There." I point at the breathtaking collar, layers of carnelian, lapis lazuli, and turquoise.

"You have a good eye, Sesha." Bebi picks up the necklace as I begin wandering the room, seeing where one might hide a scroll.

"What are you doing?" she asks.

"Looking for a papyrus." I open and browse through a wardrobe filled with elaborate dresses, pushing some aside. The citrusy, floral fragrance of neroli oil wafts out, and I break into a sweat at the queen's scent.

Confusion crosses Bebi's face. "Why?"

"It is an important medical document." Nothing here. I close the wardrobe's doors and continue scanning the room, lifting items, looking behind and under furniture.

"I do not understand. Would it not be at the temple?"

"I believe Queen Anat took it, by mistake." Methodically, I lift her bedding, look under her head-rest. Nothing.

"Sesha." Bebi's tone is intent. "Queen Anat does nothing by mistake. Will you tell me what is going on?"

"The document is mine," I say, turning to look at Bebi defiantly. "I want it back."

"You are stealing from the queen?" Her voice trills in shock, and I bring a hand to my lips to shush her.

"I am not stealing. I told you, it is mine."

All traces of her usual good cheer are wiped from Bebi's expressive face. "You used me to get into the queen's chambers?"

That was not the original plan, but I do not deny it. Bebi has been a good friend, and I owe her that much. "It is for a just cause."

Her eyes widen. "One person's cause can be an-other person's ruin," she whispers, putting her free hand on my arm.

"Yes, Bebi," I say, fighting the urge to blow through the queen's chambers like a desert wind, longing to tear drawers from their chests, rip linens from their beds, flip chests upside down. Anger at all she has taken from me bubbles beneath the surface of my skin, leaving me flushed and shaking. I take a calming breath, then another. "You are right. I am sorry, my friend. I had a long journey and am not thinking clearly." Pepi's advice to do so comes back. "Let us leave and you can be on your way with the necklace."

She looks relieved, and with difficulty I make myself follow her out of the chamber.

"Bebi," I say. "My apologies for putting you in such a position. May I have your forgiveness?"

She nods, perhaps remembering a long time ago when I was at my father's side, helping to save her mother and new sister as she was brought into the world.

"I must beg one more thing of you," I say. "Do not mention my appearance to anyone. Especially the queen. No good can come from it."

"I will do as you ask."

"Thank you, my friend." I kiss her briefly on the cheek. "Please do not think too badly of me."

"Of course," she murmurs. She turns with the dazzling collar to return to where the queen waits, where her duties and loyalty lie, an invisible collar around her own neck tethering her to the kingdom and the royal family.

I run into Pepi outside of Ahmes's chambers.

"Did you find your brother?" he whispers as we slip into the room.

"No." I force the word past the lump in my throat. "Did you search Pharaoh's room?"

"I found nothing," Pepi admits. "We should ask the healer." We debated earlier whether to ask Ahmes if he's seen the scroll, but I want to involve him as little as possible. I see what Pepi means by too much information being dangerous. The resentment I feel for the spy at not sharing the exact phrasing of the prophecy lessens a cubit. "As royal physician he might have had access to it and know of its location," Pepi says, as Ahmes walks in, overhearing.

"I might know of what's location?" he says.

I hesitate, unsure how protective the doctor will be of the document. Just as I feel responsibility for it, he, too, recognizes it for the rare treasure it is. He will also need it for Pharaoh's troops, should battle come; though that is a big part of why I am here: to suggest that it never does.

"The scroll," I say at last, looking at my father's former student. "We need it to save a friend."

"Imhotep's scroll?" Ahmes says, incredulously. "The one you found for Pharaoh?"

"The same," I say, sending up a prayer that my words do not endanger him overmuch. "As you used it to heal Ky, we wish to help another suffering from an injury it addresses."

Ahmes shakes his head. "I have not seen a copy since the night we performed the surgery on your brother."

"The original must be in Wujat's chambers," Pepi says. "That is the only place we have not looked. A document like that will not lie far from either the vizier or the pharaoh."

"I thought you wanted to speak to the council," Ahmes says slowly. "But you are just here to take the scroll?" Like Bebi, he is tethered to the palace, to these people, as I once was.

"No," I say, exchanging glances with Pepi. "I speak the truth. They need to be informed of the Hyksos's weapons."

"I do not believe the pharaoh wants war," Ahmes says, eyeing Pepi, wary. I remind myself the spy is a stranger to the royal physician. My friends and I were also once distrustful of the Hyksos. Paser still is. "It is your tribe who stirs rebellion." The doctor has figured out who Pepi is. "You came to spy on us. Your chieftain threatens battle and took the princess."

Pepi narrows his eyes. "The princess was *given* to the chieftain by her parents."

"Enough," I say sharply. Ahmes's words worry me deeply. The council will likely feel the same as the doctor toward the spy: suspicious, mistrustful. "Perhaps you should remain hidden," I say to Pepi. "These are my people and they respected my father. They may listen to me."

He shakes his head. "I am coming with you."

I try to reason with him. "They will throw you in the pits the minute you start speaking."

"You can always fish me out again." He gives me a reckless smile. Like Paser, his taste for adventure is apparent. A taste I seem to be developing as well, as addictive as the poppy plant.

"You need to trust that I can do this," I say, indicating with my eyes that he can also investigate Wujat's chambers while I'm gone.

His look is piercing, like the gods' when weighing a person's heart against a feather to see if they are worthy of entering the Field of Reeds. "Very well," he says finally. "If you think this is the wisest course of action, I will do as you say."

I give a brief nod, even though the thought of not having Pepi at my side makes me feel like I'm caught in the middle of a sandstorm again. Exposed. Scared. In danger.

"We should be on our way," Ahmes says. I take a deep breath, then follow the physician out of the room.

Pepi calls after me, "Tread carefully, Sesha. In my experience, people often turn on the messenger, whether you consider yourself one of them or not."

49

AHMES AND I WALK DOWN the darkening hallways to where Pharaoh's court is held. Memories of the last time I was here wash over me. It was the start of the Festival of the Inundation, when Paser and I found the scroll and the man beside me performed a risky operation on my brother, one that saved his life. Now, if we can find the same document, I will help a Hyksos physician do the same for another. It strikes me, the courage Ahmes must have had, to carry out such a dangerous procedure.

"Ahmes," I say. "I cannot tell you how much I appreciate what you did for Ky and me."

"It was my duty as a physician." He gives me a sidelong glance. "One that you shared once?" I do not miss the question in his voice and think of my recent patients. Of Amara and her baby, of Akin. They are part of the reason I am here.

"I still share it."

"One might think you traded in your healer's tools for those of a spy," Ahmes says, pointing to the obsidian blade strapped to my leg. "Are you an agent of the Hyksos now?"

"I am an agent for peace," I say.

We've almost reached our destination and my heart pounds at where my next steps will lead me. I try to slow it with my breath, making each inhale and exhale long and steady. Controlled breathing calms the body, which calms the mind.

At last we reach the grand chamber, passing people in the hall as they stream in for the engagement ceremony. None take note of me, whether it's my sun-darkened skin or hennaed hair, or the way I keep my head down and gaze averted. Some have been celebrating for weeks and many may not have realized I was missing, or even that I returned to the palace after my parents' death. We enter the room with the crowds. It is full of faces I grew up knowing. Coming home is a strange thing; the place I once knew intimately, though familiar, is altered somehow. Or maybe it is me who is different. Things stand out that I took for granted before: the bend in the river, the structures, even the members of my own tribe, each of their faces resonating in the smallest spaces of my body. I come to warn them, my people. My eyes are drawn like a magnet to north, to one face in particular. My person.

Ky.

He stands on the large dais with the royal family. I am overjoyed to see he looks healthy and has put on some weight. It also appears as if he's grown taller, so he remains slender. His skin gleams with freshly applied oils, and his eyes are boldly lined with kohl. Dozens of gold anklets and bracelets adorn his wrists and ankles, and his linen skirt is pleated finely. He looks so much like my father, whose scarab necklace rests around his neck, as he stands at Pharaoh's side.

Ky, I say silently in my head. *Ky, look at me. I am here for you!*

But he does not look in my direction. Instead, he looks over at his best friend, Tutan, who is dressed just as finely, if not more so. The boys stand proudly in front of Pharaoh and — my heart skips — Queen Anat, who holds little Tabira's hand. Wujat stands on their right. The vizier is speaking, welcoming everyone, his hands open wide. He thanks the gods for the recent rains and for the royal family's influence.

I tear my eyes from the dais and scan the room, looking for entrances and exits and escape routes and familiarizing myself with any other potential hazards.

Everyone seems to be here. At least Pepi will have an uninterrupted exploration of Wujat's chambers.

"Today we are honoured to announce a new member of this great and illustrious family. Young Ky, son to Pharaoh's former royal physician Ay and his wife, whom the gods took too soon." Ky straightens at the mention of his name, and Tutan grins behind him. I wonder if Ky's being named an heir will affect their relationship. As Pepi says, members of ruling dynasties do not always do well with threats to their reign.

Pharaoh and the queen step forward; she looks as terrifyingly beautiful as ever. She pulls Tabira with her, and Ky, looking uncertain and nervous, holds his hands out, palms facing up. Tabira looks at her mother, the falcon collar sparkling around her neck, and obediently puts her own small hands on top of Ky's.

Wujat continues. "We ask the gods to witness this ordained arrangement and vow to see it come to fruition, when the time comes."

The crowd cheers wildly for the new son of the royal family, a family that does not do such things lightly. Ky is now theirs in every way that matters and will be treated accordingly.

But he is still your brother. A fierce voice whispers the words at my ear, and I recognize my mother's spirit at my side after a long absence.

The queen bends down and plants a kiss on Ky's forehead. My skin crawls, as if covered in Min's caterpillars. I feel nauseous and hot and suddenly the room is stifling, the crowds pressing, and I cannot quite catch my breath.

Air. I need some air.

Heading for one of the exits I noted earlier, I rush through the masses, all jostling to get a look at the new prince and his future wife. I bump into someone and hear a rough exclamation.

Crooked Nose.

He looks like he's just seen someone come back from the underworld, a reaction I'm becoming familiar with. He reaches for my arm. Pale or not, he is still menacing, and malevolent energy comes off him in waves. But like the apparition he imagines me to be, I slip through his outstretched grasp and dart for the exit. The crowd, still trying to get a better view of the royal family, blocks him from following.

The smaller chamber off the large room is not as congested. A few high-ranking nobles and courtiers mill about, likely awaiting the council meeting and not overly interested in the formalities of a betrothal announcement.

My breath coming fast again at my narrow escape from the soldier, I look for a place to hide and wait for the council to start their meeting, but the room is fairly open and I feel exposed. Spotting a tray of food on a small table off to the right, I pick it up and put it on my shoulder, keeping my head down, assuming the posture of a servant making the rounds. I pray that Crooked Nose thinks he only saw a spectre and does not pursue me. Besides, his place is by the queen and he will not leave her unattended.

Cheers from outside ring loud and the numbers in the room swell as important officials and members of council make their way in. Pharaoh and Wujat enter, conversing. I am relieved to see Queen Anat is not with them. Congratulations are offered to the king, food and wine are consumed, and then comes a subtle shift in the air as people make their way to their seats. It is time for business.

Another servant enters the room. I see the woman looking around, presumably for the ebony tray I'm holding. When she spots me, her brow furrows and she starts determinedly in my direction. I do my best to appear as if I am supposed to be here. Her cheeks are flushed from the heat of the crowds, and possibly from her own indulgence in the beverages provided.

"What are you doing here?" she asks. "I am to serve the council."

"Beket sent me," I say, naming the head of the kitchens. "And it's a good thing, because you are late for your duties. The lords here would be most unimpressed at being kept waiting for refreshment." I have learned that putting someone on the defensive is a good offensive tactic.

The flush in her cheeks spreads down her neck. "I had to relieve myself," she says.

I've become so accustomed to bluffing, I recognize when someone else is doing it. "Because you have been indulging?" I guess — correctly, from the alarmed expression on her face. "Do not worry. I will say nothing. But we are running low on food. Go to the kitchen before people start criticizing the pharaoh's hospitality." She nods gratefully, hurrying out the doors and back into the crowds.

The council members take their places, settling onto low stools and reed mats, and finally the meeting begins. The first items on the agenda concern the rains and stores of food, which are still dangerously low after all the recent festivities. I stay out of Pharaoh's and Wujat's sight, hiding at the back of the room. The conversation eventually makes its way round to the Hyksos.

"Have you had word of your daughter?" one of the nobles asks Pharaoh.

Merat.

"I am sure she fares well," Pharaoh says heartily.

"She must be keeping the chieftain busy," another says, and the men laugh in that way some do when they talk of a woman as if she were merely an object for someone else's amusement, instead of something precious, which Merat most definitely is. "With any luck, she will turn his thoughts from battle and we will have no more trouble from his rebellious regiments."

It is time. Taking a deep breath, I step forward, still holding the tray.

"The Hyksos rebels may not be so easily dissuaded." My voice rings out clearly and loudly. It carries over the residual chuckles of the men, and a hush falls over the room. "They are not to be underestimated."

THE COUNCIL MEMBERS LOOK AROUND, confused at who is speaking. Many of them stand to see what is happening. I look directly at Pharaoh, and though he, too, looks shocked at my appearance, he holds my gaze steadily. Encouraged, I walk forward with the tray as the standing men part without realizing they are doing so.

"Sesha," Pharaoh says, blinking. "You seem to have a habit of returning from the dead."

"Who told you I was dead?" I ask.

"I did." Queen Anat steps into the room and all the heads swivel toward her. I am not the only one who has a way with entrances. "And you *are* dead, my child. You are dead to Kemet, to our kingdom, to our *family*." I flinch at her emphasis of the word; I know she refers to Ky.

Crooked Nose must have informed her of my presence, as she does not seem surprised. Not so Wujat, who also steps forward, looking stunned at my appearance. The queen must have lied to him as well. He recovers quickly, though.

"How *do* you know that the rebels are not to be underestimated?" The vizier rises to his full height as he speaks, towering over everyone in the room.

"I live among them." There are gasps and murmurs from those watching the scene unfold, like they are caught up in one of Namu's stories back at the fire.

"Why would you live among those people?" Wujat says, disdain lacing his tone.

Because the queen wanted me dead, I think. Instead, I say, "They are good enough for Princess Merat."

A shadow crosses Pharaoh's face, perhaps for the child he and Queen Anat traded away for a temporary reprieve.

"They took me and my friends in, on the word of another." Pepi's word. "Their weapons are impressive," I continue, making my voice loud enough to be heard over the council members still murmuring. "With new technology, and equipment that is much stronger and faster than that of Pharaoh's armies."

"You dare insult the armies of the pharaoh?" Crooked Nose steps forward, clutching the spear at his side, hunger to attack contorting his face. But he makes no move to assault me — for once — as no official word has been given.

I ignore the soldier. "They have an astonishing metal called bronze. It is tougher and cuts deeper than our copper. And an incredible bow, made of horn, wood, and sinew. Its lightness and advanced design help the arrows fly farther, their aim truer." Some of the men still look skeptical, but a few are listening intently, including Pharaoh and Wujat, who are both probably wondering why the queen told them I was dead. "Their axes can take off a man's head with one blow. And they have a creature … they call it a horse. It runs as fast as Set's winds and can transport men quickly across the sands."

"Where stands Avaris?" Pharaoh calls over the clamour. "Do they support these rebels?"

"No, they do not," a new voice says.

Pepi.

My eyes narrow at the Hyksos. So much for staying hidden.

"Who are you?" Pharaoh demands. Pepi's bald head is an effective disguise. It still catches me off guard.

I quickly walk over to him. "A friend."

Crooked Nose spits. "It is the spy from the pits. I guess we know how he escaped."

"Sesha is right, I am a friend." Pepi walks forward, hands raised to show he carries no weapons.

Where did he appear from? He must teach me that trick. "We come to warn you, for the sake of your people, that you do not want to enter into conflict with mine. While those at Avaris are not presently inclined to attack, they may be convinced otherwise should you offend or anger them. Continue to honour these rulers with your tribute and we will continue to live peacefully in the delta, as we have done for many years."

"Continue to pay tribute?" Crooked Nose bursts out. "You think we are afraid of your people?"

"You would have little sense if you were not," Pepi says mildly. "Do not think that if we wanted Thebes, we would not take it." The murmurings turn angrier at Pepi's slight. "We have allies in the Kingdom of Kush and we hold the delta. Consider your tribute a tax for allowing you to govern from this city."

I look sharply at Pepi. Is he deliberately inflaming tempers in the room?

"Is my daughter not tribute enough?" Pharaoh rises, colour coming into his cheeks. He looks at his queen. "Her mother persuades me to make the ultimate sacrifice by giving her to your brutish chieftain, and the man is still not satisfied? Our people have ruled these lands for thousands of years and you, *Heqa-Khasut*, rulers of foreign lands, presume to tell *us* what to do?"

Pepi makes a polite bow. "We are the ones with the weapons."

"Shut your insolent mouth," a nobleman cries from the crowd, probably hoping to incur favour with the king.

Queen Anat steps forward. "Since you speak of tribute, perhaps it is time this tradition comes to its end. If my daughter" — her voice catches on the word — "cannot satisfy your people's greed, it is doubtful anything can."

Were the queen and Pharaoh really counting on Merat to sway the chieftain from war? Is this what the princess meant when she said she should accept her fate?

Pepi turns to the Great Royal Wife. "Unfortunately, my lady, I know of an oracle who holds a differing opinion regarding this matter."

I study the queen to see her reaction. Queen Anat stills. "An oracle? Where is this oracle?"

"Yes," Pepi says, ignoring her second question. "And it says there is still more tribute to be paid." I realize he is stirring the hive, creating confusion.

"I have heard enough," Wujat shouts over the outraged exclamations. "You say you come here to warn us, yet you insult us." He looks at me. "Your father would be ashamed at the company you keep, Sesha."

"My father believed we are all the same. No matter the lands we come from, the languages we speak, or the gods we worship," I say to the vizier. "And I am not the only one who keeps others company." I look pointedly at the queen, which does not go unnoticed by Pharaoh. Unsure of the exact nature of Queen Anat and the vizier's relationship, I feel a prick of guilt for blowing smoke, but follow Pepi's lead in distraction.

"Throw this lying traitor and her spy in the pits," Queen Anat snaps, eyes flashing. She pushes her dark hair back over her shoulder, a gesture so like Merat it disconcerts me. "We will march to Avaris and consult with this oracle ourselves, leaving carnage in our wake."

I glance at Pepi. This is not going so well.

Crooked Nose, who has been eagerly awaiting this command, makes a move toward me.

"One more step and I'll straighten that nose of yours!" I shout, still clutching the tray in my hand, ready to let it fly like a discus at the soldier's face.

He lunges and pandemonium breaks loose as cowardly noblemen dive out of his rampaging path. Before I can blink, Pepi is at my side grabbing the tray from my hands and swinging the solid wood through the air, smashing it into the charging soldier. Crooked Nose spins around, dazed, one hand still clutching his spear, the other his split cheek. Other men attempt to grab us. There are too many, and I find myself caught in pawing, grasping hands, struggling to get loose, when I hear a familiar voice.

"Let her go!"

Ky.

51

MY LITTLE BROTHER STRIDES forward with an unfamiliar confidence, and I wonder if Prince Tutan has been teaching him how to swagger in a son-of-the-pharaoh sort of way. How did he know I was here? My mind, still clear despite the chaos of the last few moments, supplies an answer: Bebi.

"Ky!" I shout, breaking free of the hands that restrain me, tearing my dress in the process. I run to my sibling, throwing my arms around him. A crack in my heart fills and seals, as if with the wax of Pentu's bees.

"Sesha," he cries, and for an instant it is just me and my brother, whom I love as much as a person can love someone, who has been my companion since the day he was born. I have hunted down an ancient document for him, stood by him and saw him cured, crossed a desert for him. Tears spill down my cheeks as I squeeze him, and he pats me as if to reassure himself I am solid.

The queen's commanding voice interrupts our happy reunion. "Ky, my child, your sister abandoned you, abandoned our people and the land you may one day inherit. You are a member of *our* family now. We took you in as one of our own." She puts a hand on his shoulder. To see her standing there behind him, looking concerned, pretending he is anything more than a pawn to her, burns worse than being stranded in the sands with no protection.

"Sesha did what she had to in order to survive," Pepi shouts. He struggles against the men who are holding him. "It is you who wish to abandon your people."

Crooked Nose has recovered and holds his spear at the Hyksos's throat. I shoot Pepi a look to hold his tongue while he still has it. Antagonizing the queen further by revealing her treachery will do no good. I know what a provoked Queen Anat is like — the spear will be sticking out of Pepi soon.

"Ky," I quietly say to my brother, pleading. "Ask Pharaoh to release my friend."

He turns to Pharaoh, entreating. "Can you release him? No blood should be spilled on the day of Tabira's and my engagement. It is a bad omen."

The pharaoh does not look convinced.

"Our father served you well," I say to Pharaoh and Wujat. "He saved Tutan's life and the lives of your loyal subjects, over and over, a thousand times over." I implore these men whom I once believed to be honourable and good. "All we came here to do was warn you. Having done that, let us leave in peace."

"Do not listen to her," the queen says, now walking over to her husband. He looks at her in a way I've never seen before. Apparently, Queen Anat has not either — she pauses midstep. Pharaoh glances at his trusted friend and vizier and, seeming to make up his mind, turns back to me.

"Release the Hyksos," he says to the men. "You speak truly, Sesha. Your father served me well, and your brother is now my own son." He smiles faintly. "You also accomplished a most difficult task others twice your age and esteem could not: you found me the scroll. For these reasons I give you both your freedom, though you, Sesha, needn't go with the Hyksos. You are welcome to stay here, with us." He nods at Ky.

I look at my brother. His face is lit with the glow of a thousand beeswax candles, and I know he'd love nothing more than for me to accept Pharaoh's offer. One likely made to atone for a daughter Queen Anat apparently induced him to give away. But the queen is behind him, and despite a temporary fall from grace, she remains an enormous threat, perhaps even more so with a thorn in her paw. I think of Paser. Of Reb and Merat. Amara and Akin. All awaiting my return.

"I thank you for your kind offer, Your Highness," I say, looking at Ky with helpless remorse. Silently begging him to understand. "But I cannot stay."

The pharaoh nods at my words, accepting them as final, no further invitations extended. He speaks to two of his guards. "Take them to the edge of the city and leave them there." Turning back to Pepi, he lowers his voice. "Do not take advantage of my goodwill. If I find you in Thebes after sundown, you will be back in that pit faster than a blink of Ra's eye." Pharaoh looks at Ky. "My son. Join your brother and go celebrate. The people will want to rejoice in your happy news."

Queen Anat has stayed silent but she now offers her hand to Ky. "Come, my prince." Hesitatingly, Ky takes it, and it is like a thousand bee stings to the heart to see him walk away with her. He casts a final glance over his shoulder, a look of confused hurt at my rejection of Pharaoh's offer, and at what he likely thinks is a rejection of him.

"Ky," I shout, unable to stop myself. "Come with us."

"That is not wise, Sesha," Pepi murmurs beside me. "He should stay where he has plenty and is well cared for. Our lives are rough and dangerous."

Deep down, I know Pepi is right. Can I really take my brother from the luxury and comforts of the palace, from his newfound inheritance, from safety? Ky looks up uncertainly at the queen, and I see in his face that she has burrowed her way into his heart, like the dung beetle into the sands, a surrogate mother who he thinks loves and cares for him.

Tears stream down my face as I watch my brother walk away, hand in hand with the queen, the blistering despair in my own heart dissolving the wax seal that was only ever temporary.

The guards leave us at the edge of town with a sack of food and a canteen of water. I pick up a stone and hurl it as hard as I can into the distance.

"Why are you so angry?" Pepi asks. "We did what we came to do, with our lives intact."

"What?" I stare at him. "Not only was that a disaster in diplomacy, I am leaving my city yet again, without my brother, without a scroll." I grit my teeth to hold back a scream of frustration. The frenzied desert winds echo my emotions, whipping my fiery hair this way and that.

Pepi reaches into his clothes and pulls out a familiar cylinder-shaped papyrus. "You mean this scroll?" It is my copy, the one Queen Anat took from me.

"What in the name of Horus? How did you get that?" I blink in disbelief, clawing at the scroll, the one my father started and I tried to finish. Pepi graciously passes me the document and I inspect it, hands trembling, convinced that I am dreaming.

"The vizier gave it to me."

"Wujat?" I cannot be hearing right. I shake my head like there is sand in my ears. Pepi is an even better spy than I give him credit for. "How? When?"

"I encountered him on his way to the ceremony," he said. "It is fortunate that he, too, despite his flawed taste in women, has a deep respect for the instructions and teachings of one of the greatest men in history. Of course, a little persuasion from my friend here —" he grins and brandishes his knife "— did not hurt our case."

Relief and joy sweep through my body, soothing the wounds caused by leaving Ky. After everything we have been through, we finally have the scroll. We will return to the oasis and heal Akin. The chieftain will have to let my friends and me go to Avaris and we will escape. It also soothes me somewhat to think that Wujat, former High Priest and Chief Scribe, appreciates the value of

Imhotep's papyrus and would not see the physician's knowledge destroyed. For he would not have given it up on Pepi's threat alone. Whatever else he is, Wujat is not a coward.

I wonder how he obtained my copy. "Do you think Wujat is with the pharaoh, or with the queen?" I muse out loud.

"Perhaps both," Pepi responds, ever philosophical. "The currents of our hearts and minds sometimes come into conflict. It is not always clear from the surface which way they flow."

I fervently examine the scroll, still unable to believe I hold the document I'd thought forever lost. Pepi, seeing that I am overcome with emotion, smiles. "Remember when I said I would not tell you whether you pass or fail as a spy until the time comes?"

I nod, gripping tight the treasure in my hand. One man's key to life, the key to freedom for my friends, and the key to a prophecy.

"As we are both alive and our mission a success," Pepi says with a grin, "you pass. Congratulations, Sesha, you are officially a spy. That was smart thinking, letting the crumb drop regarding the vizier and the queen. Though we blow smoke to calm the bees, not enrage them."

"Me?" I exclaim. "You are the one who said that the Hyksos could take Thebes if they wanted it!" But I am not too fussed. My heart flips like one of the palace dancers at his announcement and at accomplishing a task that was near impossible.

Pepi shrugs. "We could. But that is neither grapes nor raisins. Now come. Let us go and find our donkey."

52

THREE DAYS LATER WE MAKE IT BACK to the oasis. I am becoming comfortable with the sensations of hunger, thirst, and extreme exhaustion. Or if not quite comfortable, I have at least learned to tolerate them. Our high spirits at retrieving the scroll also make the journey bearable. Though never easy, there is triumph and elation in this crossing. Pepi and I laugh and tease one another as we traverse the harsh desert. The gods, as if sensing our jubilation, send some light rain on our last night, a celebratory shower that quenches our thirst. I cannot wait to see my friends and tell them the good news, to show them the document, to help Min heal Akin, to at last liberate the people I love.

All except one, that is.

When the oasis comes into view, my heart, downcast at having again left Ky with the queen, flaps like a bird whose broken wing is starting to mend. But as we draw closer, something does not seem right. There is an unnatural stillness about it that is unsettling. Pepi senses it, too.

"Be on your guard," he says softly, and I reach down to grab the obsidian blade from its bindings at my leg. The village appears deserted.

"There," Pepi points. A small wisp of smoke curls up through the palm fronds. "Down by the lake."

We make our way quickly along the paths. A foul stench hangs in the air as we venture deeper into the heart of the oasis. All my instincts are screaming that something is very wrong. At last the water comes into view. As do the bodies.

I am relieved to see that the people lying spread out along the shore are all still alive, though in an extreme state of ill health and varying degrees of distress. There are only a few on their feet; Min is one of them. The healer looks as if he's aged ten years and is barking orders at two young men: Paser and Reb.

Paser sees me. "Sesha," he cries, dropping the bucket he is carrying and hurrying over. He sweeps me up in a tight hug, his arms strong, and immediately I feel safe. At home.

"What has happened?" Pepi is there beside us. Paser sets me down as Reb strides over, Min close behind. The three appear exhausted and are smeared with filth, vomit, and sweat.

"There has been a sickness," Paser says. "We moved the people to be closer to the water, as many are dehydrated."

"Has everyone taken ill?" Aghast, I glance around, scanning for Amara and her baby. I do not see them. Nor Merat.

"Many," says Min grimly.

"Where is Yanassi?" Pepi asks, one hand at his brow, searching the masses.

"He left for Avaris," Paser says. "He —"

"Did he take Merat with him?" I interrupt. Fear at not seeing the princess among the ill has me thinking the worst.

Paser nods and I praise the gods, though it seems they can never let us be content for long.

"What of Amara and her family?" I say, worrying for my friend and her fallen soldier. Their baby would be particularly vulnerable to an illness like this.

"They, too, went with the chieftain."

"How?" I say, stunned. "Akin was in no shape to travel."

"I advised against it," Min admits. "But Yanassi insisted his second-in-command remain by his side." That would not have been a comfortable journey for the soldier.

"Why did Yanassi abandon the oasis?" Pepi demands. "What is so important that he would leave before our return?" I see one of his hands go to the scroll, safe in its protective casing.

"A messenger came, the morning after you left, summoning the king's son and nephew to Avaris," Paser says. "The king is ill and wishes to announce his successor." He gives Pepi a curious look. "The chieftain told us to accompany you, upon your return here, to meet him in your capital with the scroll."

"I cannot believe my cousin would leave his people like this, even for the chance to be named king." Pepi looks at me and I shake my head helplessly, trying to work it out. The whole objective was to retrieve the scroll for the chieftain and heal Akin.

Reb shakes his head. "The village was not ill when the chieftain and his band of men left. We think the messenger brought an unwelcome companion along with his summons from the king — the disease itself. He sickened first and it spread like wildfire through the oasis, burning up those who remained behind."

Pepi gives me a look as if to say, *See, the messenger is always blamed.* Though in this instance, it sounds deserved.

Sick king or not, I, too, am surprised that the chieftain did not wait for us to get back with the scroll, especially considering how important it is to him. Unless he thought we might *not* return? Perhaps he had doubts about our success. Or — more ominously — perhaps Yanassi believed his "cousin" would go directly to the Hyksos capital once the scroll was in his possession, and hoped to beat us there. Amara said that Akin did not fully trust the spy, which likely means neither does the chieftain. Is it possible that Yanassi thought Pepi would present the papyrus to the king, in an attempt to court favour and make a play for the throne? And, assuming both the scroll and I, Pepi's betrothed, were also in Avaris, the surgery could be performed there. Another harrowing thought occurs to me. What if the chieftain tries to marry Merat before we get there?

"We are cresting the peak of the illness now," Min is saying, wiping the sweat from his brow. "The healthy tend the ill, but your healer's hands will be much appreciated."

"Who is that?" Reb interrupts, pointing at the far end of the lake where a disheveled figure is attempting to take a drink and glancing furtively around. "Did you bring someone with you?"

"Not intentionally," Pepi says darkly. Letting out a shout, he sprints to the other end of the oasis and we race after him. The stranger, a Theban by his looks, turns to run away. But he has no energy left and Pepi overtakes him, tackling him easily to the ground. We reach the pair, out of breath, and look down at the spy and his captive in astonishment.

53

"**WHAT IS YOUR BUSINESS HERE?**" Pepi demands, forearm pressing against the man's throat.

"He cannot speak if you are crushing his wind tube," I say, putting a hand on Pepi's shoulder. He eases the pressure. But only slightly.

"Who are you?" Pepi demands again.

The man wheezes, some colour returning to his face. "None of your concern."

"I believe it is," I say. Still holding the dagger, I put it to the man's throat.

Pepi removes his arm. "Are you a spy?"

The man looks at me defiantly and I apply pressure to the blade. The tip sinks into his skin and his eyes widen.

"Answer me, and I will leave you with your throat intact." I will my hand to remain as steady as my voice.

"Yes," he croaks. I pull the blade back. A small drop of blood runs down the man's neck. One of his hands goes to his throat to massage it.

"Why did you follow us?" Pepi asks, but the answer is becoming obvious. Pharaoh, Wujat, or even the queen will have sent him after us, desperate to know the location of the oasis, a prize jewel along the trading routes and the cradle of the rebellion. It is always advantageous to know where the nests of your enemies lie.

"Thebes will put down this rebellion like the wild dogs you are!" the man coughs.

"How?" Pepi asks with scorn. "You think we will allow you to go free so you can stagger back to spill the grain about our location?"

The man gives Pepi quite a contemptuous look for one who finds himself in the hands of his enemies, but he says nothing.

"There were two of you," I say, heart plummeting again.

"Your companion left you behind?" Pepi demands. I know he is probably cursing himself for not being aware we were followed. Our elation at retrieving the scroll made us careless.

"There were only enough supplies for one to return," the man says, lip curling. "For the sake of my city and my king, I deliver myself into your grasping claws so my partner can return with the oasis's location."

"He will not make it." Pepi spits on the ground beside the spy.

"He might," Paser says, coming over with some linen bandages to tie up the spy. "And he may bring an army back with him."

"Let them come," barks Pepi. "They will arrive at our camp, beaten down by the desert. Our weapons will make short work of them." I can tell he is very angry at Yanassi for leaving. He binds the spy's wrists together and then his legs, leaving him trussed like a goat for sacrifice.

"And who will wield these weapons?" I say, gesturing at the sick gathered around the main water supply. "The chieftain left with most of his guard, gone to claim a crown." And likely to prevent Pepi from doing the same. "Those left behind are weakened by sickness. These are not good odds."

"Then we must go to Avaris," Pepi says, his tone brooking no argument.

"All of us?" Reb is skeptical. I see his friend Zina in the distance, giving water to some of the ill.

"We will take the horses." Pepi turns to Min. The healer is breathing hard from his sprint and looks ready to collapse. I do not like the look of him. Nor Paser. My friend is pale and sweat dots his brow. "How long will this illness last?" Pepi asks.

"It seems to have a short lifespan," Min wheezes. They will have had no break from tending the ill. "The risk isn't so much the sickness itself, but that the affected are unable to keep food or water down. We will need a few days to tend the sick, so they may regain some strength before the journey."

"Some may not survive," Paser says quietly.

"They will not survive at all if they are left behind to face an army unprotected." Pepi's voice is terse.

"If we are to leave for Avaris, then there is no need to conserve anything," I say, not knowing if we made Pharaoh more or less inclined to attack with our visit. "We can use all remaining supplies to improve the condition of the sick. Pentu has many stores of honey. We will feed them a reviving elixir."

Min nods. "There are a lot of medicines. The challenge is having enough hands to get them into the mouths of the ill." I remember the plant the caterpillars were so fond of. We prepared a fresh large batch of medicine with it before I left. I still have our bottle.

"Gather those healthy enough and we will tell them our plans," Pepi orders. With the chieftain gone, he is now in full command here. Reb, Paser, and Min stumble off.

"What about him?" I nod at the prisoner.

"We will leave him here, so that when the Thebans arrive he can tell them to meet us in Avaris. If they dare."

"Our people will cast your people out, like the plague of locusts you are," the spy says, defiant to the last. "And you." His gaze falls on me. "You and your friends will rot for eternity for deserting your homeland."

"I did not desert my home," I say, looking down on him. I've learned that home is not just territory; it is the people who make it so. And I will never desert the people I love, no matter where they reside, no matter where I live. I think of Ky. I know I will see him again and that he will always be my brother, wherever our bodies fall on a map.

And thanks to the endless whims of the gods, it looks like my body is finally going to Avaris. The gods seem to enjoy playing with my fate. We sought the scroll to save Akin so that the chieftain would take us to the capital, where we might escape. Now we are travelling there of our own accord, to seek out Yanassi himself.

"Sesha." Pepi leads me away from the sullen spy. "Now is not the ideal time, but there is something important I must tell you." The tone of his voice has me turning to look at him.

"What is it?" I say, wondering at the tautness of his body, the hesitation in his expression.

His eyes lock with mine. "It concerns a prophecy."

"Regarding the scroll?" I demand. We pored over the document during our crossing, looking for clues, studying the cases pertaining to Akin's injury. Pepi feels the need to go into details *now*?

"No," Pepi says, and the way he looks at me makes all the hairs on my body stand on end. He eyes the blade still in my hand, as if wary of where I might stick it. "There is another prophecy. An older one. One that has monumental implications for our kingdom and was made by the same oracle, an oracle who has never been mistaken." He pauses and then, as if surrendering his soul to the gods, takes a deep breath. "It concerns you and your brother."

I stare at him. I've grown accustomed to his shattering pronouncements, but this one takes the honeycake. Out of the corner of my eye, I see Paser step, falter, and go down like a sack of bricks. Alarm flares.

"You *will* tell me every word of this prophecy later," I say evenly, locking eyes with Pepi again. "Both of them." Then, twisting my hair back and up, I hold it with one hand while sliding my father's knife through the tight coil to secure it in place. Heading straight for my fallen friend, I survey the moaning masses beyond him, and push everything else from my mind. "But right now," I call over my shoulder, "I have patients to attend to."

ACKNOWLEDGEMENTS

THIS AUTHOR GRATEFULLY acknowledges the work of all those who contributed to *The Desert Prince*. To everyone at Dundurn, especially Kathryn Lane and Jenny McWha, who are shepherding me through this process of writing a series on a tight timeline. To superstar editors Jess Shulman and Susan Fitzgerald for helping me smooth out the divots (and a few gaping holes) in the foundation. And to art director Laura Boyle and my wildly talented illustrator, Queenie Chan, for this stunning cover.

To my author friends who keep me going on difficult days, particularly the exceptional Meaghan McIsaac and Angela Misri. To my children, Aira and Nolan, for their patience and understanding when Mommy is working. And to the one person without whom this book would not have been written at all:

my structural beam, Aaron, who's provided every kind of support possible.

To all of my incredible friends and family who support and encourage me, and finally, to those of you who read and love the books: thank you for giving my words a home; I hope they do the same for you.

May you all have as many adventures as Sesha and her friends (albeit slightly less dangerous ones).

Alisha